Murder Misread

By P. M. Carlson

Murder Misread

P. M. CARLSON

A CRIME CLUB BOOK
DOUBLEDAY
New York   London   Toronto   Sydney   Auckland

A CRIME CLUB BOOK

PUBLISHED BY DOUBLEDAY
a division of Bantam Doubleday Dell Publishing Group, Inc.
666 Fifth Avenue, New York, New York 10103

DOUBLEDAY and the portrayal of a man
with a gun are trademarks of Doubleday,
a division of Bantam Doubleday Dell
Publishing Group, Inc.

Library of Congress Cataloging-in-Publication Data
Carlson, P. M.
Murder misread / P. M. Carlson—1st ed.
p.   cm.
"A Crime Club book."
I. Title.
PS3553.A7328M87   1990
813'.54—dc20   90-39755
                                                CIP
ISBN 0-385-41642-3
Copyright © 1990 by P. M. Carlson
All Rights Reserved
Printed in the United States of America
December 1990
First Edition

M

For Jim, Mike, and Bill
Three great guys

I am grateful for the helpful suggestions of Harry Levin and David I. Grossvogel, professors and friends. Errors remaining are mine and not theirs.

—P.M.C.

CYRANO:	*Rien ne me reste.*
LE BRET:	*Jeter ce sac, quelle sottise!*
CYRANO:	*Mais quel geste!*

—Rostand
Cyrano de Bergerac

THURSDAY, JUNE 2, 1977

I

Anatomically, the thing to do was to hit the brainstem. The medulla oblongata, familiar from Intro. to Psych., skipped over quickly by bored professors because it was concerned with plodding functions like reflexes, heartbeat, breathing. The same services it had performed for eons in fish, in reptiles, in shrews, in apes. Professors preferred the neocortex, that Johnny-come-lately that surged out from the humble stem to fill the skull like an atomic mushroom cloud. The cortex had all the exciting functions —intelligence, problem-solving, language, personality, literature. And yet if you damaged the glamorous cortex, the ages-old medulla—aided by some bright young doctor with a set of machines—might still keep the frail, well-plumbed bag of bones and guts ticking along, might even re-suscitate a few twitches of consciousness from the cortical remnants. But damage the medulla, and the cortex, too, would wither helplessly on its ancient, bleeding stalk.

The gun was tiny, snub-nosed, but heavy enough to drag down the clothes a little. Or maybe it wasn't physical weight, maybe it was, as they said, psychological. The months of fear, of not knowing enough, of frus-tration at every attempt to resolve the problems, all now coalesced into a compact steel mechanism in the pocket. A solution of sorts to the insolu-ble. Something that could clip out poison mushrooms at the stem.

And afterward? Who could tell? Tracks had been covered, loved ones protected. Values conflicted, and choices had to be made.

Muggy with the humid breath of vigorous new maple leaves and young vines, the June morning sent sweat trickling down Associate Professor Charlie Fielding's heaving chest. He was bounding up the railroad-tie steps from the parking lot to Van Brunt Hall, aviator glasses bouncing on his slippery nose, making the solid world appear to hiccup with each step. Charlie was late, and heartbroken. Both Deanna's fault. He'd waited half an hour longer than he should have, hoping, but she hadn't ap-peared. Probably with her new friends. Damn her anyway. Deanna of the glinting hair, whose special magic could transform a winter afternoon into a tropical haze of laughing mint-scented delirium. No, it wasn't over. It couldn't be over. Just a misunderstanding. He was sure.

But he'd fix it later. Right now, he was late for his appointment. And

sweating like Stallone in *Rocky* under his summer tweed jacket. And, he
noted with an inward groan, his socks didn't match. One blue, one black.
Today was going to be a stinker.

His office was on the first floor of Van Brunt, an unimaginative fifties
building that had largish rooms but little else to recommend it. He
wrenched open the door and threw himself into the fluorescent-lit white
hall. A dreary rhythm of brown doors and cream walls flowed past him
like the opening zoom of some science-fiction film. Only the water foun-
tains and the little brass-rimmed door placards that announced each
professor's name broke the monotony. Charlie was glad that someone in
the Buildings Department, in a rare fit of maniacal imagination, had
painted the hall of his own wing bright Disney yellow. Poor fellow had
probably been fired instantly in retribution. True, the color was garish,
but better than the main hall's vanilla blandness. Dodging the few people
strolling through the hall, Charlie aimed at the yellow gleam and galloped
down the vinyl tunnel. Ben Hur. Usually he could park near his own end
of the building, but today he'd had to settle for the corner farthest from
his office. It was that kind of day, a Jerry Lewis day.

"Charlie!" A glum, tweedy mountain jutted suddenly into his path. Bart
Bickford, reeking of pipe tobacco.

"Sorry, Bart, I'm in a rush! I'll see you a little later," Charlie called over
his shoulder. Bart peered after him, his small eyes blinking below his
massive brow. Pithecanthropus, Tal called him at the Christmas party,
right to his face. No, Bart protested with a grin, that's Java man, that's you
with the coffee. Tobacco is my vice. Tal had hooted with laughter.

Charlie raced past the hall clock across from the main office. God,
nine-twelve already. He rounded the corner of his own hall and braked
frantically. Three people—two quite small, all upside down—blocked his
door. He caught himself on the edge of the doorjamb and lurched to a
halt. Not Ben Hur. A Mack Sennett pratfall. The little girl that he'd almost
knocked over returned her sneakered feet calmly to the floor and straightened out of her handstand. Luminous brown eyes, black curls, a mischievous grin. " 'Scuse me," she said.

"Ditto." The tallest of the three, a lanky young woman in her twenties,
had bounced upright from her handstand too. Black curls again, and an
infectious smile, but this time the eyes were jay-blue. He generally didn't
like tall women, but this one had an endearing gawkiness that made him
think of Big Bird. She pushed her hair back from her face with both
hands. "We were just practicing our gymnastics. Didn't expect anyone to
come around the corner so fast."

"Yes, I'm sorry. I'm running late." Charlie pressed his aviators up on
his nose and glanced at the young woman doubtfully. "Are you, um, Dr.
Ryan?" Big-boned and slim in her blue jeans and loose sky-blue shirt, she
might be student, faculty, or visiting townie.

"Right. Maggie Ryan. And you're Dr. Fielding?"

"Charlie." He nodded as he pulled his office key from his pocket.

The third and smallest member of the trio still had his hands on the floor, kicking one short leg out behind him in vain imitation of the handstands. Now he stood, toddled toward Charlie with a broad grin, and announced, "Da!"

"Will thinks all men are named Daddy," Maggie Ryan explained. She grabbed both children, their dimpled fingers disappearing into her bony hands. "Will and Sarah, this is Dr. Fielding. He's the man I'm going to be working with this summer."

Charlie smiled at the children and was rewarded by twin grins. "Hi," said Sarah.

"Da!" insisted Will gleefully. Sarah rolled up her eyes.

"All right, pick up your stuff," Maggie instructed Sarah, swooping up Will with a practiced arm. "What's next, Charlie?"

"Checking in with our efficient Cindy Phelps in the departmental office. She's supposed to have a sitter ready. Let me just stow my briefcase and we'll take the kids over there."

"Stow mine too." Propping Will on her hip, Maggie handed the briefcase to Charlie. He slid them inside his office door while she helped Sarah tuck a book back into her satchel.

"This way." Charlie offered Sarah his hand, but she held his finger for only a few steps before bouncing ahead to turn a cartwheel. Charlie laughed. "You've got an energetic pair here!"

"Yeah. I really sympathize with my own mom now! Do you have kids?"

"No, I'm not married. But of course I like kids. You see quite a few of them around an education department. Even one as theoretical as this one." He nodded at an open door with a sign painted on it: Main Office, Educational Psychology. They all trooped in. The no-nonsense chairman, Reinalter, had kept the drab vanilla-modern decor provided by the university, but nevertheless a few tools of the trade had drifted onto the bookcase shelves: a Montessori block, a carousel projector, a 3-D model of a statistical bivariate normal surface. Little Sarah headed straight for the life-size plastic head with a cutaway, take-apart brain in tastefully muted pinks and purples. Its name was Eric, after the long-dead founder of the department.

The quiet tapping of the Selectric halted. "Hi, Charlie." Cindy Phelps was freckled, muscular, with a Farrah Fawcett-Majors tumble of highlighted hair and a shell-pink dress. She ran the department like a high-fashion spider tending her web.

"Hi." Charlie cleared his throat. "Cindy, this is Dr. Ryan, the project statistician. You've probably got a form for her to sign."

Cindy's prominent blue eyes swept eloquently to the ceiling. "God, yes! I've got forms for every occasion. And to match any color scheme.

Today's special is buff and canary." She nodded toward a chair in the corner. "I've also got you a sitter. One of our undergraduate majors. Liz!"

Charlie watched his new statistician size up the tanned, broad-shouldered young woman with unfashionably short, dark hair who came toward them. "Hi, Liz, I'm Maggie," she said. "This is Sarah, and this is Will. I hope you like reading stories and climbing trees."

Liz grinned. "Yep. Also Play-Doh and swimming."

A trace of caution in Maggie's blue eyes. "Swimming?"

"I'm on the team here. And I work as lifeguard at the state park on weekends."

Maggie relaxed. "You're hired! I won't have to tell you about energetic kids, I see. Here, Will, meet Liz." She handed over the little blue-jeaned boy, who looked up somberly into Liz's face. "Don't let them run off too far just yet, okay? I want to talk to Dr. Fielding a little while, then I want to talk to you and set up a schedule. Will needs a nap after lunch or he's whiny and nasty all afternoon."

"Can do. Why don't you come out to the preschool area when you're done? Northeast corner of this building." Liz gestured with her free hand.

"Fine."

"Come on, Sarah, want to go to the playground?" Competently, Liz bustled the children from the office.

Charlie turned back and saw the inner office door open behind Cindy's desk. Bernie Reinalter came out holding a sheaf of papers. Bernie was lean, very fair, no taller than Charlie but with an aloofness that was suitable for the chairman of the department. "Good morning, Charlie," he said.

"Hi, Bernie." Charlie started to smooth his hair but stopped himself. Bernie was always carefully and conservatively dressed. Even now, in shirtsleeves for summer, he was in a pale yellow button-down shirt, and there was a crease in his gray trousers. "Uh, Bernie, this is my statistical consultant for the summer. Dr. Ryan. This is our chairman, Professor Reinalter."

"Glad to meet you," said Maggie.

"Sorry I don't have time to talk to you just now," Bernie told her. "I'm just bringing Cindy some material to type up. I'm meeting a couple of Japanese scientists for lunch, so it helps to have it in written form too."

"Sure, we'll have time to get acquainted later."

Bernie disappeared back into his office. Cindy glanced at the stack of papers he'd left on her desk, then turned back to Maggie. "You'll be using the corner office in Charlie's wing. Professor Schiff's office. He's moved out, but the custodian says he won't be finished cleaning till late this afternoon so I'll give you the key later."

"Okay."

"And now forms. All assembled in one color-coordinated packet. Unlike socks," she added, with just a hint of a glance at Charlie. In his pocket, his fist tightened on his keys. *Bitch.* Cindy continued smoothly, "Why don't you take them along, Dr. Ryan, and fill them out when you can? I'm here till four-thirty."

"Fine. And please call me Maggie." She scooped up the packet. "The checks come to this office too?"

"Right. I'm the money lady."

"You sure are. Another day, another dollar, eh, Cindy?" said Charlie.

"Now, where have I heard that before?" Cindy turned her shell-pink back abruptly and resumed typing.

"Dismissed," said Maggie. Her smile was as mischievous as her daughter's.

"She rules us all," explained Charlie as they walked back toward his yellow hall. "Money, keys, typewriters—she controls the mainstays of life."

"I'll treat her with proper deference," Maggie promised. "Okay, now. Tell me about this project of yours."

"Fine." Charlie pushed his door open and kicked the wedge under it to hold it open. He hung his jacket on the wooden coatrack, then picked up his briefcase and pulled out a stapled manuscript. "You've seen the proposal?"

"Skimmed it." She slid Cindy's varicolored forms into her own briefcase. "But my experience has been that proposals often get altered as the first results come in."

Charlie laughed ruefully. "You've got us pegged, all right. A lot of the details have changed. But we're still hacking away at the same basic question: How does a skilled reader read? When we know what the best adult readers are doing, we can start thinking about how to teach kids to do it too. I mean, just think what happens when you read." He gestured at the papers in his hand. "You pick up a sheet of paper with funny little marks on it, and your eyes look at the marks. Not all the marks—your eyes bounce from one fixation point to another, usually hitting just a few spots per line."

"Right, I remember the basics. You process hundreds of words per minute. More like picking up thoughts instead of letters."

"Something like that. But remember, all you have on the page is letters, grouped, with spaces between groups." He pushed his glasses up on his nose and waved his proposal eagerly. "So an efficient reader must have some sort of plan, or he'd be misreading all the time, having to go back and check. Obviously your peripheral vision will have some blurry information about what's coming up next on the page, so when you know how, you can bounce your eyes to the best possible next fixation point." His fingers stabbed at the pages he held. "The point that will give you the most information about the thought that the writer is developing. We're trying to figure out what kinds of points are chosen for fixation by skilled readers. How the hell do we do it? What blurry peripheral cues do we respond to? It's not easy. As you guessed, we've already given up on half of our bright ideas about how to measure this process."

Maggie cocked her head, her hands thrust into her jeans pockets. "But the other half must be working or you wouldn't have sent for an expensive New York statistician like me to help analyze it."

He couldn't help responding to that smile, a sudden glow like Diane Keaton's. "Well, I have hopes." Boy, did he ever! He'd been promoted on the basis of work that had grown out of his long-ago thesis. This was his first major project since then, his bid to prove that the department hadn't been wrong to choose him to fill the famous Professor Chandler's shoes as reading researcher. If this multitude of interconnected studies didn't work out—well, he'd still have tenure. But he'd seen too many professors scorned and patronized when their early promise had fizzled out, human deadwood in their own departments. Last year, two of his pilot studies in a row had failed, and for a week he'd had nightmares: rigid shoulders marching out the door, little Charlie screaming, "Wait, wait!" unable to follow.

But he'd succeeded on the next experiment and dared to hope again. "At least we've got a usable method," he told Maggie. "Here, let me show you." He flicked on the television that sat on the side table, and went to the bookcase-covered back wall. The books in fact sat in carefully organized stacks on the floor, crowded out by rows of plastic videotape containers. Charlie selected one and fed it into the machine. Uncooperatively, the screen began lazily to flip up horizontal bars.

"What we're using is basically a double-exposure technique," he explained as he struggled with the controls. "Camera one is recording the reflection of a light on the cornea of the reader's eye. You see the reflection as a white spot on the TV. Camera two is on the page he's reading. So the white spots you'll see superimposed on the page are the places on the text where the eye fixates." The bars were rolling down the screen now.

"Ha! I told you it'd never replace the horse," declared a cheerful new voice.

Trust Tal to be around when anyone new appeared. Charlie turned. "Tal! Hi!"

Tal Chandler was bald, a wiry, twinkling old gnome with knobby nose, knobby chin, knobby red cheeks, as though his face had been constructed of little hard apples. He reminded Charlie of a Walt Disney dwarf. He wore shapeless gray trousers, a heather-gray tweed jacket with leather elbow patches and sagging pockets, and a wide grin. He nodded toward Maggie, who was studying the video controls. "And who is the lovely learned lady?"

"Dr. Ryan. Our statistical consultant, just arrived from New York," said Charlie. "Maggie, this is Tal Chandler. The Meredith Professor of Educational Psychology. Emeritus."

"Talbott Chandler! Of course!" Maggie turned from the video. The screen was behaving itself now, showing a clear page of text with white spots hopscotching across it. She extended her hand enthusiastically, and Tal dropped his bookbag to shake it. "You did that famous stuff on how kids learn French!"

"A linguist as well as a statistician! Delightful!" Tal beamed. "Tell me, are you related to the small children I saw a few minutes ago in the preschool playground? The younger announced that I was 'Da.' The elder told him, I believe, *'Fiche-moi la paix.'* "

"Oh, God." Maggie clapped a hand to her forehead in mock dismay. "I'd hoped that if I did my swearing in French they wouldn't pick up nasty words to shock innocent bystanders. Not a good strategy around a university, I see."

Tal's smile widened, his little round cheeks bunching even tighter. "Fear not, I shan't translate," he assured Maggie.

"Hey, c'mon," protested Charlie.

Tal rolled his eyes at Maggie, beckoned Charlie closer, and whispered in his ear, "It means 'shut the hell up.' "

"Mm. A truly useful phrase," Charlie admitted.

Tal turned back to Maggie. "And where is the lucky father of these phenomenal infants? Will we have the pleasure of his company?"

"He's still in New York, but he'll join us a little later this summer. He'll be acting near here, at the Farm Theatre again."

"Ah, the Farm Theatre. Good outfit, that. Saw a splendid *Cyrano* there a few years back," Tal reminisced.

"That was Nick!" exclaimed Maggie. "He did Cyrano!"

"He did? Send him my congratulations!" Tal snatched up Charlie's borrowed ruler left-handed and waved it on high. "What moments, eh? 'Let death come! I wait, standing proud, with sword in hand!' *Debout, et l'épée à la main!*" He hopped onto a chair, commenting aside, "My wife can do this all in French, you know. She makes a far better Cyrano than I. You must meet her. Let's see . . . something about old enemies . . . ah—"

Maggie's blue eyes were dancing. " 'Despite you all, old enemies that round me loom . . .' " she prompted.

"Ah yes!" Right hand cocked behind him in a fencer's pose, he thrust the ruler at the air. " 'Despite you all, old enemies that round me loom, I bear aloft unstained, unyielding—my white plume!' "

He swished an imaginary hat and bowed extravagantly. Maggie applauded, laughing. *"Quel geste!"*

Charlie said, "Tal, you're bouncy today!"

"Yes. The delightful company, of course. And I'm celebrating!" He twinkled down at them. It had been months since Charlie had seen him so ebullient.

"Celebrating what?"

Tal shook his head vigorously. "That's a secret! Tell me, Dr. Ryan, will you be free for lunch today?"

"I'll probably have to meet the kids."

"Tomorrow, then! And you must meet my wife. She can't come today either." He jumped down from the chair, stumbling a little but catching himself by grabbing at the jacket on the rack. "But Charlie, you must join today's celebration! Not the cafeteria. Someplace on College Avenue, with proper champagne. Plato's, all right? At noon?"

"It's a deal," agreed Charlie.

Tal's cheeks bunched in another grin. "A celebration! I'll see who else can come. Of course I asked Cindy, but she had another appointment. I told her I'd save her some champagne. But now perhaps you should tend to your tapes." He gestured theatrically at the TV screen, where little white flashes continued to bounce silently across the displayed text. "Do you know how we used to do eye-movement research, Dr. Ryan?"

"No, I'm afraid not."

"One brave fellow, Professor Ahrens, actually stuck a tiny cup on his eyeball with a thin marker attached, so as he read, the pattern of eye movements was traced onto a smoked drum in front of him."

"God! That's hideous!" Maggie shuddered. "How could he read normally?"

"Yes, indeed, that's what the rest of us all said! You see, we didn't want to have to do experiments like that ourselves. We scientists like to think that we can endure anything in the search for truth, but really we hate to sacrifice our little comforts and little vices. But luckily, in this case someone eventually thought of bouncing light off the eye and photographing it, and bright young folks like Charlie here are refining the methods all the time. Though I don't know about Charlie." He shook his head in mock sorrow. "This young sprat thinks we make up hypotheses as we read, whereas anyone sensible knows we look at the words."

"This old geezer says we struggle along word by word without any coherent ideas about what they mean," Charlie returned.

"You see what I mean?" Tal appealed to Maggie. "He twists simple statements of fact. Why, according to him there's no need to look at the page at all, just open the book and start hypothesizing. Daydreaming."

Charlie laughed. "Tal, who's twisting now?"

"Well, wait'll you hear my paper at the MPA convention!" Tal glanced at his watch. "But right now, I'd best return these books to the library. Now that I've finished daydreaming my way through them." He hoisted his bookbag and whisked out as quickly as he'd come.

"Famous scholars never look the way I think they will," said Maggie, amused. "His publications are very sober."

Charlie nodded. "He was a little giddy today, though he's always cheerful. He's been retired four years now, and still bustles around. Publishes a lot even now. We have great discussions about the control of eye movements. And he's curious about everything. You notice the grilling he gave you already!"

"Yeah. A man after my own heart. Now, what do we want to find out from those little flashing lights on the screen?"

They returned to their chore.

II

Sunlight sifted through the trees. The creek giggled below. A little child galloped down the path, paused to pick up a pebble from the mud, ran back to her smiling mother. They moved on past, until their happy chatter merged into the rustling of the leaves.

A sweet day for a murder.

In the end, Maggie decided to join Tal's celebration lunch. The athletic baby-sitter was getting along well with the children, Maggie reported back to Charlie. "Liz is even willing to take them to McDonald's. A place I avoid whenever I can," she explained with a disdainful wrinkling of her nose. "And Will needs his nap afterward, so she can take them back to my apartment. Meanwhile, if it's okay, I'll tag along with you grown-ups instead."

"Great! Let's go, then. It's about time." He locked his office and led the way down the stairs to the parking lot. "Tal will be glad you can come. Though you won't get out of meeting his wife tomorrow too. He seemed bent on that. Did you work out a schedule with your sitter for tomorrow?"

"For the next week, until Liz's classes start, there's no problem. And when Nick gets here he'll have some time too." She smiled at him as he locked the office door behind them. "It's refreshing to be working in a place where people provide for children. Most of my clients assume that parents' plans can be adjusted at the drop of a hat."

"Well, in this department so many people are working with children it's hard to forget. Frankly, I'm glad my own work is with college students at this point. It's a hell of a lot easier to schedule."

"And they're easier subjects, statistically. They know the test-taking game, how to play by the rules, much better than the little ones do. So you don't get too many squirrelly answers to skew your data."

They had walked past the end of the parking lot. A deep wooded ravine cut raggedly along this edge of the campus, separating it from the congestion of the town. Long-legged Maggie, swinging easily along the uneven ground, unhesitatingly chose the right path from among the several that meandered down into the woods. "I see you still know your way around," Charlie observed.

"Yeah, it comes back. It was only seven years ago that I left."

"Did you ever work in this department?"

"No. I worked on a neurology project out at Carroll Lab once, but mostly I hung around the math building and the psych building at the other end of campus."

"Yeah. Education is a little world of its own." Charlie pushed aside a branch that overhung the path. Norway maples had taken over the steep hillside here; except for a few malnourished vines, other species found it difficult to cope with the shallow, greedy maple roots and the dense shade of the broad leaves. The rough earth, still dark from yesterday's rain, sported only a skimpy undergrowth of baby maples. But the sun, sloping through the shifting leaves, dappled the warming earth, and he felt an irrational stirring of cheerfulness. Deanna would come back, he was sure. She had her moods, but who didn't? And what they shared was so special. Maybe after work today, he would—

"Which way do you prefer here?" Maggie paused at a fork in the trail, where one path led to a green-painted metal pedestrian bridge, and another wound lower and under the bridge along the edge of the little creek that had patiently carved out this gorge.

"The lower one's prettier if you don't mind steps. But it may be soggy still from the thunderstorm yesterday. I generally use this upper path."

"Fine, let's be prudent." That warm Diane Keaton smile again as she turned toward the bridge. "I love this walk, don't you?"

"Yes. I'm a hiker. You must miss the woods, living in New York."

"Not as much as I expected. We're only a block from Prospect Park, so we've got plenty of woods and meadows and ravines to explore."

"Aren't those big city parks dangerous?" He had to stretch to keep up with her athletic strides.

"Well, I don't wander through them alone at night." She hesitated, glancing at Charlie with an ambiguous smile. "Somebody did try to rape me once. But it wasn't in Prospect Park. It was only a few miles from this very spot, when I was a student here."

"God!" What could he say? What a horrible experience, to have someone forcing himself. . . . He mumbled inadequately, "That must have been terrible!"

"Yeah. Well, help arrived fast and we sent him up for ninety-nine years. Happy ending." She didn't sound happy, her shoulders hunching under the sky-blue cotton. "Anyway, I've learned to stay alert. Did you notice the guy under the bridge just now?"

Charlie looked back, frowning, and pushed his glasses up on his nose. The ravine was a visual crazy-quilt patched from dark earth, green leaves, splashes of sunlight. The original camouflage design, quivering as the breeze riffled the leaves. Below, the little creek gurgled and glinted through the shadows; trunks and branches traced irregular dark lines through the trembling foliage. Near them, the artificial pea-green of the bridge shafted straight-edged across the little chasm. "I don't see any-one."

"See where the trail widens? That muddy patch? Maybe thirty yards up the trail?"

"Yes. Oh!" He saw him then: standing nearly hidden by a clump of bushy young maples, only a bit of gray sleeve and a dark shoe visible from here. "Wonder what he's up to?"

"In Prospect Park he'd probably be a birdwatcher," Maggie said lightly, turning back up the path toward College Avenue. "Either that or one of the homeless mental cases the state has so kindly liberated from institutions so they can find their own New York apartments. A task that drives the sanest of us batty."

"Yeah." Charlie glanced back uneasily. He could no longer see the shadowed figure. "You've got sharp eyes."

"Yeah. Half Irish, half eagle, that's me." She flapped her arms in the loose shirt clownishly.

They emerged from the woods into the abrupt tar and concrete world of College Avenue. Temporarily depopulated until summer school began, it seemed spacious today in the sunlight. Only a few blue-jeaned students drifted along the sidewalks. Maggie pulled an envelope from her brief-case. "Is the branch post office still up the street there?"

"Yes, next to the shoe store. We could—"

"Be right back!" Without waiting for him, she sprinted across the street toward the storefront post office. Charlie scuffed slowly along, enjoying the sun after the shadows of the ravine. The street was lined with nine-teenth-century commercial buildings of brick or stone, two or three sto-ries high, their carved cornices still bulking proudly against the sky but their upper windows peeling and decked with the tacky detritus of cheap student apartments: a row of Genesee cans on one sill, a T-shirt drying on another, an Indian cotton curtain knotted in the center to let in some light in a third. Below the second story the Victorian facades had disappeared completely behind layers applied in more recent decades—storefronts of glass and fake brick, or turquoise panels, or neo-colonial white plastic columns supporting white pediments. Up to a level of eight feet or so most nonglass surfaces had been sprayed with graffiti.

After a few minutes Maggie rejoined him. She was reading the walls too. "The messages change, don't they?" she observed. "When I was here it was all anti-Vietnam, down-with-Nixon stuff."

"Yeah, I remember. Jimmy Carter just doesn't inspire the same emo-tion in our graffiti artists."

"Yeah. Who cares about human rights? They've reverted to more eter-nal concerns."

She jerked a thumb at one elaborate message and Charlie smiled. The wall proclaimed, "Whiskey makes you frisky, brandy makes you randy, rum makes you cum." He said, "There must have been a few slogans like that, even then. There certainly were on my campus."

"Yeah, I have to admit. But we extolled drugs besides alcohol. We would've said 'pot makes you hot' or something, right?" She pushed open the door of one of the fake-brick fronts and Charlie followed her into Plato's.

A wide mahogany bar ran halfway back into the restaurant. Wooden booths lined the walls under a trellis decked with bunches of plastic grapes. Only a few people sat in the booths or at the tables clustered in the rear. Plato's did not attract the rowdier undergraduates; the plump, dark-mustached owner purposely priced his beer high and never featured all-you-can-eat specials as did the other College Avenue eateries. "Sure I lose a little money," he had once explained to Charlie. "But I don't have to replace the chairs those animals break, or mop up where they've thrown up all over the rest rooms. If Sal wants to do all that, let him make the profit. Besides, I get the nice people."

"I don't see Professor Chandler," said Maggie. "But we're early."

"Yes." Charlie squinted at his watch, which was hard to see in the dimness. Looked like ten of. He'd allowed more time for the walk than necessary, given Maggie's long-limbed energy. "Why don't we just sit in a front booth, so he'll see us when he arrives?"

"Great. I'm famished! How about some dolmas to start now, and we'll have something else when the others arrive?"

Her eager appetite reminded Charlie of Deanna, how she studied the menu with a tense little smile of ravenous anticipation, her long lashes blinking dark on her cheek as she puzzled over the choices. He tried to brush the image away and looked up at the too-plump blond student waitress to tell her he'd wait for their friends to arrive. She nodded pertly and went to fetch Maggie's order. Bouzouki music strummed through speakers high in the corners, attempting to cover the pops and clatters from the kitchen. Maggie leaned back into the corner of the booth, one rangy leg stretched across the seat, and studied Charlie. The sky-colored shirt made the darker blue of her eyes seem electric.

"How long will it take you to finish coding your videotapes?" she asked.

"A couple of weeks. I'm a little behind because one of the grads who was supposed to help code them had to leave right after spring classes ended. Family problems. But the other two coders are slogging away. Already have a couple of the experiments ready for you to look at."

"Good." One bony finger poked idly at the salt shaker. "So tell me, how did you get interested in studying reading?"

"I wanted to help kids learn to read. I know my stuff seems pretty far from that, working with adults in this project, but we have to know how skilled readers do it before we can help kids learn the skill."

"Makes sense. But, I mean, why not help kids learn math? Or become an optometrist or a statistician or some other useful thing?"

"Well, reading is so important! Absolutely basic to life today. If you can't—well, I've known people—" He broke off, gulped some of his ice water.

Her blue eyes were intent on him. "People who had trouble learning?"

He shrugged. "My Aunt Babs. She pretty much raised me after my mother left. She was so embarrassed about not being able to read. Always pretended she could . . . you know, claimed she'd forgotten her glasses or something. She'd bring home papers she had to sign and ask me to read them. I was only eight or nine then. Had to share what was treated as a filthy family secret. A couple of times I tried to teach her but she gave up right away. And I thought, if only I knew how to teach. She said she was stupid and that was that." There was a blur on his glasses, and he took them off and rubbed them with a paper napkin. "She, uh, committed suicide. I came home from hockey practice and found her."

"God, Charlie!"

"Yeah. Well, later I realized she wasn't stupid at all. She'd pretty much run the drugstore where she worked. The pharmacist was the owner and he did the ordering and so forth. But she rang up sales and knew every box and bottle in stock. She always talked to the salesmen. Could give the pitches herself. Amazing woman."

"Yes." Maggie straightened, flashed a grateful smile at the plump waitress, and greedily devoured one of the stuffed grape leaves set before her. "Want one?" she mumbled, pushing the plate toward Charlie.

"Thanks." It was good, the savory rice filling set off by the faintly bitter stringiness of the grape leaf.

Maggie reverted to their conversation. "What did you mean, you realized it later? When you were small did you believe your aunt when she said she was stupid?"

"Everyone in the family said that. Her parents, her brother—my father. He always said so too. How he hated to leave his son with . . . And if I did anything he didn't approve of, it was because I was stupid the way she was."

"But you could read."

"Yeah, I didn't say he was consistent. And for me, reading was a good escape. I was happy reading. But he said—" Charlie replaced his glasses. Why the hell was he nattering on about olden days? No need to present his statistical consultant with his whole life history. He said, "Anyway, there you have it. The reasons this knight decided to slay the dragon of illiteracy."

She smiled. "Good reasons. But it's a big and complex dragon."

"Yes. There are so many theories about, so many complexities. But if we . . ." He trailed off, becoming aware of Maggie's gaze fixed behind him, of a strong stale-smoke scent, of a massive tweed elbow by his ear. "Oh, hi, Bart!"

"Hullo." Bart Bickford's small eyes, set deep in their bony sockets, scanned the interior of the restaurant. "I was supposed to meet Tal Chandler here. Have you seen him?"

"We're waiting for him too. Sit down." Charlie slid across the seat to make room. Bart needed a lot of room. "Maggie, this is Bart Bickford. Teaches development of creativity. Maggie Ryan, our project statistician."

Maggie murmured, "Mmph," pleasantly around a mouthful of dolmas, swallowed, and asked, "What kind of creativity are you interested in?"

"Last couple of years I've been working with verbal creativity. There are musical prodigies, math prodigies, but it's harder to set criteria for poets or story-tellers at very young ages."

"Are you finding the criteria?"

Bart shrugged diffidently. For such an immense man he always seemed to Charlie to be apologetic, even timid. He said, "We're developing a couple of criteria. Long road ahead." He glanced back at the door. "Do you have any idea what Tal's up to?"

Charlie suggested, "Probably got another book accepted for publication."

"Yeah." Bart continued to stare at the door. He drummed his fingernails on the tabletop almost imperceptibly to the rhythm of the bouzouki. "Probably. But he seemed so excited."

"Well, maybe he'd had good news from the doctor."

"Yes, but—did he say anything to you about old enemies?"

Charlie frowned. "Enemies? Tal said something . . . a quote, wasn't it?"

Maggie, having swallowed, nodded agreement. "From *Cyrano*. 'Old enemies who round me loom.' But the enemies he's talking about are pretty abstract—falsehood, cowardice, prejudice."

"Well, Tal has certainly always been against those," Bart said, fumbling in his jacket pocket. "Still, it seemed odd."

"He could still have been talking about the cancer," argued Charlie, warming to his own idea. "It's in remission, but a couple of years ago it was a very real enemy."

"Could be." Bart was fussing with one of his buttons, winding a loose thread around the shank. "I suppose there are academic opponents too, though I don't know a hell of a lot about research on reading."

"Yeah, that's true," Charlie admitted. "A couple of younger guys at MIT are attacking his theory."

"And your work?" asked Bart shrewdly.

"It's not exactly an attack," said Charlie uncomfortably. "More a development. Anyway, you know Tal, he's always ready to argue almost any side of an issue. Though he claims to be flattered that his work is still being noticed."

Bart squinted at the button, seemed to approve, and looked back at the door. "Hell, I'm probably reading too much into it. Look, there's Nora!"

Charlie twisted to look back over his shoulder at the door. Outside the plate-glass windows, the sun glinted on College Avenue's boutiques and trash cans, on bicycles, motorcycles, aging rusty Fords and gleaming Camaros, on blue-jeaned students strolling languidly through the sleepy, sparkling vacation day. One of the figures, not blue-jeaned but dressed in navy skirt and jacket, pushed open the door and stood for a moment blinking at the dimness.

"Over here, Nora!" called Bart.

Her head turned with a little puzzled frown at Maggie, then she saw Bart and smiled. A knot of apprehension gathered in Charlie's stomach. Nora was okay as a colleague, but after hours . . . Well, she hadn't referred to the incident since, and they managed to behave civilly enough in their daily interchanges. But he still cringed with embarrassment to think of last fall's Halloween party. He'd parted his curly hair in the middle, removed his glasses and added a tiny mustache and tramp clothes. "My God, it's Chaplin!" everyone had exclaimed. Nora, a little tipsy, had declared herself so smitten she wouldn't leave his side. And she hadn't. He'd had to drive her home, practically push her weeping out of the car. But she wasn't tipsy now; she was her usual businesslike self. Nora's skin was fine, tight, as though a size too small for her facial bones. Her eyes were brown and intense, and her dark hair was scraped back smoothly from her brow, softened only by the first streaks of gray.

At the Halloween party, she'd been wearing a slinky thirties gown and a platinum wig. Jean Harlow, he supposed. Though at one point she'd borrowed someone's shawl and claimed she was the blind girl in *City Lights*.

"Hi, Bart," Nora said, squinting at them. "Oh, and Charlie too! It's hard to see anything in here at first."

"You want my thumbnail lecture on dark adaptation?" teased Charlie, pleased that she was keeping her distance.

"Not in the least! One of my few joys in life is that I don't have to worry about physiology anymore. I'm Nora Peterson," she added, turning abruptly to Maggie.

"Maggie Ryan. Statistical consultant for Charlie's project. If you're waiting for Tal Chandler too, have a seat." She slid farther into the corner, patting the space next to her.

"Thanks." Nora took off her dark jacket, folded it carefully, and placed it with her briefcase on the seat beside her as she sat down. Her cream-colored blouse, though simple, had an unexpected tiny edging of lace that reminded Charlie of Deanna's underthings. He forced his eyes up to focus on Nora's thin, smiling, talking lips. "Well, things must be going well with your project, Charlie! Getting the statistician signals phase two, right? Are you going to give us a report soon?"

"Can't give much of a report until the numbers are properly crunched." Charlie smiled at Maggie. "But now that the cruncher is here, it shouldn't be much longer."

The plump waitress arrived, dealt out menus like blackjack cards, and asked Maggie hopefully if she wanted anything else.

"You bet! But I'll wait until Professor Chandler comes."

The waitress beamed. "Oh, good! I'm glad he'll be here. Okay, I'll be back soon." She bustled away.

"How's your brother doing, Nora?" Bart asked.

"Fine."

"It's a different world for teenagers these days. Hard to stay out of trouble. Drugs and all . . ." Bart shook his head.

"He's twenty-two, and he's doing fine." Nora turned to Maggie. "You're not from NYSU, are you?"

"I'm partner in a New York City consulting firm now. But in fact, I got my Ph.D. here a few years ago. So it's not completely new."

"A nostalgia trip?"

"Partly. Mostly business, some pleasure. What's your field, Nora?"

"How children solve problems at different ages. I'm applying some of Piaget's theories to moral dilemmas that I pose to children. Though I'm not ready for a statistician yet!" Her taut face split into a smile.

Maggie smiled too. "Good. I'm not looking for more work. I want to have time to enjoy the beautiful country summer." She gestured at the window. "Sunshine, trees, graffiti—"

"Now there's a moral dilemma," said Bart. He shifted in his seat, causing a small earthquake at Charlie's end of the booth. "Tell me, Nora, if a person knows someone who sprays the walls, is it moral to turn him in? I mean, weighing the relatively trivial nature of the crime against—"

"Excuse me." Maggie stood up on the seat of the booth, placed one sneakered foot neatly between the salt shaker and the dolmas plate, bounced across the table, and landed on the floor running. She was pulling open the door before Charlie could turn his astounded head.

But then he heard it too, still partly masked by the bouzouki music but getting louder. A woman screaming: "Help! Oh, my God, help! Help!"

III

Anne Chandler's wandering attention was caught by her own stubby fingers pulling yet another Gauloise from the pack. Unwillingly her eyes slid to the ashtray: this would be number seven. No, eight, damn it. She tapped the cigarette back into the pack regretfully and tucked it into her jacket pocket.

"So, uh, do you suppose you could give me the extension?" asked the pimply student sitting stiffly on the other side of her desk. His Adam's apple bobbled in his scrawny young throat. Knot, the French called it; *noeud de la gorge,* knot of the throat. And *noeud de la question,* the crux of the matter. The crux was that this poor kid wasn't suited for college at all. Anne wanted to pat his downy cheek, set him on a tractor, let him earn a living in the healthy open air with no need to decipher any more funny-looking French words.

But no doubt he was pursuing some other, less suitable goal. Ambitious parents, perhaps. It would be kindest to get it over with. Anne squashed her maternal instincts and said briskly, "Three more days. But that's it, Bill. I can see that it's a problem for you to get the paper in by next Wednesday"—somewhere in his maundering account he had made some excuse or other, she remembered vaguely—"but I really have to close the books on this course. It's already a week past the final." She stood up to signal the end of the conversation.

"Yeah, okay, I'll try, Professor Chandler." He stumbled to his feet glumly.

"I'll look forward to getting your paper," she lied with her best inspiring-teacher smile. His gangly height loomed a good twelve inches over her own stocky bantam figure. "See you later, Bill."

"Thanks, Professor Chandler." He shifted his bookbag apologetically and ambled out.

Anne fingered the cigarettes and looked at her phone.

It didn't ring.

What the hell was he up to?

With sudden decision she plopped back into her chair, picked up the receiver, and dialed Ken Little.

"Ken, sorry to call you so late, but I can't meet you for lunch today. Could we reschedule?"

"Sure thing, Annie. I have some kind of bug anyway, woke up feeling woozy, and I wasn't really looking forward to lunch that much. You know, with the food at the Union—"

"We really should get the film schedule set soon, though," she broke in, paging through her calendar. "How about tomorrow, at ten?"

"No good. Eleven?"

"Fine. I'll start my office hours late."

"Okay. Do you know if there are any bugs going around? I mean, this just came out of the blue. When I woke up—"

"You'll feel better tomorrow, Ken. See you then." She pressed down the cradle before he could reply and, without letting herself think, dialed Tal's office. But again, it rang fruitlessly, over and over.

Dr. Lambert, then.

God, why was it so difficult? She had muscled her way brashly into the academic world long before women were welcomed. *La plastronneuse,* some catty old professor had nicknamed her: the pushy one, the show-off. Or, more literally, the starched shirtfront, the breastplate, the chesty one. Tal had been delighted with the pun, burrowing his nose into her ample bosom and murmuring lasciviously, "Mmm, *la plastronneuse!*" and they'd both giggled like kids. Well, pushy she'd been, she'd had to be. She had defended countless papers at conventions, had traveled alone in France and French Africa, had force-fed the glories of French literature to generations of linguistically lazy students. But now, instead of making a simple call, her fingers were again twitching at the Gauloises.

She pulled her erring hand from her pocket, placed it firmly on the receiver, made herself dial the well-known number.

"Can you hold a moment, Mrs. Chandler?" asked the receptionist.

And in a moment, miraculously, John's voice: "Dr. Lambert here."

"John, it's Anne Chandler. I haven't been able to catch Tal, and I wondered . . ." She trailed off. What she wondered could not be put into ordinary English.

And didn't have to be. John exclaimed enthusiastically, "Looked great, Anne! Still shrinking. He keeps on like this another six months and he'll be good as new."

"You're . . . sure?" she faltered.

"The X rays were as clear as they could be. He's winning, Anne!"

"John . . . thanks." She hung up, dazed. Braced to deflect the worst, she found that this good news could not penetrate her defensive walls either. She was adrift, unable to believe or disbelieve.

And Tal? Maybe this was why he hadn't called, this inability to believe. Anne slung her bag over her shoulder, locked her office, and hurried out into the June sunshine.

The air was pleasantly tepid, scented with the first blooms on the rose plants around the Modern Languages building. *To hell with you, roses, with your little pink smell.* She pulled out her Gauloise and lit it defiantly, sucked the delicious stinking smoke deep into her chest, then spewed it contemptuously at the blossoms.

To hell with you, too, cancer.

The Ed Psych office was locked when Anne arrived, the halls nearly deserted in this peculiar between-semesters slack. *Les vacances,* the French said: vacation, vacancy. Tal's office, as it turned out, was vacant too, locked and dark. Puzzling over her next move, she wandered back toward the door. Maybe she shouldn't have canceled that meeting about next year's French film season. But she couldn't face Ken and his need for mothering today.

At the door she met Cindy Phelps approaching from the library walk. "Oh, Cindy! Just the person I wanted to see!"

"Really?" Cindy's light blue eyes looked kindly at Anne from under shelves of enhanced black lashes. She dragged her rose-colored cardigan from her shoulders and tossed it over her forearm, then reached into her bag for the office key. "What can I do for you?"

"I'm looking for my wayward husband."

Cindy glanced over her shoulder at the hall clock. "Twelve-thirty. He'll still be at lunch."

"Yes. But do you know where he is?" Anne followed Cindy into the departmental office. Eric, the plastic brain model on the shelf, stared at them with blank blue eyes.

Cindy stowed her bag and hung up her cardigan. "For once, yes. He said he'd be at Plato's. Invited me to come with him and celebrate."

"Celebrate?" An avalanche of hurt battered Anne's heart, stirring buried memories of that horrible long-ago winter when she'd discovered Tal's affair with that bosomy premed student.

Cindy laughed, preening. "Oh, God, that sounded wrong! This wasn't like a tryst or anything. A bunch of people went. He asked Bernie too, but Bernie had to have lunch with some computer people from Japan. I couldn't go, so Tal said he'd save me some champagne." The hand patting her exuberant hairdo into place slowed, and she frowned at Anne. "Are you okay? I mean, he said you had an appointment. How come you're here?"

"Oh, it got canceled." Anne smiled at Cindy, the weight lightening. It was true—Tal had known about her lunch with Ken. Still, why hadn't he called? "So he's at Plato's?"

"Right. Say, what's he celebrating? His birthday? Seventieth, right?"

"Right, you might say that. Cindy, I tried to call him this morning but he didn't answer."

"Well, he got in late." Cindy lifted the cover from her typewriter. "And he was running around the halls, in and out of everyone else's office. Busy busy. So you didn't have much of a chance of getting through."

"Well," decided Anne, "I'm going over to Plato's. If I happen to miss him again, tell him I want to talk to him, okay?"

"Sure thing."

"Cindy, how are you doing?"

For an instant their eyes locked. "Okay," said Cindy. "It'll be okay." Then her gaze slid away and she glared at the smiling man who was pushing a wire cart laden with manila envelopes into the office. "Oh, damn, here comes the mail to sort."

Anne waved good-bye and walked back out into the sun. She was jumpy today, wasn't she, unable to make phone calls, thinking of that curvy premed for the first time in years. Well, months. She crossed the parking lot, surprisingly full for vacation time. Probably people who usually had to park at the peripheral lots, taking advantage of *les vacances*. A high proportion were the old rusting hulks driven by grad students, instead of somewhat newer Toyotas or Vegas favored by the faculty. The undergraduate Porsches were probably off to the beach.

The woods were lovely, washed by yesterday's rain, each leaf defined in the chiaroscuro of June sun and deep shade. The noises of civilization —motors, sirens, voices—faded rapidly as she descended. Birds called, a squirrel ranted in high-pitched hoarse indignation, foliage rustled. Almost nice enough to take that old bastard Rousseau seriously, all his drivel about getting close to nature. Anne tramped stolidly down the path, her bag swinging from her shoulder, her face turned up to catch the occasional dazzle of sky beyond the rippling leaves.

She heard the voices first, from the fork in the path. Men's voices, gruff working-class voices, down by the creek. As she hiked along the upper path, she tried to peer down through the ragged screen of young maples to see what was happening. Nearing the bridge, she could glimpse flashes of light and paused, squinting. A photographer of some sort? She pushed aside a young branch so she could survey the activity.

The photographer was squatting, stretching, clambering onto logs and rocks, even into the stream in a strange ritual ceremony around a quiet heather-gray form on the path. Well outside the circle of his dance, others stood watching: men in uniforms, the gray of the campus safety officers, the navy of the city police, the white of ambulance attendants who stood with a stretcher vertical between them. Beyond them, clumps of university people—tweeds, blue jeans, Aran sweaters. A tall black man in a blue blazer was talking to the largest of the tweedy ones. Looked like Bart, Anne thought. Next to them, a lanky young woman with black curls had a comforting arm around a sobbing female student in a jeans jacket.

Anne stepped back onto the path, letting the branch spring back across the view. With shivering hands she pulled a cigarette from her pocket, lit it, and inhaled deeply. Then she marched back to the fork in the path and down toward the crowd.

She was stopped after a few yards by a big gray-jacketed safety officer, young, taut-faced, a trace of acne on his jaw. Dixon, said his badge. "I'm sorry, ma'am," he croaked hoarsely, and cleared his throat. "Please use the other path. This one is closed."

"Someone's hurt?" asked Anne, drawing in the sustaining smoke. She knew it was a dumb question. The ambulance attendants had been standing idly by, waiting.

"Someone's been shot and killed!" confirmed the youthful officer, his murky blue eyes troubled and lively in his stiffly held face. "So we have to ask you to go the other way until they're finished with the body."

"But you see," explained Anne, enunciating carefully for the benefit of his dazed young ears, "I think I'm married to that body."

IV

Charlie stood smacking his fist rhythmically into his other hand, an ineffectual release for his fury and confusion. Tal could not be dead! "I just saw him this morning," he'd protested stupidly to big Sergeant Hines, a line from a million B movies. But he couldn't accept it. He'd taken one look at that lump of gray tweed and turned away. Couldn't be zesty little Tal. Tal had been like a father, no, more like a playful uncle, from the time Charlie had first joined the department. He couldn't be dead. This was a nightmare. A horror flick. Not real.

But the cops were real enough. There were gray-shirted men from the Campus Security Office, and solid fellows in navy uniforms from the Laconia city police. And there were plainclothes detectives moving through the little crowd. Sergeant Hines was in charge, a big black man with a light blue summer blazer stretched across his muscular shoulders. As Reggie Hines he'd been a running back for Syracuse, Charlie remembered someone saying. A smart player, not quite good enough for the pro leagues but graduating with a good record and working his way up through the Laconia police steadily. He'd been calm and efficient questioning Charlie, his face stolidly neutral, as though carved in ebony, but his questions were alert and to the point. O. J. Simpson turned cop.

Charlie was standing at the bend where the trail angled up, partly because he couldn't look at the crumpled heather-gray heap farther down. The cops had shooed everyone back up the trail, gray uniforms and blue uniting in their insistence that civilians keep their distance. Hines had arrived soon and taken charge. He'd set his own men to work measuring, photographing, cordoning off a large area of the path and woods, searching the trail and creek banks. He'd rounded up the witnesses and put them under the supervision of a couple of Campus Security cops, telling them all not to discuss the scene. One at a time, he drew the witnesses aside and asked them his questions.

Near Charlie, the young woman student who'd found the body had stopped sobbing at last. She had caramel-colored hair and square-framed glasses. Dorrie something, she'd said. Maggie's arm in the loose blue shirt lay across her denim jacket like a soothing wing. Maggie was murmuring comfort, but her keen blue eyes were panning across the scene, checking trail, woods, cops. Half Irish, half eagle, she'd said. She saw Charlie looking at her and gave a small sad shake of her head. He realized that she believed Tal was dead and suddenly he began to believe it too. He smacked his fist into his hand again and glared at Hines. What the hell was the man doing? Why wasn't he chasing down Tal's killer instead of talking to Bart? Tal deserved police helicopters, bloodhounds, search-lights, SWAT teams. Instead Hines was asking Bart Bickford the same calm questions he'd already asked Charlie and Maggie and Dorrie. He'd taken Bart a few yards down the trail, but Charlie could still hear most of it above the gurgling creek and the whispering leaves.

"Yes, he'd asked me to meet him for lunch," Bart said. He was fidgety, his big hands knotted in his jacket pockets, his heavy brow thickened in a frown.

"Did you pass this part of the trail on the way to Plato's?"

"I used the upper trail." Bart nodded at the green-painted bridge, dull against the sun-sparkled foliage at the top of the ravine.

"This was a few minutes before noon?"

"A quarter of, maybe," Bart amended. "I went early because I wanted to drop off some film to be developed."

Hines was making notes. "In Collegetown?"

"Yeah. That place around the corner on Jefferson. A block off College. Quick Prints."

"And then you went to Plato's?"

"Yes. Pretty damn close to noon." Bart shifted his weight to his other foot.

"Did you meet or see Professor Chandler on your way?"

"No. Saw a woman with a little girl taking a walk down here on this trail. They were the only ones on it."

Hines's expression didn't change, but Charlie sensed a new tautness in the broad shoulders, a brightening interest. "Can you describe the woman?"

"Young, slim, brown hair, about—God, it's hard to judge height from above, isn't it?" Bart's sunken eyes squeezed closed with the effort to remember. "Some kind of a checked shirt. Bluish, I think. Blue jeans. Gray sweater tied around her waist."

"Good." Hines seemed pleased, scribbling in his notepad. "And the child?"

"About five, I'd guess. Red sweatshirt, jeans. Brown hair. Kept running over to throw stones in the water."

"Fine. And no sign of Professor Chandler?"

"No. Nor of anyone else. They were the only people I saw."

"Was anyone entering the trail from the Collegetown side?"

"No. Only a few people on the street this time of year."

"Right." Hines turned the page. "Is there anything else you can add?"

Bart blinked at the big detective. To Charlie Bart seemed a big, sad creature out of his element, a Neanderthal puzzling over Cro-Magnon behavior. He said, "No, I can't think of anything. But if I do—"

"Right. Let us know. We'll let everyone go in a few minutes. Bear with us a little longer. We'll want a formal statement later. You'll be back at your office today?"

"Yes, until six o'clock or so."

"Fine. Give your phone numbers and address to Officer Porter." Hines nodded at the blue-uniformed cop who was taking notes nearby. Bart lumbered toward Porter as Hines consulted his notes for the next witness. "Ms. Peterson?"

"Yes. Here," said Nora.

Charlie had hardly been aware of her, standing silently in the shade of the maples nearby, her navy blue suit as dark as the shadows. Now she stepped into the dappled sunlight of the trail.

"Just a few questions, Ms. Peterson." Hines smiled at her, but his quick glance was sizing her up professionally. Height, weight, hair color, eye color, any distinguishing marks—Charlie could almost see her being converted to checkmarks in boxes on official police forms.

Charlie had already talked to Hines, so he'd been converted already.

"Yes, he invited me to lunch too." Nora was businesslike, only a quiver of her eyelid betraying stress. "He said it was some kind of celebration. I figured maybe he'd had a book published."

"I see. Now, what route did you take to the restaurant?"

"The upper bridge."

"What time was it?"

"Noon, maybe even a minute or two after. I was a little late because I wanted to finish some exams I was grading. Essay type, they take a long time to grade."

"Right. Did you see anyone on the lower trail?"

She shook her head slowly. A couple of strands of her scraped-back hair had come loose, making her look strangely vulnerable. "I'm sorry, I was in such a rush because I was late. So I just hurried straight to Plato's."

"You didn't glance down?"

"I probably did. One does when crossing a bridge. But nothing registered as any different from the last hundred times I walked across."

"You didn't notice a man by those trees?" Hines nodded at the clump of maples that Charlie and Maggie had identified as the place the unknown man was lurking.

"No. I didn't."

"A woman and child?"

"No."

"Was there anyone else on the upper trail?"

"I passed a couple of students just as I entered, coming out on the campus side. Young men."

"Good. Could you describe them, please?"

"I didn't really notice. Well, jeans, of course. Sweatshirts. Backpacks, maybe. One of them was blond."

"How tall? As tall as Officer Porter?"

"Yes, roughly. Not as heavy."

Charlie became aware of a murmur farther up the trail. A gray-uniformed Campus Security officer was talking to a city cop. The campus officer was escorting a short, stout woman—oh, God, it was Anne! He hadn't thought about Anne. She'd always awed him a little despite her good humor, because of the keen intelligence and brusqueness wrapped in that solid matronly little figure. But Tal doted on her, proud of her accomplishments, even bragging that he'd married the prettiest professor on campus. "None of these wispy little model types for me," he'd confided to Charlie early on, man to man. "I go for a real woman. A huggable woman." He'd tactfully stopped those comments when Charlie had gotten engaged to slim Lorraine, a grad student with big blue eyes and enormous ambitions that eventually had drawn her away from Charlie to New York City. Lorraine had been sweet and brainy and understanding, but definitely on the wispy side by Tal's standards.

Back then Charlie had thought she was just right.

Well, that was over and done with. Better luck next time.

Anne Chandler was smoking those smelly French cigarettes of hers, her hands moving jerkily to her mouth. She was dressed in lightweight brown tweed. She and Tal always looked like a British couple about to go out for a tramp on the heath. Her hair was salt-and-pepper gray, cut short and ruffly around that intelligent face. The Campus Security officer led her straight to Hines. The big detective's impassiveness had melted a little. "Mrs. Chandler? Professor Talbott Chandler's wife?"

"Right." A puff on the cigarette. "He's dead, isn't he."

"I'm afraid so, Mrs. Chandler."

Her shoulders sagged at the confirmation. "May I see him?"

Hines squinted down the trail. "We won't be finished for a while yet. Do you want to sit down?"

"Been sitting all morning. You want to ask me questions?"

"Yes, but I don't want to cause you further distress. I can talk to you somewhere else, later." Hines's voice was full of compassion. "Just let us have your address, phone—"

"You're saying you don't want me to see him now." She lost interest in Hines. "Hello, Nora."

Nora nodded bleakly.

Anne took a card from her bag, handed it to Hines, took another puff and turned away. Her gaze lit on Charlie. "Hello, Charlie."

"Anne, I'm so sorry." He shoved his hands into his pockets awkwardly. What the hell did you say? He felt as awkward as a nine-year-old, trying to tell Aunt Babs he'd lost her fifty dollars.

"Thanks," she said brusquely.

Hines looked at the card she'd given him and nodded. "Thanks." He turned back to Nora.

Anne marched over to Charlie. "What happened?"

He avoided her savvy dark eyes. "Well, we were going to have lunch with him at Plato's."

She nodded. "Yes, Cindy told me."

"Well—" He felt ridiculously relieved, as though she might have challenged his statement. Heartened, he went on, "The rest of us had already arrived at Plato's."

"Who's the rest of you?"

"I arrived with Maggie, and—"

"Maggie?"

"Me," said Maggie. Anne turned to look her over. "I'm Maggie Ryan. Statistician for Charlie's project. I just met your husband this morning, Professor Chandler. I'm so sorry—"

"Thank you." Anne brushed off her sympathy with a wave of her cigarette and inspected Maggie clinically. "You're not in the Education Department."

"No. I'm just here for the summer this time."

A cloud of smelly French smoke billowed past Charlie's nose. "Were you here before?" Anne asked her with a little frown.

"Yes. Got my Ph.D. here seven years ago."

Anne nodded curtly and glanced back at Charlie. "So you two arrived at Plato's first."

"Yes. We were a couple of minutes early." He cleared his throat. "Then Bart arrived, and finally Nora."

"Tal asked Cindy too," offered Maggie, "but she couldn't come, because of another meeting she had."

"Mm." Anne was looking down the trail again.

Maggie said, "Tal said you had a meeting too."

"Canceled it," said Anne, then looked sharply at Maggie. After a moment she said, "So everyone was up there at Plato's, except Tal."

"And Cindy, and you, and the rest of the campus."

"Right." Anne dropped her cigarette stub onto the trail and ground it out with the toe of her crepe-soled walking shoe. "What happened then?"

"We were waiting for Tal," said Maggie, "and I heard Dorrie here calling for help. So I ran out of Plato's to see what I could do. She said there was a man hurt on the gorge trail."

Dorrie nodded mutely. Anne studied her a moment, then asked gently, "What did you see?"

Charlie looked apprehensively at the Campus Security men. They weren't supposed to be talking about it. But the guards had edged closer to Hines and Nora, avidly listening themselves.

"I was coming down the trail . . . ," Dorrie began, tugging nervously at her honey-brown hair.

"From College Ave.," said Maggie.

"Yes. And I saw this jacket lying there. And at first I didn't know what it was, you know? And then I saw his head. And all the blood. And I screamed, and, well, I just ran back to get help."

Anne's inquiring eyes turned to Maggie.

"I brought her into Plato's to call the ambulance and the police," Maggie said. "Charlie and the others helped her."

"Maggie ran on ahead," Charlie explained.

"I know a little CPR," said Maggie. "But when I saw him it was clear that it was too late. So I tried to keep people away until the cops came."

Anne nodded, looking down at the brown toes of her shoes. Then she raised her eyes to Maggie, and for the first time there was a catch in her voice. "He was shot?"

"Yes," said Maggie gently.

Anne looked back at her shoes.

Dorrie said in a wondering tone, "I guess I heard it. I was just starting down the trail and I thought it was a car backfiring." Her eyes were wide behind her square-framed glasses. "God, I never thought—"

"You told the detectives about the backfire?" Maggie asked.

"I don't remember what I told them. I was so confused."

"Well, that's normal. But be sure you tell them first chance you get." Maggie gave the girl's shoulders a squeeze.

Charlie noticed that his fist was hitting into his palm again. He felt so damn angry and frustrated. He wished Hines would let them go, so he could think. He thrust his fists back into his pockets and looked at the detective, who was conferring now with a gangly man in a pinstripe suit. Hines took a couple of notes, then came over to where his witnesses were gathered. "Mrs. Chandler?" he said gently. "Could you answer a few questions now?"

Anne squared her shoulders, her face a mask. A tough woman, Charlie thought. She'd always seemed a little frightening. "I'm ready," she said brusquely.

Hines led her a few steps down the path. Dorrie said quietly, "God, I never thought about him having a wife, you know?"

Maggie nodded but didn't answer. She was watching Anne intently, her lower lip caught behind her teeth. Reluctantly, Charlie followed her gaze. Hines towered over the squat little woman but she seemed to be the dominant one as she answered his murmured questions. Then, suddenly, her calm shattered. "No!" she exclaimed, her voice indignant.

"But you see, he was holding it—"

"Doesn't matter!" Anne was still agitated but as confident as ever. "It just won't work. He had no reason for suicide. None!" She was fumbling in her pockets, pulled out a cigarette. Hines lit it for her, bending over her like a lion tending a cub.

"I had to ask, Mrs. Chandler," he said. "Because he was holding the gun."

Anne shook her head stubbornly.

"Excuse me," Maggie called.

Hines looked around with a frown. "Just a minute."

"No, you see, there's a problem," Maggie insisted. "The gun was in his right hand."

Hines continued to frown, but Anne exclaimed, "There! You see?"

"See what?" Hines asked.

"Is she right? Was the gun in his right hand?"

"Yes."

"Well, Tal's left-handed."

Hines snatched out his notebook eagerly. "You're sure? Well, of course you're sure." He wrote it down. "Now, Mrs. Chandler, I'll have someone drive you home, and—"

"Look, Sergeant Hines, I want to do something," Anne said crisply. "You say he wasn't robbed. I know it's not suicide. I can't think of any reason someone would do this, but I can't just sit around fretting. I could help you check his office. That's where he spent the morning. Something may occur to me."

Hines checked the pugnacious tilt of her jaw and acquiesced. "Okay. I've got some things to finish up here, then we'll go to Van Brunt Hall and—"

"Sergeant Hines!"

The speaker was a handsome, square-faced, graying man with a mustache and sharp blue eyes. His gray uniform strained around a beer belly, but Charlie sensed power yet in those muscles. Burt Reynolds at sixty. Hines turned, but didn't seem impressed. "Captain Walensky," he acknowledged, but Charlie could hear quotation marks around the *Captain*.

Walensky scanned the group, nodded at Charlie and at Nora before returning his attention to Hines. He wasn't as tall as the black detective, but he wore his age with a solid dignity. His eyes fastened on Anne Chandler. "Hello, Mrs. Chandler," he said solemnly.

Anne gave him a curt nod.

He cleared his throat and said, "What have we got, Reggie?"

"Suspicious death, Wayne," Hines snapped back.

Walensky's Burt Reynolds eyebrows furrowed. "My man said suicide."

"Yeah, but you know how things are, Wayne. You never know how things may turn out."

"It was Professor Chandler?" Walensky said softly, his eyes sidling to Anne.

"I'm afraid so," said Hines.

Walensky muttered something under his breath, then, "I knew him. Great guy."

"Yeah." Hines's expression didn't change.

"Well, I'd better get at it." He took a step down the path.

Hines's arm shot out, hand up in a traffic-cop stop. "I'll show you."

Walensky paused. "It's on NYSU property."

Hines said softly, "And you're calling us in, right, Wayne? Even if it's your side of the line. How about we go look together?"

Walensky's frown swept over the watchers. He jerked his head toward the body. "C'mon, Reggie. We gotta cooperate."

"Right. That's what I'm saying."

"All right." Walensky looked at Anne again. "Mrs. Chandler, I'm sorry."

Anne nodded, unsmiling. The two policemen moved down the trail.

"Little bit of friction there," Maggie observed.

Charlie nodded. "Yeah. Dorrie called the Laconia police but the Campus Security people usually respond to campus problems so I suggested calling them too. Didn't know they'd all show up at once."

Anne said, "They're supposed to have an agreement now. The administration got together with the city police chief and with Walensky." Her voice was crisp, detached, scholarly. "Worked out some arrangement; I don't know the details. The campus police handle campus complaints, but they're supposed to call in the city department when it's serious."

"I remember in the sixties the city cops tried to break up an antiwar demonstration," said Maggie. "Roughed up some students and made the thing twice as bad."

"Right," said Anne. "That kind of thing was why they worked out the agreement. Basically it means student demonstrators are called before campus judiciary committees."

"Instead of getting real rap sheets. I see," said Maggie.

"But major crimes are turned over to the city police, right?" Charlie said uneasily. "Like that kid who stole the NYSU Film Club receipts?"

"Right," said Anne. "He was caught by Walensky's people but turned over to the city courts. What the hell are they doing down there?" She gestured with her reeking cigarette.

Charlie looked too. Walensky was squatting, with some effort, inspecting the muddy bank of the creek. When he straightened he looked grim.

"Footprints," Maggie informed them.

"What?" asked Charlie.

"Someone walked through the creek, came up the bank at that point, then back down into the creek."

Anne's sharp eyes were on Maggie. "You were down there?"

"I went down while Dorrie was phoning the police and ambulance, just in case I could help. I couldn't, but I did take a quick look around."

"And what did you see?" Anne asked dryly.

"The gun in his right hand. Powder burn on the right side, behind his ear. Footprints along that muddy section. Some very small ones, maybe that little girl that Bart saw. And big ones, deep tread like a man's boot. No overlap. Don't know which came first."

"A good observer," said Anne.

"Just curious. Anyway, you're right. As a suicide it looks pretty fishy."

Anne nodded vehemently. "Impossible."

Hines and Walensky had apparently agreed to a truce and were ambling back up to the group.

"Thank you all for waiting," Hines said. "Mrs. Chandler—"

"Yes?"

"We'd appreciate it if you'd identify him for the medical examiner downtown. In about an hour, if that's all right."

"I can't go with him?"

"It would be easier for us to take him. We'll send someone for you soon. Meanwhile—"

"Meanwhile," Walensky broke in firmly, "we'll take you all back to Van Brunt Hall. Take some preliminary statements for our own records while we wait for Sergeant Hines to finish up here."

Hines's face had that carved-wood look again. "Thank you, Captain Walensky. See you all soon."

Charlie trooped up the hill with the others, following Walensky and his men. His mind churned, images and worries flashing by in a rapid-sequence montage. Tal, expansive, inviting everyone to lunch. Hines's careful reconstruction of the traffic on the trails. The shadowy figure among the trees. The obvious disruption to come as two different police forces took statements and snooped through Tal's things and Tal's friends. He had so much to do, and this was bound to louse things up. Things wouldn't get back to normal until the cops had tracked down the killer. Could be weeks. And he had so damn much to do. But God, that was a selfish, callous thought. Tal came first.

Anne was trudging up the hill next to him, smoking, her face as wooden as Hines's, trying to escape grief behind an Eastwood-tough exterior, trying to distract herself.

And you, Charlie Fielding, trying to distract yourself too.

An image pushed itself to the fore: Tal pretending to be Cyrano, the ruler-sword waving, yes, in his left hand.

Something seemed to be caught in Charlie's throat.

V

Captain Walensky handed Anne into the backseat of the pale gray Campus Security car. Her mind, hunting distractions, cataloged the smooth plastic upholstery, the floor carpeting scrubbed but still stained faintly yellow by some accident or other. "There you go, Mrs. Chandler. Are you comfortable?"

"Fine," said Anne shortly. She hated to be fussed over. Disguised condescension, most of it. Men holding doors for you and then shocked when you insisted on attending the meeting instead of fetching them coffee. Better these days, or better disguised. But Wayne Walensky was old-style, *un vieux birbe.* She'd have to bear with him. And, she reminded herself, he meant well. He knew her, knew Tal, knew and loved the whole damn campus. That was worth a lot.

Charlie's new statistician slid in next to her without waiting for directions while Hines and Walensky stood talking to the student outside. Anne could hear their voices dimly, making arrangements to get the young woman's official statement. Anne felt distant, an observer only, suspended above the petty world on a jet of pure white rage. She'd have to cope later, she knew. Pull out her shredded heart and hold it up to the light. But for now the job was to find out who the hell had done this to Tal. To *her.*

Outside, Walensky was telling the student they could drop her at the library, and the girl climbed in next to the statistician. Strangers both. Just as well. Charlie and Nora and Bart would just ask what they could do for her. Fuss over her. But hell, she'd better get used to that. Everyone would fuss.

The back door slammed, then Walensky climbed into the front passenger seat next to his driver. Seemed to be the same young fellow Anne had met on the path, though it was hard to tell from the back of his neck. He needed a trim, looked almost shaggy next to the captain's neatly clipped head. But Walensky's gray short-sleeved shirt was sweat-stained and wilting, she saw as he plopped one arm along the top of the seat back. There was a scar on the back of his upper arm, a long red line dotted on both sides with stitch marks so that it looked like a ghostly zipper. And these sweating, scarred fellows were supposed to catch Tal's killer. God. She looked away, out the window.

Walensky said to the younger man, "Library first, Pete."

The car moved smoothly from the curb, passing a second Security car where Bart and Charlie were being invited to climb in. Walensky swabbed his forehead with a rumpled handkerchief, frowning at them, then glanced back at Anne. "Sorry about that Hines fellow, Mrs. Chandler," he said. "Those city cops are clumsy as elephants."

"It's all right," said Anne.

"Those guys don't understand," Walensky went on. "A campus community is different. Where young Hines comes from, downtown, well, a little head-bashing may be necessary. But up here on campus we've got a basically law-abiding community. Strong feelings about politics, sure, but even that's cooled off in the last ten years. Anyway, that's not involved in a case like this. Get a lot more information with kid gloves than bludgeons."

Anne felt far away, looking down at Walensky as though at an insect, a life-form whose little hungers and desires were pitiful compared to her own enormous need. He buzzed on, "See, Hines is a real stickler for all the rules. Doesn't realize the rules are for a whole other class of people. Now, your campus community, you don't want to force things into pigeonholes. These are bright people. You want to let them make some connections. Let them think things through. Speed things up in the long run."

"Captain," said Anne bitterly, "just catch the killer, all right?"

"Sure!" He shifted on his seat so he could see her better. "That's what I'm talking about! I'll do my best, but that Hines—still, the guy who did it is probably from downtown. Hines's territory."

"Maybe cooperating is best," said Charlie's statistician pacifically.

Walensky snorted. "Cooperate? That's a new word to Sergeant Hines. Muscle his way in, is more like it," he grumbled. "Here's the library. Pull over, Pete."

Anne's eyes had wandered to the statistician. She looked so familiar. Anne's mind snatched eagerly at the distraction: who was this woman? Charlie had said Maggie something. That seemed to fit. But fit what? Something dim in her memory. She watched her say good-bye to the student Dorrie, who was climbing out of the car. Then Maggie pulled the door closed and settled into the far corner, stretching lanky legs toward the middle of the car. She glanced at Anne. Deep blue eyes in a pleasant squarish face, a mass of feathery black curls. Anne saw that face suddenly in black and white. Newsprint. Tragedy. She blurted, "Jackie Edwards."

Maggie nodded. "You taught one of Jackie's favorite courses. French drama."

"My God. You're her roommate!"

"Yes."

"The one who caught the guy."

"I helped, yeah." Sorrow shadowed the blue eyes.

Walensky had been leaning out his window, giving some kind of instructions to the student they were leaving. Now he turned to look at Maggie. "What guy? Wait a minute—Margaret Ryan. Not the Triangle Killer?"

Maggie nodded again, her mouth grim.

"Christ," said Walensky. "Small world."

Anne remembered Jackie Edwards. A lively, pert young grad student, full of promise and enthusiasm. That beast of a man had raped and killed her. Suddenly Anne's eyes were brimming. She bumbled blindly into her bag, looking for a tissue. Then one was pressed gently into her hand. "Here," murmured Maggie.

"You all right, Mrs. Chandler?" asked Walensky uneasily from the front seat. A question so silly it was unworthy of consideration. Anne blew her nose noisily into the tissue while her mind splashed about searching for something solid so she could haul herself out of this undignified sea of tears.

Maggie, more pragmatic than the policeman, provided a second tissue and a lifeline. "You know, it might help the police if you thought about some of the things Tal was doing this week."

Walensky said, "Now, Miss Ryan, this isn't the time to trouble her with—"

"Oh, shut up, this is exactly the time!" Anne barked at him. She blew her nose again. "Only reason I'm coming along is to try to speed things up! Now, do you have a notebook?"

"Uh . . . yes, ma'am." Walensky glanced hastily at young Pete. Probably wanted to be sure the younger man understood that he was buttering up the university community rather than capitulating to an old bitch. Well, Anne didn't care what Walensky thought of her, as long as he got the information.

"All right. Tal's projects. Today is what, Thursday? Well, he was expecting to hear back from a publisher sometime this week. They'd accepted his book but it was conditional on some revisions. He'd sent them in a month ago but hadn't heard yet. He was also working on an article, finishing the statistical analyses. He was thinking about a grant proposal, but I don't think he'd actually started work. Depressing things, grant proposals. Like writing a book or monograph but it doesn't count as a publication. But as I say, he hadn't really started on that except to collect some reprints on the subject." Anne found a dry corner of her tissue and scrubbed the last vestiges of those embarrassing tears from her eyes. "That's all the campus stuff I remember. Did you get it all, Captain?"

"Yes, ma'am. Though the car doesn't help my penmanship much."

"Well, do your best," Anne said resignedly. C-student, no doubt,

Wayne Walensky. Tal deserved better. "Ask his colleagues about it too. Now, do you want me to tell you about his home projects?"

They were pulling into the Van Brunt parking lot, but Walensky said, "Yes, please."

"Okay. He had a doctor's appointment this morning, regular checkup. Doctor said he was absolutely fine. And Tal was trying to get last year's taxes straightened out. We were in France for spring break and sent in an application for late filing. But some half-wit at the IRS lost it, so Tal was busy making copies of everything he'd sent just to prove we were law-abiding citizens. Aside from all that, just the usual stuff. Getting the car washed, clipping the hedge. What everybody does."

"Fine, Mrs. Chandler," said Walensky heartily. "Anything else?"

"Got nothing to add now. I'll tell you when I think of something. Now, you'll give all that to Sergeant Hines too, right?"

"Yes," said Walensky without enthusiasm. "We'll cooperate, best we can. But be sure to call on me if he gets obnoxious, all right? Both of you."

"All right." Maggie opened her door and hopped out onto the blacktop, unfolding her long frame, stretching. Walensky shoved the notebook back into his pocket and climbed out too. Anne allowed him to hurry around to open the door for her. Men like Captain Walensky functioned best when they were being protective, and she needed him at his best.

Inside the building, Cindy looked up in surprise to see Walensky. When she heard his news, she clapped a hand to her mouth. "Oh, no," she moaned. "Oh, no. Oh, no."

Anne didn't want to hear Cindy. She stalked over to the window. Parking lot view. Here came the second car, the one with Charlie and Bart and Nora. Anne pulled out a cigarette and lit it. But it tasted flat, tired. *Ereintée,* fagged out. A pun in English. Tal would've liked it. She turned back to the room.

Bernie Reinalter had appeared at his office door and was staring at Walensky with barely disguised shock. The department chairman was a tall, pale man with fading blond hair. Silver hairs among the gold. His family was Swiss, he'd told Tal once. Tal, who had done a stint as chairman himself, grumbled about Bernie's insistence on meeting deadlines and budget restraints. But under Bernie the department had done well enough, hiring some good people, winning expanded support for the preschool lab facilities. We could do a lot worse, was Tal's judicious overall assessment.

Walensky was taking notes, talking to Cindy. "Now, what time was this?"

"It was late for Tal. Nine-thirty, maybe. He's usually in an hour earlier."

"And what did he say?"

"The usual hello, how are things, very jolly—God, I can't believe this!" Cindy was dabbing at her mascaraed eyes.

"Did he mention any plans?"

Bernie Reinalter had noticed Anne. The chairman strode toward her decisively but paused before he reached her, with an awkward, helpless movement of his well-kept hand. "Anne, I'm sorry. If there's anything I can do—"

She nodded curtly. "Thanks, Bernie. I'll let you know."

"Please do." His hand made another ineffectual gesture. This was something efficiency and planning couldn't fix. He looked back at Walensky. Anne ground out the tasteless cigarette on the inside of the metal wastebasket.

"He was going to return some books to the library after he checked his mail," Cindy was explaining. "Had a bag full of them. He dropped them on the chair there and went into the mail room. I called after him that the mail hadn't come yet today, but he reminded me that he still had to pick up yesterday's. See, he'd left at lunchtime yesterday. And today he had to go to the IRS office, he said."

Walensky nodded, writing it down. "And then what?"

Cindy glanced at the door. Anne saw that Nora and Bart and Charlie were coming in, all looking tense and drawn. Funereal faces: Nora's smooth face tight with worry, Charlie anxious behind his glasses like his favorite Woody Allen, Bart enormous and sloppily mournful. Cindy nodded a greeting at them and answered Walensky. "And then he came out, even happier than before. Something about a publisher. That's when he invited me to lunch. I couldn't go, but just then Professor Bickford stepped into the office and Tal started talking to him."

Bart Bickford nodded. "That's right. We walked across the hall to my office." One beefy hand was fidgeting with the button of his jacket. Twice as big, and looked twice as haggard as anyone else. Suddenly Anne understood his problem. Or a big hunk of it, at least. She crossed the room toward him as Walensky asked, "Any special reason he went to your office?"

"I wanted some advice about a grant proposal I'm writing." His hands were in his jacket pockets now, clenching and unclenching. Anne held out her pack of Gauloises. Too quickly, his fingers sprang from his pockets, twitched out a cigarette, snatched the lighter from her other hand. "Uh . . . thanks," he said when it was kindled. Didn't seem to taste flat to him.

"Did he mention anything that he was worried about?" Walensky asked.

"No," said Bart, exhaling smoke slowly and ending with a little cough. "On the contrary, he was very upbeat. Patted me on the back, told me I'd get my grant if their committee had half a brain. Then he wanted to know if I'd seen Charlie, and I said yes, maybe twenty minutes before. He'd been rushing toward his office, said he was in a hurry."

"Yes, I was late to meet Dr. Ryan," said Charlie.

"So Tal said not to forget, noon at Plato's, and zipped off. I figured he was going to talk to Charlie."

"Now, about what time was this?" Walensky asked.

Bart frowned, but Anne noticed that his hands were moving more steadily now. "I can only guess. I'd say nine-forty."

Walensky's light eyes moved to Charlie. "And did he find you, Professor Fielding?"

Anne inspected Charlie. A shy young fellow, no taller than Tal, earnest and eager to please. He looked sorrowful too, like Bart, but without suffering the added edge of nicotine withdrawal. Charlie said, "Yes, he came into the office while Dr. Ryan and I were discussing my research. I introduced them. We talked for a minute, he invited us to lunch, then off he went. To the library, he said."

"Did he give any indication of his mood?"

"Like everyone says, he seemed very happy. The lunch was to be a celebration, he said."

Walensky peered at Maggie Ryan. "Do you agree, Miss Ryan?"

"Oh, yes, he was full of enthusiasm." Maggie had taken Anne's place by the window. The lights played in her black hair, cool blue fluorescent glints from the room, and a bright warm edging of sunlight. "I don't know what he's like normally, but today he seemed very bubbly. He was jumping onto chairs, quoting Cyrano, bragging about how much better his wife could do it."

Anne's heart squeezed tight as a fist. What a ham Tal was. She could see him, swishing his imaginary sword, telling them she could do Cyrano better. She forced the image away and concentrated fiercely on Walensky's questions.

"And what time was this?"

"Maybe a quarter to ten," said Maggie.

"He was going to the library?"

"He said so. But when did he talk to Nora?" Maggie asked.

"Must have been about then," Nora said.

Walensky was dutifully taking it all down. Probably none of it would help, Anne thought. They should be out questioning people about the trails, about strangers, about—But Hines was doing all that, she supposed. And of course it was true that they ought to make sure it wasn't somehow connected with one of Tal's projects, make sure it really was a mugger.

Nora added, "He brought me a cup of coffee."

"That's right!" Cindy exclaimed. "He popped back into the office for a cup of coffee."

"Coffee?" Walensky asked, looking around.

"Right by the mail room door." Bernie Reinalter, eager to be of help, indicated the big aluminum urn on a table by the door. Jars of instant coffee, whitener, sugar, and tea bags were arrayed next to the urn, and stacks of foam plastic cups.

Cindy said, "He asked me if I wanted any and I said I'd just had a cup. Well, he said, he'd save me some champagne instead. And off he went again."

"Did he usually bring you coffee?" Walensky asked Nora.

"It was a sort of joke," Nora replied. She spoke flatly, but a tiny flutter at the corner of her eyelid betrayed her tension. "I'd complained once after a departmental meeting that women made up forty percent of the department but they were asked to get the coffee eighty percent of the time. Tal overheard and told me Anne had made almost the same observation about her department, so he was going to bring me coffee eighty percent of the time. Reparations, he called it."

"I see." Walensky wrote it down.

"He spilled it," Nora blurted.

"How do you mean?"

"Well, I opened the door for him. He came in past me and put it down on my desk, and was explaining something—the lunch at Plato's, I guess. And he made a big gesture and knocked the cup over. He rushed around and mopped up the desk and even the drawers. He used the Kleenex I keep on the windowsill. Very thorough. He said he'd get me another cup, but I said not to bother. He promised solemnly to make it up to me at lunch. Then he picked up his bookbag and rushed out."

"Was he sad?"

"No, no. I mean—he was sorry for spilling the coffee, but he was still cheery. Exclaiming about how lucky he'd been not to knock it on the stack of student papers I had sitting on the desk. Joking about what a clumsy old codger he was, about how he'd mop up every drop. It was a very upbeat kind of apology, if you see what I mean."

"Did he tell you what he was celebrating?"

"No, just that—" She stopped abruptly and stepped back.

Anne had to step back too as Sergeant Hines strode into the room, followed closely by Officer Porter. The officer was carrying a large cardboard box and several sealed plastic bags. Evidence bags, Anne realized with a tightening of her stomach. She couldn't see the contents clearly, even though she was near as he rested his burdens on Cindy's desk. Little white plugs—cigarette butts. A little spiral-bound notebook. Something else—was it a pipe?

Hines said, "Ladies and gentlemen, I'd appreciate it if you could all go to your offices. There are some items here I'd like you to try to identify, and I'd rather have each person react individually."

Maggie said, "I'm told my office isn't ready yet. And Professor Chandler's is in the French department across campus."

Hines said, "I'll be talking to Mrs. Chandler at home later. Is there an office Ms. Ryan can use?" Automatically, he looked at the right authority: Cindy, not Bernie Reinalter.

She said, "Dr. Ryan will be using the corner office in Professor Fielding's wing. Room 104. It's empty, it's just that the floor hasn't been waxed. Might as well use it."

"Fine," Hines agreed. "We'll start with Ms. Ryan, then."

Cindy selected one of the keys in her desk drawer and handed it to Maggie, making a note on a card. Anne was impressed that she had followed procedures even under this pressure. The ideal secretary for Bernie.

Cindy was eyeing Porter's plastic-wrapped items on her desk, and Anne saw her lips curve a little as Porter picked them up carefully. Had she recognized something? Anne saw her gazing thoughtfully at the people by the hall door.

"Well, Charlie," Cindy inquired mildly, "did you drop something?"

VI

Damn Cindy!

An adrenaline sweat of rage, fear, and mystification flooded Charlie. In the murky swill of his memory childish horrors stirred: Dad's rigid accusing shoulders, the fly on Aunt Babs's dead staring face, Lorraine naked, holding a white sock, eyes boring into him like Cindy's now. A Hitchcock moment, shocking ancient fears from sleep, even though he'd half expected it. He'd glimpsed the little spiral-bound memo book too, with its black-and-white Chaplin design glimmering inside the plastic bag. Surprised, he'd reached in his jacket for his own memo book. Not there. He'd slithered his fingers through his pockets in desperate hope. But it was gone. No one else had a book like that, not around here. But how could his book be in an evidence bag? And then came Cindy with her insinuations, in front of the cops, Tal's formidable wife, the department chairman! What the hell was going on?

Well, stay cool when attacked, Coach Wilhelm used to say. No need to feel defensive anyway. The explanation, whatever it turned out to be, couldn't hurt him. He tried to keep his voice light as he said, "Maybe I did lose something. You've probably misplaced things yourself, Cindy, sometimes."

The skin tensed around her pale blue eyes, but the little smile on her face didn't change. He noticed that Maggie was studying both of them with unconcealed interest.

More to the point, so were Hines and Walensky.

Hines said, "There's something here of yours, Mr. Fielding?"

"Now, Reggie," said Walensky, "let's go slow. He can't tell you the answer to that until he sees the items, now, can he?"

"That's right, Wayne," said Hines, his jaw tight. "So let's go let him have a look. Mrs. Chandler, I'll see you right after. We'll look at your husband's office together. Professor Fielding, what's your office number?"

"103," said Charlie. "Around the corner, down the hall."

"Fine. Porter, see these other people to their offices and get McConough to stay with Mrs. Chandler for a few minutes. Then bring the stuff to 103. Everybody else can go to their own offices and I'll be along soon. Please stay in the building."

Charlie glanced at Walensky. His mouth was tight, his bushy brows contracted. "I'll be glad to interview them, Reggie. I know Peterson, Fielding, Bickford, Reinalter . . ." he said in a surprisingly mild voice.

"Thank you, Wayne. Go right ahead. But I'll take Professor Fielding right now." Sergeant Hines offered Walensky a hint of a smile, and Charlie's tiny remaining hope faltered. Maggie had been right: the two policemen were engaged in combat, and losing that damn memo book had dropped him right in the middle. Well, nothing to do but cooperate. Find out the truth. For his own sake now, as well as Tal's.

Hines accompanied him down the hall and around the corner to his office. Charlie, walking on unsteady legs, wished Walensky had come along. He knew Walensky, and maybe he wouldn't have felt quite so friendless and threatened if the paunchy captain had been along. On the other hand, the last thing Charlie wanted was to be the football in this game the two cops were playing. Well, help them both. Find out the truth. He unlocked his door.

Hines scrutinized the office professionally as he followed Charlie in. Charlie felt revealed, almost violated, as the dark gaze hit each item, riffling through his life. The bookshelves, crammed with videotapes instead of books. The wood coatrack with his shabby plastic emergency raincoat and an old black umbrella. The file cabinet bearing the videotape machine, the television, the sixteen-millimeter projector. The screen rolled up in the corner. The vintage Wizard of Oz poster, half obscured by a stack of books that had been crowded out by the videotapes. He worked so hard to keep things orderly, but under Hines's cool gaze it seemed a sty. On his desk, reference books. A mug containing pencils and his Donald Duck pen, a silly gift from Deanna. Student schedules. The grant proposal he'd been discussing with Maggie that morning was spread out in the center of the desk. Near the edge lay the ruler that Tal had been waving only a few hours ago. It seemed like years.

Porter appeared and placed his packages on the oak chair Tal had used as a soapbox, then closed the door and leaned against the jamb. Hines said, "Let's sit down for a minute, Professor Fielding." He waved a hand at Charlie's desk chair, and Charlie sat down uneasily while Hines sank into the chair that faced the TV screen. He said, "You do educational TV?"

"No." Charlie had to clear his throat. "It's reading research. How people scan a page of print most efficiently. The letters are on the TV screen, and we measure their eye movements while they read."

"Pretty complicated. But kids probably like the TV."

"Maybe. We aren't working with kids yet."

"I thought this was an education department, like how to teach school."

"Sure. But first we have to find out how adults do it. Then we can try to reconstruct how it's learned. And then, finally, we can design a way to help kids who are having trouble learning.''

Hines nodded. "So the idea is to find the facts about how it's done, before telling kids what you think they're doing wrong?''

"That's right.''

"Good idea. Facts before theories. Same thing we tell rookie cops. Porter, let's see that book.''

Porter selected one of the bags and placed it on the desk.

Charlie nodded and pushed his glasses up on his nose. "It's mine," he said unhappily.

"You're sure?" Hines asked.

"As sure as I can be when it's in a plastic bag. You see his ear?" He pointed at the Chaplin cartoon on the cover. "That little tear's been there for months. Of course, I'll have to look inside to be a hundred percent sure, but still—''

"Okay. Thank you. Now, when did you see it last?''

"Let me think. This morning, before I left home. I checked the time I was supposed to meet Dr. Ryan. Then I put it in my outside jacket pocket.''

"Right or left?''

"Right.''

"And you haven't looked at it since?''

"No, there was no reason to. I'd saved the whole morning to talk to Dr. Ryan, and nothing else came up that I had to note down.''

"Not the lunch appointment?''

"I could remember that without writing it down." Charlie's glasses had migrated down his nose again. He pushed them into place, wishing Hines would show some reaction, some emotion, any emotion, instead of regarding him with that impassive gaze. Porter too was unmoving, leaning relaxed but attentive against the doorjamb.

"Well, now, Professor Fielding, we found that book on the lower trail. Can you tell us how it got there?''

Charlie's mouth was bone-dry. "I don't know. All I can think is that it fell out of my pocket.''

"You were on the lower trail?''

"No. Well, yes, when we all went to see . . . to see Tal. I told you before.''

"Yes, we have to keep going over things. Now we want to know exactly what happened.''

"Well, Maggie—Dr. Ryan—ran out of Plato's. Then in a minute she came back in with the student, um . . .''

"Doris Keating.''

"Yes. Dr. Ryan said there had been an accident and to help Dorrie call the police, and she ran out again. So we got Dorrie to the phone, and she called you people and you told her to wait at Plato's. But Bart thought we might be able to help, so he and I left Nora Peterson with Dorrie, and we ran down to the lower trail."

"Which way? Across College Avenue from Plato's?"

"That's right. The steps that come up next to the College Avenue bridge. We ran down those steps and followed the trail down toward the creek. We crossed that little stone footbridge and went on—"

"You turned right or left after you crossed the stone bridge?"

"We turned right. We could see Maggie from the little bridge."

"Okay. So you're on the lower trail, right next to the creek now."

"Yes. We ran along a little ways. We could see there was . . . something on the trail." Charlie licked his parched lips. "But Maggie was waving at us, yelling to us to stop. So we did. She said to stay where we were and keep anyone from coming down the trail until the police arrived. We asked her what happened and she said Tal had been killed. I couldn't believe it!" The shattering horror of her words, his own instant defense against them: *No, not true, not possible.* Charlie shuddered.

"That's a natural reaction, Professor Fielding." But there was no special glimmer of sympathy from either policeman. "Now, we'll get back to Dr. Ryan in a minute. Right now I want you to focus on where you were on the lower trail when you stopped."

"I was . . . well, it's hard to remember. Maybe I could show you."

"Okay. Just for now, give me a rough idea if you can. Try to visualize yourself standing there, where Dr. Ryan told you to stop."

"Okay."

"Now, there are three bridges over the gorge in that area, three different heights. The lowest one is the little stone bridge you crossed."

"Yes."

"Next one up, to the north of the little stone bridge, is the metal footbridge you cross if you use the upper trail."

"Yes. That's the one I crossed on the way to Plato's."

"The highest one is the vehicular bridge, the College Avenue bridge. That's south of both the other bridges. That's where the steps go down to the lower trail."

"Yes."

"Now, you're standing there looking at Dr. Ryan, right where she told you to stop. The stone footbridge is behind you."

"Yes, and the College Ave. bridge is even farther behind me. You want to know if we'd passed under the metal bridge of the upper trail."

"Just to get a rough idea of where you were standing."

Charlie squeezed his eyes closed. It came back to him, the sense of horror, the rippling water nearby, Bart's heavy breathing right behind him. He said, "Well, I can't be certain, but I think the metal bridge was almost overhead. A little bit ahead of us, maybe. Check with Bart. Professor Bickford. He might remember."

"We will." A noncommittal nod of the dark head. Charlie, hungry for a reaction, couldn't tell if the detectives believed him or not. Porter, too, was listening without a flicker of emotion, as though this were some goddamn poker game. Where the hell had they found his memo book? Hines said, "So you didn't pass under the metal footbridge?"

"I don't think so. But—well, you know, I did cross over it before, when we were on the way to Plato's." Charlie leaned forward, forearms on his desk, eager to explain the idea that had just come to him. "And you know, we stopped a moment to look down at the lower trail. When we saw the man hiding down there. So it could be."

"You're suggesting it may have fallen from the upper trail at that time? Do you remember any moment when it might have happened?"

"Well, no, not really. But I don't remember any other time I dropped it, either. Damn it, if we're going to go by my memory, that book is still in my pocket!"

"I understand, Professor Fielding." Hines's voice had slowed, but there was nothing lazy about the sharp eyes that were measuring Charlie's discomfort. "It's difficult to remember all these details, I know. But we have to try. Now, back to Dr. Ryan. You and Professor Bickford were standing on the trail where she told you to. Now, where was she?"

"Next to—to the body."

"Which side? Left, right? Near side, far side?"

"Uh, far side. And to the left, away from the creek."

"You said she was waving her arms."

"Yes, she had on that light blue shirt, waving both arms, and yelling for us to stop. After she told us to keep people away she said she was going a few steps farther along the trail to head off anyone coming from the campus."

"So she went on, farther away?"

"Yes."

"How far?"

"Well, we could still see her so it was probably just this side of the bend. You know, where it angles up again."

"Yes. And you and Professor Bickford were where?"

"Where we were stopped. Not quite under the metal footbridge."

"Did either of you move away from there?"

"Well, Bart was pretty nervous. Guess we both were. He said we should go check the other branch of the lower trail, beyond the little stone bridge, to see if anyone was running off that way. But Maggie was right that we should keep people away until the police came. So finally we decided he should stand on the stone footbridge to stop anyone coming down from College Ave., and I'd look farther along the trail."

"I see." Hines glanced at Porter, then back at Charlie. "He stood on the bridge, and you went along the trail by the creek, away from the body?"

"That's right."

"How far did you go?"

"Not far."

"You went under the high bridge? The College Ave. bridge?"

"Oh, yes. A few yards past it." Palms damp, heart pounding like the soundtrack of a western, praying that the killer would not be there. "Then I heard sirens and when I looked across the creek I could see police coming down the trail from College Ave. So I went back to where Bart was, and we talked to them."

"Right. You'd seen no one when you went to investigate the trail?"

"No. But of course it wouldn't be hard for someone to hide, really, because of all the bushes and the bends in the trail."

"Okay. So at the time of the arrival of the first officers at the stone footbridge, you're on the left branch of the trail. Ms. Ryan has gone along the right branch all the way past the body and is waiting on the trail beyond it, and Professor Bickford is standing on the bridge."

"Yes, that's right." It was vivid yet—the bubbly water, Bart's lumpy hulk on the bridge. Charlie added, "Also, while you people were talking to us I looked over at her and saw a Campus Security guy talking to Maggie."

"So he'd come down from the campus side. Okay, thank you, I've got the picture." Hines switched topics abruptly. "Now, I'd like you to look at some things here, see if you recognize them."

Charlie licked his lips again and tried to concentrate on the objects in the evidence bags that Hines was showing him. A red baseball cap. A muddy pipe. A plastic ball-point pen. A card-sized scrap of paper with a fragment of a bibliography printed on it. A pair of big black rubber overshoes in the box.

"Does anything look familiar?" Hines prompted.

"Well . . . Bart has a pipe of that general type, but lighter colored, as I remember. And the little card looks like what you find in the library for scrap paper to jot down call numbers. They cut up excess copies of old handouts and leave them in little boxes for people to use when they're looking up books."

"I see. The boots don't look familiar?"

"Not really. I've seen that kind before, it's common enough. They're a pretty large size, aren't they?"

"Size twelve."

"I'm a size nine."

"Thank you." Hines pulled his own large oxfords under him and stood up. Porter, at the door, shifted to attention too. "We'll be back to you soon, Professor Fielding. I'd sure appreciate it if you could remember exactly when you misplaced your memo book."

Charlie shook his head. "I've told you all I can remember."

"Well, let me know if anything occurs to you. We'll have to hold onto it for the time being, I'm afraid. See you soon, Professor Fielding."

Charlie nodded weakly and watched Hines and Porter out the door.

What the hell should he do now? Tal shot: unbelievable. His own memo book on the lower trail. How had it gotten there? And where was it? He'd been unable to tell from Hines's impassive expression whether his movements down the trail with Bart could account for where it had been found. He closed his eyes and tried to reconstruct those terrible moments. Tracking shot: Charlie Fielding hurrying down the steps next to the College Avenue bridge. Down into the leafy gorge, Bart crashing along close behind. The damp earth packed behind railroad-tie steps, the jar of each footstep—that could have bounced his book from his pocket! Would Hines have worried about something found so far away? Maybe. But Charlie had gone much closer to Tal. Could it have fallen out closer? Think! On down the trail, still very steep but sloped now, no actual steps. Across the little stone footbridge, three feet wide, gray stones assembled in a gentle arch over the creek, WPA project, the aging mortar cracked in places. Maggie's distant figure off to the right, sky-blue sleeves flapping like semaphores. But wait a minute. Coming off the footbridge, two stone steps down to the trail. Could the book have jounced from his jacket then? Would Hines be interested in something found by the footbridge? Maybe.

Tracking on: moving toward Maggie, noting the lump of gray tweed at her feet with no conscious understanding of what it was, but looking away hastily even before she spoke, some inner director crying, *Cut! No more, no more!*

Don't think about that. Stick to the memo book.

If it had fallen from his pocket earlier, while he was looking down at the lower trail from the upper footbridge, it might have landed closer. Pushed by the breeze, maybe, or ricocheting off a branch. But he couldn't remember any time that—

"Hi," said Maggie. She glided into the office and dropped a flat white box onto his desk. A puff of air from its landing lifted the pages of his grant proposal. "I bribed what's-his-name, your assistant—Gary, right?— to go get us a pizza. Want some?"

"God, I hadn't thought about eating." But the aroma of onions and sausage set his recently parched mouth to watering.

"Yeah, I'd forgotten too," she said soberly. "But my ridiculous stomach never quits. It told me a couple of dolmas were not enough for lunch no matter what. Go ahead, have some." She perched on the edge of the chair Hines had used.

"Thanks." Charlie grabbed a napkin and took a piece, careful of the warm cheese dripping from the sides. "Maggie, can you think of any time my memo book might have fallen from my pocket onto the lower trail? Maybe when we were standing on the bridge looking down at that guy?"

"So that Chaplin-design memo book was yours, huh?" She frowned, hooked an ankle under the rung of the second chair, and pulled it closer to prop her feet on it. "I don't remember you dropping anything. I was looking down at the guy in the bushes, but I think I would have noticed if you made a sudden movement big enough to dislodge something from your pocket."

"Yeah," Charlie agreed gloomily. "I can't remember anything like that happening either. But how in the world did it get down there?"

"Mm." She was chewing vigorously, her cheeks lumpy, her eyes clouded with thought. "Well, I think of two things," she said indistinctly. "First, don't worry about Hines. After all, we were together almost the whole time."

"That's right." But Charlie was not completely soothed. Hines hadn't reacted as though he believed he had an alibi. But then Hines hadn't reacted at all. He wasn't stupid, though; he'd know Charlie hadn't been down there. Maybe he was merely curious, just as Charlie was, about how it got to the lower trail.

"But no one knew beforehand that I'd be with you, did they?" Maggie mused. "I'd told Tal I had to have lunch with the children. Hell, even I didn't know I was going with you until the last minute when Liz offered to take them to McDonald's."

"Yes, but the important thing is that the police know I was with you."

She paused, a fragment of pizza still held in her hand, studying him intently. "Charlie, could someone be trying to frame you?"

"Frame me? My God, no!" But even as he spoke his stomach clenched in cold fear. She was right. Someone must have stolen his book. That's how it got there. But who the hell hated him that much? Hated Tal that much? It wasn't possible. He said wanly, "So you think I didn't drop it at the bridge."

"Maybe, maybe not. I'm just a statistician, looking at another hypothesis that we haven't yet disproven. I'm thinking that you were racing through the halls when I first saw you this morning. Could the book have fallen out then?"

Charlie nodded unhappily. "Sure. Or outside in the parking lot, or running up the stairs."

"Did you have it in the same pocket as your keys?"

"Yeah. Right outside pocket." He patted his jacket.

"I don't remember anything falling out when you pulled out your keys. But the kids were there and we were both distracted." She swooped another wedge of pizza from the box, stringy cheese trailing behind it.

She spun the cheese spaghetti style onto her forefinger, lifted it high, and ate it like Chaplin savoring his boiled shoelace. "But," she mumbled, mouth full again, "we've got a real possibility that someone got hold of your book and used it as a backup plan."

"Backup to what?"

"Okay. Someone decides to kill Tal. Doesn't want to get caught. Drops your memo book there so the cops will think it was you."

"Yeah, I understand."

"But the guy has a high opinion of you. Knows if you did such a thing you'd cover your tracks. So he figures you would stage a suicide to throw the police off. Okay so far?"

"Uh . . . yes. So the killer puts the gun in Tal's hand. And that's supposed to implicate me too!"

"Right. The killer probably knew Tal was a cheery man and that his friends couldn't accept suicide without insisting on further investigation. And further investigation would turn up your memo book."

"But why me?"

Maggie swallowed the last bite of pizza, peeked regretfully into the empty box, and lounged back into her chair again. "I don't know why. Maybe nothing more than opportunity. There was your book on the floor, just when he needed it. And you'd be walking across the bridge alone, or so he thought. Tell me, was it generally known that Tal was left-handed?"

"I can only speak for myself. I knew, yes, but I didn't think about it much. You don't spend a lot of time watching other people write."

"Yeah. It certainly wouldn't be at the top of your mind if you'd just shot someone and were arranging the scene to look like suicide."

"So you think Tal's killer waited in the bushes. Tal came along, he ran out and shot him, stuck the gun into his hand, and ran off again. And he dropped my book to make it look as though I'd tried to stage it all. But why not keep the gun and hide it in my stuff somewhere?"

"Maybe there wasn't time to hide it. Maybe he had to establish an alibi. So it was easier to leave it, make it look as though you'd staged a suicide. Now, you see, we've learned a lot about this killer."

"Well, we know he picked up my book somewhere."

"Not any old somewhere. Probably here, because he knew about Tal's lunch. Knew Tal would be on the gorge trail on the way to Plato's. Thought you'd be using the trail too, but alone. So you *know* this person, Charlie."

"Me? But . . . well, yes, you're right." Charlie took off his glasses and rubbed his nose. "Somebody I know killed Tal. God, I don't believe it!"

"Killed Tal. And tried to frame you with something you dropped right around here this morning. So, next question: Who was around this morning who might want to kill Tal?"

"God." Charlie put on his glasses again and leaned back in his chair. "I was going to try to think about that. But then Hines started asking about the memo book and, I don't know, I started feeling defensive."

"I know what you mean," said Maggie. "It's happened to me, even worse than this time. Of course I was already upset because someone had died, and the cops came in like big computers, processing what I told them as though it might not be true, checking my actions as though I might have done it. I mean, that's their job, they don't have any choice, but it's still scary as hell."

"Yeah." Charlie found her words comforting. It was their job, after all. They had to check everyone. But he'd felt so damn defensive. He noticed he was holding his Donald Duck pen. He replaced it in the holder and said, "But who the hell . . . well, I guess if a person is willing to kill someone they won't hesitate to frame someone else."

"Right. It's still Tal at the center of this. Can you tell me anything about his work? He was retired, right? That's what emeritus means."

"Yes, officially. Here, a professor emeritus doesn't have to do a thing if he doesn't want to. But if he does want to stay around, he can have office space, hold seminars, and so forth. Most of them wind down slowly, do a little research, come in to catch up on the news a couple of times a week. Tal was much more involved than that. In every day, doing research, even teaching a seminar once a year. Loved students, and they loved him."

"So his retirement was on paper only."

"Right. Of course his chair was awarded again, to Kenton, the personality development man. And Tal didn't have to serve on university committees anymore."

"He probably didn't miss those."

"You said it!"

"Who were his friends in the department? Who did he talk to?"

"God, everybody! Well, you met him. He made the rounds of everyone in the department who was on campus, just about every day. From Reinalter down to the lowliest student. And he'd made a lot of friends in other departments. Often had lunch at the faculty club across campus."

"And was he always as curious as this morning?"

"Usually. He was always asking questions, skimming grant proposals and papers, gossiping."

"About things he'd learned from other people?"

"Yeah, the usual things. Where Nora was going on vacation, how Bart had the flu, what kind of car Reinalter was thinking of buying—that kind of stuff. But he and I talked about reading research, mostly."

"So he didn't seem to know anyone's dark secrets?"

"Never passed any on to me. But, uh, are you suggesting someone told him something and then . . . but what could possibly be that dangerous?" He pushed his glasses up his nose. "And if it was, why would anyone tell Tal?"

"And what would Tal do with the information? Would he—oh, hello, Captain Walensky." Maggie's head turned toward the door. "Have you come to tell us not to talk about this case?"

"Not at all, Miss Ryan." Walensky, baggy-eyed and drooping, seemed older than when he'd first appeared just an hour ago. "Just wanted to apologize for the city police. Hope they haven't been hassling you too much."

Charlie said, "They've been asking about my damn memo book when they know I was with Maggie and couldn't have done it."

"Christ," Walensky growled. "Just filling up their files. I might be able to stop them if I could prove it was suicide, but they've got this idea it might be homicide and so my hands are tied."

"Well," said Maggie, "Charlie's memo book was found at the scene of the crime. They have to ask. As soon as they find out who did it they'll leave us alone."

"*If* they find out," Walensky corrected her. "Now, you'll tell me if you think of anything that might throw light on this. Anything about his enemies, or about worries that might lead to suicide?"

"In fact," said Maggie, "we were just wondering if someone in this department might have something to hide. Professor Chandler was so curious and sociable, he might have learned something that someone didn't want known."

Walensky's brows bunched skeptically. "This is a campus, Miss Ryan, not a hangout for criminals. I say that, and my job shows me the worst of it."

"That's true, I'm sure. You probably spend most of your time on parking violations instead of grand larceny."

"Yes. And if it turns out not to be suicide, damn it, we should be hunting down in Sergeant Hines's town, not up here on the hill."

Charlie thought of his memo book, of someone deliberately leaving it to point blame at him. Maggie's idea made a lot more sense than Walensky's. Whoever dropped his book in the gorge was someone from this department.

Unless it really had fallen from his pocket somehow . . .

Maggie was standing up, folding the pizza box, cramming it into Charlie's wastebasket. "Well, I'm going back to my desk before they want to question me again," she said. "I'll be next door in 104, Captain Walensky."

"Okay, fine," he nodded.

"But we should all probably be thinking about the possibility that someone from this department had a reason to kill Professor Chandler," she added gently. "Because in my experience, professors can be just as naughty as any other group of people. They just use bigger words to explain it."

She bobbed her head politely to Walensky as she went out.

VII

Anne stood at the window of her living room, gazing at the back lawn, bright green streaked with long shadows in the late sun. Tal had mowed it a few days ago and it looked neat enough, although it was already spangled with a few yellow dandelions. *Dent de lion,* lion's tooth, from their jagged leaves. But they were not lionlike, not regal. They were sneaky little weeds with long strong roots. No matter how often you decapitated them some sprang back, eager as students in September.

"So this is a pretty generous policy," observed Sergeant Hines from the sofa. Anne glanced over her shoulder at him. His long legs were angled wide to fit behind the coffee table, knees far apart as he leaned forward to inspect the papers he had fanned out before him. Porter, standing at the end of the table, gazed down at the papers too.

"TIAA-CREF is supposed to be a good program," said Anne.

"So would you say you'll be pretty well set now?"

Well set! If she weren't so tired she'd be angry. She said, "Sergeant Hines, I was already pretty well set, as you put it. I'm covered by exactly the same program as Tal when I retire. The house has been in my name for several years. I've got a good job, with tenure. Whatever comes to me now is not going to make a hell of a lot of difference."

"What are your plans for the money?"

"No plans." She looked back out the window. Some prewar designer's idea of Tudor. Pseudor-Tudor, Tal called it. Dark oak woodwork around the diamond panes framed the late-afternoon lawn, the evergreens at the back property line, the metal swing set left over from when Paul and Rocky were small. "Probably save it for my children," she told Hines. "I haven't thought much about it."

"Yes, of course, Mrs. Chandler." She heard him rustle the papers behind her. Out on the lawn, a flock of starlings landed and marched across the grass, glossy black in the sun, searching for grubs or whatever unpleasant thing it was that appealed to starlings.

When Hines spoke right at her elbow, she jumped. "Nice yard. Did your husband take care of it?"

"Most of the time. I'd do it if he was busy or feeling sick. And of course if there was a major project like planting a tree, then we'd get someone with the right equipment to come in." She looked sideways at Hines. He was inspecting the yard with his flat intelligent eyes, his chocolate skin picking up a sheen from the reflected sunlight. "Not a very complicated yard," she added. "Mow the lawn every week or two and hack down the bushiest bushes a couple of times a year. We never had time for flowers."

"Vegetables?"

"No. We go to the farmers' market."

"Still, it's fun to do it yourself. Nothing like a tomato still warm from the garden." Hines turned back into the room. "Well, are we done?" he asked Porter.

"For now."

"Mrs. Chandler, I appreciate your help very much. We may have to come back to you if new questions develop."

"Please do. I want to help," said Anne. Not that she thought they'd find anything now. If they were asking her about insurance it showed how far they were from a solution. And she hadn't heard for hours from Walensky. Maybe he was following up an idea somewhere. He knew more about the campus, after all. But she suspected he was off somewhere tut-tutting. She led the way to the other end of the living room and into the little hall. "Do you have everything?"

"Yes, we're all packed up. Will you be all right, now, Mrs. Chandler?"

"I can call Laura Brand next door if I need anything." Laura had already been over twice, first to ask what she could do and to invite Anne to dinner. Anne had refused. But soon Laura had come back with a casserole from her own freezer.

"Good," said Hines. "Be sure to do that. And call me if you remember anything at all that you haven't told me."

"I will. Thank you, Sergeant Hines."

She closed the dark oak door behind him and leaned her forehead against the varnished wood, her hand still on the knob. God, the house seemed empty. She was exhausted and at the same time numb, distant, as though it were someone else's eyes that felt sandy, someone else's legs about to buckle, someone else's grief trying to storm its way in.

Maybe Laura Brand was right, maybe she should eat something.

Or drink something.

She went into the kitchen and opened the refrigerator. There was the white burgundy she and Tal had started last night. A new label, not great but okay. She poured herself a glass and took it in to sit on the sofa, with a vague plan of organizing the facts she knew. There were the insurance papers spread all over the coffee table. Dollars and cents, the prize money for reaching this age or that age, for having a partner who reached this age or that age. She'd have to go through the motions, she supposed, file for benefits. Benefits! Cindy would help. Cindy understood all that trash, or at least could send her to the right administrator.

The house seemed so empty.

At Van Brunt Hall, she hadn't had time to talk to Cindy. When Hines had gone haring off after Charlie Fielding, both Walensky and Bernie Reinalter had descended on her, full of useless solicitude. She'd taken a cup of coffee for politeness' sake while she waited for Hines to finish with Charlie, then left it behind, undrunk, in her eagerness to join Hines when he finally reappeared. Hines and Porter had taken her to Tal's office. Not the big corner one he used to have. The new Meredith professor had moved into it. But Tal had shrugged. "So now I've only got one window for looking at the parking lot," he'd said. "That's more than enough. The important thing is bookcases."

And he did have plenty of bookcases. She'd looked them over carefully, searching for something that would jog her memory, or for something unusual, something that didn't fit with the projects he'd shared with her. But nothing stood out. It was his familiar collection of books, classic volumes on perception, language, testing, education, reading. Ranks of journals on the same topics lining the lower shelves. She went to the shelf nearest his chair. "These are new," she said, looking at the crisp bindings, the unfamiliar titles. But the names were all reasonable additions: *Eye Movements and Psychological Processes, Cognitive Development, The Psychology of Reading.*

Determined to find something that would point to his killer, she'd flipped through his notes, his mail, even the stack of mimeographed bulletins. All the usual. Announcements of lectures, of new textbooks, of conferences. Requests for letters of recommendation, for reprints of his articles, for his assistance on committees. Nothing odd. She'd shaken her head, suddenly weary. "Nothing," she said. "Exactly what I would have expected yesterday, before anything happened."

"Well, thank you for looking it over, Mrs. Chandler. Now, I'd like to speak to the others here, and see you at home later. Would about five o'clock be all right?"

It was more command than request. Anne said, "Of course."

"Do you have a car here?"

"Yes, at my building. Harper Hall."

"Did you drive your husband to campus this morning?"

"Oh, I see what you're asking. No, we took both cars today. He stopped off for that checkup first, and I drove straight to my office. His is probably in the parking lot here. Black Volks bug."

Hines wrote it down. Walensky said, "I'll be happy to drive you home, Mrs. Chandler."

She wasn't about to be carried home like some invalid, but she'd allowed Walensky to trundle her off as far as the Harper parking lot because she thought Hines would be more efficient with him out of the way. She'd driven home numbly, occasionally aware that she'd just done something reckless, such as making a turn without really checking the traffic. But there were few cars on the road at intersession and she was lucky.

Once home, she'd made some calls. She'd called her secretary, only to find that Cindy had already spread the news. She'd called Rocky in Chicago and Paul in Houston. Shocked and disbelieving, Rocky weeping, they'd promised to come. She'd called a funeral director. Then Laura Brand next door had appeared with her casserole. Finally, Hines and Porter. They'd stayed a long time, asking about Tal's life, touring the house with her and looking over his den with special care. As they checked through the rooms she realized that Hines was inserting other questions, finding out where she'd been all day, what she'd been doing. And he'd been interested in every detail of those bankbooks and insurance policies. It was his job; she shouldn't be angry. But how the hell could he be challenging her? She, who had lost . . . And besides, it was wasting time. Pointless. Frittering away hours they needed to catch a killer.

But at last they were gone.

And the house was very empty.

She knocked back the rest of her wine and went out to pour herself another glass.

Couldn't face that damn casserole, she decided as she returned the bottle to the refrigerator. But maybe some cheese. She hadn't bought any bread today, but there was a half box of crackers left over from an end-of-term party they'd given two weeks ago. Better eat them; they were already going stale. She sat at the kitchen table and made herself cut a few slices of cheese. What she ought to do was organize the facts she knew. Maybe in black and white something would leap out at her. Maybe she'd notice something that a stranger like Hines wouldn't. She got a pad of paper and placed it by her chair. Then she crossed the kitchen to turn on the radio. The cheery young voice that couldn't quite pronounce Mussorgsky was annoying, but the well-worn music, *Pictures at an Exhibition,* filled the empty air. Helped keep feelings at bay.

Okay. What were the facts? Time: just before noon. Place: lower gorge trail. People in the area at the time: could be anyone, really, unless they could prove they were elsewhere. But she knew some. Nora, Charlie, Bart, Maggie. That student, Dorrie.

She stared at the list. Now what?

Mussorgsky marched on through the exhibition.

It was a relief when the doorbell sounded. Maybe Laura Brand back with dessert.

But, astonishingly, it was Maggie Ryan. She stood on the porch, each hand holding a child's. Little girl about four, toddler not much over a year. All three with black curly hair and blue jeans.

"I'm sorry to bother you," she apologized. "But I thought it might be better to catch you now than later, when more people will be here. I just had a question."

"Come on in. Maggie, right?"

"That's right. This is Sarah, and this is Will."

"Hi." Anne grinned foolishly down at the bright-eyed youngsters. Cute. She opened the door wider. Sarah stepped in to look inquisitively around the oak-beamed hall. Little Will spied something and beelined for the living room with Maggie in hot pursuit.

"Come on, Will!" She scooped him up as he passed the coffee table and asked Anne, "Where do you want us?"

The little boy was pouting, making grasping movements toward the brass fireplace poker with his pudgy hand. Anne said, "How about the kitchen? I'm trying to finish up a box of crackers."

"Great." Maggie put Will down and herded the children after Anne into the kitchen. She sat on one of the chairs and plopped Will into her lap. All three accepted the crackers.

"Yum!" said Will, cramming one into his small mouth, the delights of brass pokers forgotten.

"Yum," Maggie agreed.

Anne sat down at the other side of the table. "Well. You had a question?"

"Yeah, about my new boss. I'm sorry to barge in like this, Professor Chandler, but—"

"Oh, God, call me Anne. You have as many degrees as I have. As many children, too."

"Anne it is. You have children?"

"A boy and a girl, like you. Paul and Rocky. A man and a woman, I should say."

"Your daughter is named Rocky?"

"Roxane."

"Oh, of course!"

"She decided at age ten that Rocky was more suitable. Tal complained, of course. He's—he was such a romantic at heart, wanted his gorgeous daughter to have a gorgeous name. But she played first base for the Laconia Lions and he had to agree that Rocky was a better name for striking fear into the hearts of the opponents."

"A good dad." Maggie's smile was warm. "Will Paul and Rocky be joining you soon?"

"Yes. Rocky should be here by Saturday night. Paul thinks he can get here Sunday."

"Good."

"Yes. Now," Anne pursed her lips sternly, "you're avoiding the question you came to ask. What is it?"

"Well, I was talking to Charlie Fielding. And I wondered if someone might be trying to frame him. Look, please tell me if you don't want to talk about it."

"Frame him? What do you mean?" There was no question of not talking about it. Ancient habits of mind persisted. For most of the problems in her life, the most productive reaction had always been to discuss them, inspect their logical structure, think through the solution. Now, even though part of her knew that there was no solution, no satisfactory solution, the process of discussing it was comforting, familiar. Better even than making lists. And she was determined to find out what had happened.

"Did Sergeant Hines show you the items they found there in the gorge?" asked Maggie.

"Yes."

"Well, the little Chaplin memo book belongs to Charlie Fielding. But I'm pretty certain he didn't drop it there today because I was with him from about nine-fifteen on. He says he looked at it before he left his house this morning. So sometime between then and the time I arrived at the scene in the gorge, somebody dropped his book there."

"Bart," said Anne.

"Bart? Why do you say that?" With the schizophrenic skill Anne remembered from her own days of young-motherhood, Maggie was expertly doling out crackers, wiping crumbs from little mouths, and following the conversation with eager attention.

"The pipe." Anne shook her head. "But why would he?"

"That was Bart's pipe? Charlie said it was similar, but lighter—oh, of course! He didn't have his! You gave him that cigarette because he needed a smoke! He was practically sick."

"I sympathize with withdrawal symptoms," said Anne. "Speaking of which . . . you don't smoke?" She held the pack toward Maggie.

"Thanks, no. But Gauloise smoke brings back some good memories."

"You've been in France, then." Anne lit her cigarette.

"Paris, my junior year of high school. Learned a lot."

"A city full of lessons."

"Yeah." Maggie fumbled in her bag, handed a book to Sarah, and at Will's squeal pulled out one for him too. Then her blue eyes locked on Anne's again. "When I met your husband this morning we discussed French for a minute, and he said he especially wanted me to meet you. That's the other reason I came tonight."

"Because of your French? How did he know that?"

"Well, he heard my daughter swearing in French, and—"

"Mine does that too." Anne smiled approvingly at Sarah.

"And because my husband acted Cyrano a few years ago at the Farm Theatre. Nick O'Connor."

"Cyrano? That was your husband? God, we enjoyed that!" She remembered Tal bouncing around the parking lot afterward, replaying his favorite parts as they walked to the car. Anne herself had still been wrapped in the romantic pathos of Cyrano's beautiful death scene, a catch in her throat as she tried to smile at Tal's antics.

There was a catch in her throat now. Anne blew her nose into a paper napkin.

Maggie said, "I'm glad you liked it. Nick will be working at the Farm Theatre again this summer. Marc Antony and Big Daddy. He's going to join us next week after he finishes shooting a TV episode."

"Oh? Which one?"

"*Kojak.* They needed someone who could look similar to Telly Savalas." But Maggie had picked up the waning of interest in Anne's tone and returned to her first question. "Can you think why Bart, or anyone else, might want to frame Charlie Fielding?"

"Frame Charlie? No." Gratefully, Anne turned to the problem. "Can't imagine Charlie with serious enemies. He's a shy young man, always pleasant, eager to please. Very smart, good insight into scientific problems. Works too hard. Sometimes I think it's unhealthy, the way young professors have to put in such long hours for tenure. I imagine that's why things didn't work out with Lorraine."

"Lorraine?"

"His ex-wife. She'd been a student here. Very hard-working herself, ambitious. Stayed on after she earned her Ph.D. Tal was chairman then and he found a half-time instructor job for her, but of course it was pointless in terms of getting on with a career. So she finished up her research, got some articles accepted, and went off to a position at Queens College. Commuted back and forth on weekends for a while but apparently they couldn't make it work."

"Yeah, Nick and I have had to do that occasionally. Hell of a way to run a marriage. The divorce was amicable, though?"

"Far as I know. Though Charlie seemed very withdrawn for a while." Anne peered suspiciously at Maggie. "You're not suggesting that Lorraine Fisher engineered this whole thing from afar to get back at Charlie, are you?"

"Sounds ridiculous," Maggie admitted. "But you never know, some ex-wives are pretty bitter. And since I'm working for the guy, I just wondered if there was anyone who was angry at him, or would benefit somehow if he got into trouble. What about his academic situation? Any rivals?"

"Chiefly Tal."

"Tal? They seemed the best of friends this morning."

"Sure. The rivalry was strictly intellectual. The big point of contention is what guides the eye to the next fixation point."

"Oh, I remember them joking about that. Charlie emphasizes the meaning, the hypothesis a reader has about what meaning will come next on the page. Tal emphasizes the physical stimulus on the page. Letters and spaces."

"Right." Anne smiled. "The usual academic angels on the head of a pin."

"Sure. But with some practical implications all the same. I mean, besides maybe helping us understand how to teach people to read better, there's lots of grant money and other academic prizes riding on it."

"True."

Sarah was tugging at Maggie's sleeve. Maggie bent her head toward the little girl, nodded at her urgent whisper, and gave her another cracker. Will, sitting flat on the floor, was crooning to his book. Maggie smiled across at Anne. "So I was hired to help prove your husband was wrong!"

"To try to," Anne said with spirit. "He was assembling counter-evidence. Tal said this latest study would hit right at the heart of Charlie's theory. Showed the importance of word shape over meaning."

"Really? Who knew about this study?"

"I don't know. Tal only analyzed it a couple of days ago. But I don't think it was a big secret."

"So someone might have realized the problem it would cause Charlie?"

"What are you suggesting? That Charlie was framed because someone thought he had a motive to—to—But that's ridiculous!"

"Maybe. But Charlie's put a lot of years into this study. If it collapsed now it wouldn't be a small thing."

Anne nodded morosely. "So maybe someone thought it would make a passable motive. But it's irrelevant anyway, right? Charlie was with you."

"True, but . . . That's a horse, Will. Horse."

"Doggie!"

"Well, have it your way." Maggie caressed the little boy's shiny curls.

"Silly Willy," declared Sarah scornfully.

"No, not silly. He's labeling sets, Sarah. Just hasn't subdivided it between horses and dogs yet. Charlie was with me, yes," she continued without breaking stride, "but no one knew he would be. So the killer might have chosen to frame Charlie because there was a kind of motive and because it was easy to get Charlie's memo book and drop it there to point the police in the wrong direction."

"I see." A sensible plan. Would Bart be that sensible? Probably. "But I thought it was supposed to look like a suicide."

Maggie said, "Like a staged suicide. Staged by Charlie."

"Pretty complicated!"

"Yes. But I wondered—well, suppose the police hadn't found Charlie's memo book. This is an unkind question, but since there's a kind of motive for Charlie, I wondered if there might be some kind of motive for suicide."

"Absolutely not!" Anne leaned across the table, stabbing at the air in front of Maggie with a stiff forefinger. "He was happy! Celebrating, for God's sake! It couldn't be!"

"I know." Maggie didn't cringe from her anger. She reached toward Anne gently. "My husband's first wife—they thought it was suicide. He was shattered. Absolutely shattered. And it wasn't even that much of a surprise. She'd had a history of depressions and suicide attempts."

"Nothing like that!" Anne shook her head. "Two years ago, sure, in the midst of chemotherapy, Tal was depressed. Who wouldn't be? But after . . . well, he valued life that much more. And he's doing fine. His doctor gave him a good report just this morning!"

"Charlie thought that's what he might be celebrating at lunch."

"But you're suggesting that the killer thought that the police might believe suicide. If they didn't find the memo book." She leaned back, exasperated. "Sounds like an academic mind at work, doesn't it? Explanations behind explanations, in case the first explanations don't work."

"Yes. Also, it's an easy way to get rid of the gun in a hurry." She combed her curls back with her fingers. "But now I have to ask an even nastier question. You arrived on the scene pretty soon. You've got nice insurance policies in there on the coffee table. You know Tal's department well, could have set things up."

"Merde!" Anne slammed her fist onto the table. "You're worse than that idiot Hines! Look, it's true, two years ago Tal and I both had to face the possibility that he'd die. We had to face that it was out of our hands. But damn it, I wanted every instant of that man that I was granted! In whatever shape it came!"

VIII

"Yes," said Maggie. "I believe you."

"Well, then, why are you asking these things?" Anne demanded.

Sarah had moved to her mother's side at the sound of Anne's raised voice, and Maggie gave her a reassuring hug. Oblivious, Will still crooned "Doggie" to his book. Maggie said, "It's my first day on a new job, and somebody's murdered, and my boss is implicated. I want to know what's going on. And it's hard to find out without asking rude, gross questions. You see," she added gently, gesturing at Anne's clenched hand on the table, "you're on my list, Anne. Just as I'm on yours."

Anne looked at her fist. Beneath it was the paper on which she'd written the names of people who'd been in the gorge: *Charlie, Nora, Bart, Maggie, Dorrie.*

She said, *"Merde,"* and sagged back in her chair.

"Yeah. Look, it's your turn if you want. Ask me rude, gross questions. Or if you prefer, I'll leave. Up to you."

Anne glared at Maggie. The younger woman hugged her child to her side but gazed back at Anne with those frank, intelligent eyes. Anne raised her Gauloise to her lips and said, "You're a ruthless bitch, aren't you? Don't give a damn what people think. Or feel."

Maggie shrugged. "Depends on the stakes. If we're talking about murder, yeah, sometimes I'm ruthless." She released Sarah and bent down for her bag on the floor. "You want me to go, then."

"Just a minute," growled Anne. An idea was taking form amongst the clouds of suspicion and rage. "A little ruthlessness may be just what we need. And I've always preferred truth to good manners myself."

"Ditto," said Maggie, straightening. "Honest, I'm not here trying to add to your troubles. But I'm curious, and sometimes rude and gross is the only way to get answers. So I'm an oaf sometimes."

"Listen, oaf." Anne took a long draw of fortifying smoke. "I've been remembering a little about Jackie Edwards. You struck me as much more sensible than the police back then. And you found Jackie's killer." She fought down the embarrassing tremor in her voice. "Maggie, help me find Tal's."

"Hey, whoa!" Maggie arched her eyebrows at Anne, then gave Sarah a pat of dismissal. The child went to sit on the vinyl floor next to her little brother. The two children began to argue about Will's book. Maggie ran her fingers through her hair and frowned. "I'm not police, Anne. There are plenty of police."

"Too many," Anne snapped. "Hines seems to know his job, but he doesn't know the campus. City cops hardly ever set foot on it. So he's here asking dumb questions about insurance, just like you. And Walensky knows the campus but I don't think he's ever handled a murder. Even botched that hit-and-run two years ago, when the little Hammond boy got two broken legs. Tal was furious. Said Walensky was more interested in making NYSU look good than in catching the driver." She squinted at Maggie. "But you know all this! You came here to ask about Charlie. You must not trust the cops all that much yourself."

"You're right." The children were up now, wandering around the room. Maggie's gaze followed them as she spoke. "Walensky seems out of his depth. Hines is starting from way behind because Walensky isn't helping him. Also, he has to spend time checking out Charlie Fielding, and checking out me. I can take a shortcut because I know neither of us did it. I figured it wouldn't hurt to think about—Hey!" This last was directed to Will, who was opening one of the base cabinets. Maggie dove across the room like a hawk after a mouse and snatched Anne's cut-glass bowl from his plump hands.

Anne ground out her cigarette. "We've still got an hour of light left. They can play on our swing set out back if they want. And we can have a glass of wine on the terrace."

"Perfect!" Maggie's wide smile flashed. She'd found a toy for Will in her bag but apparently it didn't match the charms of the cut-glass bowl. She chucked the whimpering boy under the chin. "Will, did you hear? Do you want to go swing?"

"Swings! Hurray!" cried Sarah.

"Wing! Way!" echoed Will.

Maggie took the children out to the swings while Anne got out a second glass and arranged them with wine, crackers, and ashtray on a tray. She glanced out the window. Maggie was checking the chains and seats of the swing set, at one point shinning up to the top bar of the frame to inspect the bolts. Apparently it passed muster because when Anne came out to the terrace with the wine, Maggie loped back up the lawn to join her on the flagstones. "That'll keep them happy for a while," she said. "They're going to play astronauts, sailing through the air."

"Fine." Anne gestured toward the white mesh chairs and table. The living room and kitchen projected into the backyard a little farther than the dining room between them, and the flagstone terrace nestled between the two wings, protected from the worst of sun and wind. Tal always enjoyed having dinner out here, or even breakfast on hot days. Today had been too cool. Anne picked up her glass and sipped before seating herself.

Maggie angled her chair for a good view of the children, then pulled a snapshot from her bag. "May I borrow this photo?"

It was a group picture of the departmental Christmas party. Anne, Tal, Bart and his wife, Charlie, Nora, Bernie, all holding champagne glasses and grinning stupidly at the camera. Anne had last seen it posted on her refrigerator with a magnet. She said, "Be my guest."

"Thanks." The photo disappeared again into the bag. Maggie took a sip of wine, nodded, and asked, "Is there anything I can tell you for starts?"

"You were with Charlie Fielding the whole time, you said?"

"Yes. Well, almost. We crossed the gorge on the upper trail, and when we hit College Ave. I ran on ahead to mail a letter to Nick. Had to cross the street to the branch post office, mail it, cross back again. A couple of minutes, maybe. Charlie was just about where I'd left him. Now, he might have had time to race back to the upper footbridge and race back. But he couldn't have shot anyone on the lower trail, stuck the gun in their hand, and gotten all the way back up so soon."

"And you're sure that's when it was done?"

"Yes. We stopped on the upper bridge on our way over, and we stood looking at the lower trail pretty carefully. It hadn't happened yet. The trail was empty. But we saw someone hiding in the bushes down there. God, if I'd known—" Maggie took a gulp of wine and sat frowning at the glass, twiddling the stem in her long fingers.

"Who was it?" Anne asked, her throat tight.

"I don't know. We could just make out a sleeve and a shoe. Same color as those big boots Hines showed us, but that doesn't prove much. Too far away to see if there were already footprints in the mud." She jerked her thumb angrily at herself. "And bright girl Ryan here was maundering on about how it was probably a birdwatcher. God."

"What about the others who met for lunch?" Anne asked. "Could it have been one of them?"

"Bart or Nora? Sure. They both say they used the upper trail too. You heard them. But either one could have been on the lower trail after we moved on."

"And there's Bart's pipe."

"Yes. He was fidgety at lunch too," Maggie said. "Already missing it." She took another sip of wine, peering at Anne owlishly over the rim of the glass. "Did Bart have some quarrel with Tal?"

"No. Not that I know of. You're asking because I jumped in with his name."

"Yes."

"I was just thinking of the pipe. Well, Bart has his problems. He's not a happy man. Finding it difficult to publish these days, and because of that, Bernie Reinalter has been miserly with the pay raises."

"He has tenure?"

"Oh, yes, there's no getting rid of him unless they can prove gross incompetence. But Bernie does the budgets, and with inflation the way it's been I'm sure Bart is hurting. Tal said he was hopeful about this new grant proposal he was sending in. He'd asked Tal for a letter of support. Probably to counteract the lukewarm words he'd get from Bernie."

"I see. Well, that's not such an unusual situation. Does Bart have a family?"

"His wife works at the NYSU Press, a science editor. A couple of grown kids, moved off to the big city."

"No family problems, then?"

"His wife had an eye operation last year. No obvious marital problems, if that's what you mean. But who knows for sure about such things?" She wondered if anyone in the department had known about Miss Premed, years ago. Tal was a discreet man, apparently had never intended to endanger his marriage. It had been Miss Premed's idea to show up on the doorstep to demand tearfully that Anne release Tal to his true love. Anne, a baby balanced on her hip and fifty-three undergraduate essays in French waiting for her attention, had said, "Honey, if Tal wants anything from me, he'll have to ask me himself. I just don't have time to work through intermediaries." He'd never asked, of course, never brought it up at all, but had carefully brought home the news that Miss Premed had transferred to a New York City college next term. Poor kid . . . Anne dragged her meandering thoughts back to the present.

"I see," Maggie was saying. "Now, we figure Charlie's memo book might have bounced out of his pocket while he was running from his car to his office this morning. Several people could have picked it up."

"Bart?"

"He's one. Nora, Cindy, the chairman. For that matter, my babysitter, Liz, was in Van Brunt in the morning. But I asked at McDonald's about her, and a waiter there confirmed that my two kids had been there with a young woman of Liz's description from a quarter till to twelve-thirty."

"He was sure of the time? Not that Liz would have any reason—"

"I know. The waiter's shift started at eleven-thirty. He admitted it was an estimate but was certain within five minutes." She smiled. "We statisticians occasionally use common sense. Anyway, I believe him enough to let her take the kids again."

"Well, I'm glad someone's cleared."

"Cross one off. Right. Now, what do you know about Reinalter?"

"Bernie? But why—"

"That's what we're trying to find out," said Maggie brusquely. "Reinalter arrived at Van Brunt about nine, Cindy says. I met him just for a moment when I was getting forms from Cindy. She says he left at eleven-thirty for lunch with a couple of Japanese computer scientists at the faculty club. He could have found Charlie's notebook, and if he'd left a car at the right place near the trail entrance, he could have been at the faculty club by twelve-fifteen. Not really likely, but don't cross him off until we know a little more."

"I see what you mean. But, damn it, after what Tal did for him! He really went out on a limb!"

"What did Tal do?"

Anne stared out at the lawn. It was almost completely in shadow now, but the sky was still bright above the evergreens. The children bobbled back and forth on the swings, their chatter thin in the distance. Sarah was on the trapeze, a strong little girl who had pulled herself up nimbly to sit on the bar. She was lecturing Will about the surface of the moon. Will was paying little attention. He had thrown himself across a swing seat on his stomach and was pushing himself forward with his stubby legs, then swinging back with a giggle.

Maggie said, "It'll be even more rude and gross if I have to ask Reinalter."

Well, that was true enough. "Tal was chairman when Bernie came," said Anne slowly. "About fifteen years ago. Bernie was at some little college in the Midwest. Someplace in Iowa, maybe. He's in educational testing, and he'd just developed a new math inventory that people thought was pretty good. He applied for a position here. Gave a good talk, and the search committee said grab him. But Tal thought it was a little odd because it wouldn't be an advance for Bernie. The rank was exactly the same, the salary was actually lower. Bernie said he wanted to move to the East, to a larger university, and so forth. But Tal had an old friend in Iowa. Not at Bernie's school, but in a nearby town."

"No friends at Bernie's school?"

"It was a pretty small college. But the old-boy network came through anyway. Tal's friend did some research and found that Tal was right. Bernie was under a cloud. Apparently the local DA in Bernie's town had arrested a couple of prostitutes. And in exchange for leniency they'd named Bernie as one of their clients." Anne snorted. "Didn't name any of their cop or lawyer clients, I bet."

"Hey, they wanted leniency," Maggie said.

"Exactly. Bernie couldn't bite back. Anyway, it being an election year, it hit the local newspapers before it was dismissed by the court. It *was* dismissed," she added, to be sure Maggie understood. "Now, it would have been bad enough in a town like this one, with a big university. Parents sending their daughters off to college and hearing rumors that one of the professors patronized a bawdy house—horrors! But think of the reaction in a small town in the Bible Belt, that long ago. And think of a professor who works not just with college students, but who does educational research with the town's small children. Like your children."

"I see," said Maggie, her eyes on the little ones swinging across the lawn. "Intolerant, maybe. But you have to sympathize with the parents too. I know I'd do just about anything to keep my kids from being hurt. Anything." She glanced at Anne, her blue eyes dark in the fading light. "Tal hired him anyway?"

"Told him to shape up and design some more good tests, and probably no one would ever think about it again. So Bernie came and as far as I can tell, that's what happened."

"He looks the soul of respectability."

"He *is* the soul of respectability."

"What happened before is in those Iowa papers, I suppose," Maggie said thoughtfully. "Any industrious reporter could unearth it. So in itself it wouldn't make any difference that Tal knew and no one else did. But if Reinalter got into some new trouble—maybe minor in itself but looking bad against the background of the earlier accusations—what were they? Something kinky?"

Anne shook her head. "I don't know. Tal didn't mention it to me so I suppose the papers didn't go into it." She shivered and buttoned her jacket. It was cooling off. Hard to imagine straitlaced Bernie getting into any new troubles. She said, "I always thought of Bernie as the burnt child, grateful for a fresh start."

"You're probably right," said Maggie. "But let's not cross him off our list yet. Next is Cindy."

"Cindy?"

"Secretaries are important people in departments. Why not consider her?"

"She was at a lunchtime meeting. I met her coming back."

"Where had she been?"

"Don't know."

"Where did you see her?"

"Van Brunt. At about twelve-fifteen, just before I started across the gorge."

"Mm. Not quite good enough," said Maggie softly.

"I know. For me either," snapped Anne. "Hines went over it half a dozen times with me. I'd phoned someone shortly before I left my office in Harper, but he wasn't impressed."

"There are a lot of phones on campus. And on College Ave., for that matter. You could have been anywhere."

"Yes. Still, Cindy and I can vouch for each other up to a point." *Could it have been Cindy? Surely not.*

"And the other people at her meeting will vouch for her."

"Maybe." Would they? Anne drained the bottle of wine into her glass. "Shall I get more wine?"

"No, thanks, I'm fine." Maggie's shrewd eyes were fixed on her, curious. Anne returned her gaze flatly, and finally Maggie said only, "Can you tell me anything about Nora?"

"Another hardworking young professor, like Charlie Fielding. Already has a book out. Development of social problem-solving, Tal said."

"Family?"

"A younger brother in New York. She told me she raised him so the parents must be gone. And last year she had a live-in, a computer scientist. Brownell, some such name. He only came to a couple of departmental parties so I really don't know him."

"How about Tal? Did he ever mention that she had any problems?"

Anne shook her head. "No. That is—well, she and the computer fellow had a falling-out last year. At the Halloween party, I remember, Nora got tipsy, started chasing after Charlie Fielding. Scared the poor fellow to death. Don't know if she ever got back together with her computer scientist or not." Anne shifted on her chair. "The only other thing Tal mentioned about Nora was a student last year. Young man. Came into Nora's office, apparently threatened her somehow. Tal and Charlie Fielding were talking in the hall and heard shouts. They went to see what was going on, saw an absolutely furious stringy-haired young man beating his fist on her desk. When they appeared she told him she'd talk to him when he'd settled down, and he left. But Tal said she seemed pretty shaken for a while after that. Even mentioned getting a gun. That kid must have threatened her."

"A gun! That sounds serious. What was his problem?"

"She said it was a grade. But Tal said if that was all it was he must have had a drug problem too. He was too worked up for your standard grade complaint."

"Even failing-this-course-means-I-can't-graduate?"

"Well, in thirty years of teaching no one has ever seriously threatened me, even for that. But I suppose it's possible."

"Tal's probably right, about the drugs." Maggie pulled up one leg and propped her foot on the front edge of her seat. "God, these sunsets are gorgeous."

Anne nodded. The sky in the east was dusky now, but in the west ragged ribbons of cloud blazed pink and gold in a last moment of glory before the night. Across the lawn the children were attempting to sing "Gonna Fly Now." The world was turning. Other people's lives rolling on. Only Anne sat stunned, rigid, trying to distract herself from the void with these silly speculations. *"Et je voudrais mourir,"* said Cyrano, *"sous un ciel rose."* I'd like to die beneath a rosy sky. Well, you didn't quite get your wish either, Old Nosy.

Maggie asked gently, "Have we talked enough for now?"

Anne swallowed more wine. Stave it off a few more minutes. "Let's go on. Keep moving before I forget how."

Maggie reached across the table and touched her shoulder encouragingly. "Okay. We've talked about Tal's colleagues. About his work. Was there anything else he worried about?"

"Not really. Well, back fifteen years ago when he first became chairman, the department had serious budget problems. But he worked those out, and when Bernie became chairman everything was back on track."

"Nothing recently?"

Anne shrugged. "Nothing big. I mean, a couple of times he said there was something strange going on. But if I pressed he'd say no, he was just getting old. Make a joke of it. And then of course he was always full of sympathy for students with problems. I think that's how he—well, we're talking about recently. Let's see. Young woman with a knee problem last year, and another who lost both her parents in a car crash. Or little kids that he met when they came in for experiments. He loved to meet them in the halls, talk to them. Sometimes he'd come home saying that he should have been a classroom teacher. I'd have to remind him that he already was. He just got the kids ten years further on."

"Practically his first question to me was about my kids," Maggie said.

"Yes. That's why he was in education; he thought kids were such wonderful people. Really got involved. I remember a couple of years ago there was a little girl in one of Bart Bickford's childhood creativity studies. Jill Baker. Told a marvelous story about being chased by sharks, and about taking out her own eyeball to be a periscope, and having a magic word that made the sharks stop. Clever child. But a month later Tal told me he was still haunted by that story. I said why not? This Jill Baker may be the next Jules Verne. Though in fairness to Tal I should say that kids shared big problems with him sometimes too. They'd really open up to him. There was another little girl in Bart's study. Frannie something. Can't remember her name. She didn't react much during the testing, and Bart's student assistant was peeved. But Tal said she had such a sad expression that he sat down on the floor of the hall and explained to her that it was hard to think about everyday things when there are big problems too. Frannie agreed and told him very matter-of-factly that she had to think about dying. Turned out they'd just diagnosed leukemia."

"God!"

"I think it was especially poignant to Tal because this was during his own chemotherapy. He cried about Frannie. And at about the same time the little Hammond boy was hurt by that hit-and-run. We all felt awful, but Tal was depressed for days."

"Well, he's right. Worth mourning." There was a huskiness in Maggie's voice.

"Yes." Anne looked at the young woman across the table. Maggie's leg was still pulled up, her elbow on the cocked knee and her hand propping her forehead. The mass of black curls shaded her face. Anne said, "Those kids are probably what upset him most, of all the things I've mentioned."

"Me too." Maggie straightened her leg and shifted restlessly in her chair. "It's pretty shapeless, though, isn't it? Stresses and strains in the department, but nothing that seems wildly unusual. I mean, hit-and-runs do happen. Prostitutes do have clients. And so forth."

"Yes. Maybe we're on the wrong track."

"Maybe. You mentioned something to Walensky about Tal's taxes."

"Oh, the IRS thing. Yeah, we were out of the country at filing time so he applied to file late. Pretty automatic, we thought. But the IRS lost the application somehow, charged him with late filing. He had to go have the documents copied again. He was really angry about it."

"Right. Still, it's hard to see a motive there."

"So we're back to the department."

"Right. Don't see how we can avoid it. Well, tomorrow I'll talk to Charlie again. He may have thought of something overnight. And I bet Cindy knows a lot."

"She may. She's a bright woman," Anne agreed. She should talk to Cindy too.

Across the lawn the children were lively blurs in the thickening dusk. How often she and Tal had rested here, watching little Paul and Rocky, laughing together, sharing their days. She said, "You asked about his worries. But most of the time Tal brought home happy stories."

"Oh, I know! I met him for a moment. And he made it joyful."

"Joyful." Yes. Tal made the world joyful.

Her knobby-nosed, brilliant Tal.

Suddenly Anne was blubbering, huge wet sobs ratcheting up from her gut one after another, on and on, swamping her with their primeval urgency. It was a long, long time before they eased a little and, exhausted and shuddering, she became aware of Maggie kneeling next to her, arm around her shoulders, murmuring and rocking her gently.

The children, she saw through filmed eyes, were sitting on the terrace in a square of light from the kitchen window. They were paging through their books again.

Above, the sky was black.

FRIDAY, JUNE 3, 1977

IX

Charlie tilted up his chin. He scraped the razor along his stubbly neck and blinked sleepily at the sagging face in the mirror. Smile, Fielding. Ah, much better. Practically a Paul Newman. Suave, tough and handsome, ready to take on whatever the world threw at him, ready to take on Sergeant Hines or—

Hines. Oh, hell. Tal Chandler! Reality crashed in. Charlie's early morning brain had sent him staggering into the bathroom on automatic, without reminding him of yesterday. Hard to believe when half the night he'd tossed and turned, battered by sorrow and fears, unable to forget. At last he'd dropped into fitful sleep. A couple of hours later the alarm had dragged him partway awake. Now, in a rush, the blessed numbness was shattered and all the horrors returned.

Tal was dead. His exuberant, challenging friend had been shot.

And whoever had shot him had left Charlie's memo book nearby.

And Sergeant Hines suspected Charlie.

Who the hell had done it? Fully awake at last, Charlie swabbed the last flecks of foam from his face and put on his glasses. After dinner last night he'd tried to figure it out, making lists, puzzling over the million conflicting facts, trying to think of someone who might want to kill Tal. It seemed impossible that the friendly little man could inspire murderous feelings in anyone. But after a while some ugly possibilities occurred to Charlie.

Near midnight he'd finally admitted to himself that he was damned scared.

Some of the possibilities involved Tal knowing too much.

Which could mean that Charlie knew too much too.

Last night, for the first time in years, Charlie had gone around to lock all the windows, double-check the doors. The fragility of his paltry defenses glared at him. No burglar alarm. No gun. No Dobermans. In this development you weren't supposed to need that kind of protection. Crime was a city problem, right? Murders didn't happen in this town.

But one had. And Charlie was caught in the middle.

He'd been much too upset last night to work things out with Deanna, so he hadn't even tried. Things were touchy with her right now. There'd been no open fight, but there were too many excuses about having to work on some project or other, about having to see friends. With anyone else he might have shrugged it off, a pleasant adventure gone stale. But he and Deanna had something special, something worth saving. Not just the shared interests—films, of course, and ice skating, and silly jokes, and Italian food. But most of all, together they were explosively sensual, somehow reaching and satisfying each other's deepest needs in a way he'd never achieved with Lorraine. Away from Deanna he ached, incomplete, craving the scent of her hair, her clear honey-tan skin, her warm slender legs, her smoky eyes full of ancient wisdom and ancient hunger. She needed him too.

But he'd have to have time to talk with her, to find out what the trouble was. At the end of the term he'd probably been distracted, inattentive. The worst thing he could do right now would be to throw this hideous new distraction into the mess. So he'd contented himself last night with tucking his favorite snapshot of her under his pillow. A foolish schoolboy move, maybe. He'd hoped he could soothe himself to sleep with the idea of seeing her soon, reassuring her, savoring that sweet silken body again. But his maverick mind kept cutting back to uglier things: the gray tweed on the trail, Hines's flat questioning voice, Cindy's taut little smile.

And now, awake at last, he could see that the image in the mirror had nothing to do with Paul Newman. Just ordinary Charlie Fielding, his doglike eyes weary and anxious behind the bravado of his aviator glasses.

He went back to the bedroom and was opening his shirt drawer when the buzz of the doorbell sawed through the silence. Freeze-frame: Charlie bent, hand stretched toward the drawer. Then a rapid montage of last night's fears tumbling back in. The murderer? Was the murderer at the door? Because Charlie Fielding, who knew too little, might guess too much?

Dad, of course, would have swaggered to the door cool as Bogart, could have stared down a platoon. But Charlie didn't get the right genes, somehow.

Play to your strengths, Coach Wilhelm had exhorted them. Dry-mouthed, Charlie ticked through the possibilities. He could run out the back door to the patio. But no, because then he'd have to pass the front of the house to get to the street. Well, he could run through the kitchen into the garage. Leap into the car, gun the motor, and escape that way.

But to get from the bedroom to the kitchen and garage, he'd have to cross the front hall. And anyone standing at the door could see him through the glass.

He could use a bedroom window, crawl out through—

But it might not be the killer. It might be Hines, and trying to escape would be the dumbest thing he could do.

Charlie pulled his terrycloth robe tighter and belted it, wishing it were a bulletproof vest, a suit of armor, a Sherman tank. He pulled his hockey stick from the back of his closet, licked his dry lips, squared his shoulders, and swaggered quaking to the door.

"Maggie!"

"Hi, Charlie. Want to join me for breakfast? Or have you had some already?" She was wearing a red shirt under a slouchy denim jacket, and her smile was a splash of sunlight.

"Breakfast? Uh, sure." His knees were wobbly with relief. He hung onto the doorknob as he stepped back to let her in. "Uh, I mean, no, I haven't had any."

"Fine. I thought I'd go to Plato's. They still serve breakfast, right?"

"Yes. My assistant eats there sometimes."

"My God, Charlie! What in the world . . ." She had crossed the tiled entry hall and was staring into the living room.

Charlie stood his hockey stick in the corner, took a deep breath, and smoothed back his hair. Would she like it? "Movie collectibles," he explained.

"God, it's wonderful! Such memories!" She bounced toward the fireplace. It was flanked by bookshelves crowded with lamps, lunch boxes, dolls, autographed pictures, even a few books. On the walls above the bookcases, he'd hung framed posters: a fifties *Superman* with George Reeves, a more recent Clint Eastwood as Dirty Harry, *Rear Window*, and a couple of smaller Chaplin lobby cards, *Limelight* and *The Kid*. Maggie, at the mantel, looked over her shoulder at Charlie. "These are real costumes?"

He'd hung a light blue pinafore and a cream-colored shirt neatly above the fireplace. Charlie nodded proudly. "Judy Garland wore the pinafore in *The Wizard of Oz*."

"God! That's practically sacred! And the shirt?"

"One of Valentino's. *Son of the Sheik*."

"Incredible!" On tiptoes, she scrutinized the shirt. "Where do you find these wonderful things?"

He shrugged. "Auction houses. Ads in collecting periodicals. Place in New York called Second Hand Rose."

She moved along the bookcase, grinning as she recognized each toy. "A batmobile! I love it! And hey, you're all set for the beach, aren't you?" She gestured at the inflated vinyl *Jaws* shark and at the bright sand pail featuring Snow White and the seven dwarfs. "Oh, what's this?"

"A music box. Here, I'll wind it up for you." He turned the little key carefully and set it down again. Mickey and Minnie Mouse danced to the tinkling tune of "Yes, Sir, That's My Baby."

Maggie laughed. "I'm going to have to bring the kids to see all this! But I sent them off early with Liz because I wanted to talk to you before we hit campus this morning." She glanced at him, the side lighting from the big glass patio doors picking out the strong bones of her cheek and jaw.

"Hey, look, don't let me hold you up. Why don't you get dressed and I'll just browse around until you're ready?"

"Fine."

Charlie hurried back into the bedroom. Surprising woman, Maggie. He was pleased at her reaction to his collection. Some people said, "God, you mean this trash is worth money?" and proceeded to tell him about all the childhood nightlights and lunch boxes they'd thrown out. Maggie seemed to understand instinctively, like Lorraine, like Deanna. Of course Maggie was married to an actor, that probably helped. Charlie fished his left shoe from under the bed and decided he would ask her about some of his ideas about Tal. She was sensible, not close-mouthed like Sergeant Hines. He wished he knew what Hines was thinking.

When he returned to the living room Maggie was lounging in his leather recliner, thumbing through a Laurel and Hardy book. The ankle of one long blue-jeaned leg rested on her other knee, the book braced on her thigh. Her bright smile flashed. "Two questions."

"Okay." He shrugged into the light jacket he was carrying.

She stood up and returned the book to its place in one fluid motion. "I figured out what most of the things are. But what's the hat?"

He followed her finger. A spiffy 1940s style fedora. He said, "Al Pacino's hat from *The Godfather.*"

"Amazing. Half of Nick's friends were extras in that. That was quite a movie."

"Yeah, I was glad to find that hat. Should go up in value too. The costumes seem to climb the fastest. That pinafore is worth hundreds already." He met her blue eyes. "You had another question?"

"Yeah. All of this stuff is connected with films." She flapped a hand at the bookcases. "Where are the films?"

He hesitated. They were pirated for the most part, illegal, and he could never risk showing her his secret collection. But she seemed sympathetic; he could let her see the room. He said, "On sixteen millimeter, mostly. I'm getting a good collection." He jerked his thumb at the third bedroom. "Do you want to see?"

"Sure." She followed him eagerly. A floor-to-ceiling bookcase was filled in part with his books on film and video, but for the most part with his pirated films. A screen and a large television on a fireproof filing cabinet faced a scuffed sofa. Hastily he picked up a sock from the sofa and a couple of magazines from the floor and stowed them on the shelves. Maggie said, "This is impressive."

Charlie found himself grinning with pride. "It's not all on display." He unlocked the file cabinet and pulled a thick book from the top drawer. "This is my inventory."

"God, you're well-organized." She thumbed through it, then glanced around the room, head cocked like a robin's, looking at everything.

"Yeah. When Lorraine moved out I thought about getting a smaller place. Then I moved a TV in here, and the rest gradually accumulated." He locked the cabinet, remembering. "This room used to be Lorraine's office."

"Lorraine."

"My ex-wife. You wouldn't have known her. She teaches at Queens now." He stepped back into the hall and switched off the light as she followed. "She picked out this house. Liked the patio. But it's pretty comfortable for a bachelor too."

"Yeah. Nice place. Hey, I'm starving! Let's go eat, okay?"

He followed her black Camaro into the valley and up the next hill. College Avenue was near the top. She swerved suddenly onto a side street and parked. There was a second available slot a few spaces up. They got out and walked the half-block to Plato's.

George Zikakis spotted Charlie and lumbered over to meet him, his round mustached face set in lines of sorrow. "Terrible, terrible!" he exclaimed. "I can't believe it! Tal Chandler . . . he was like a brother, that man! A brother!"

"Yes. Yes, he was." Charlie allowed his shoulders to be clapped in hearty commiseration. Then he said, "Maggie, this is George Zikakis. Owner of Plato's. This is Maggie Ryan. She's here to work with me this summer."

George pumped Maggie's hand. "Good, good! But I'm sorry you came at such a sad time." He waved them into a booth and beckoned a waitress.

"You were a friend of Tal's too?" Maggie asked.

"Of course! He came here often. Always with a happy story. Or a compliment for old George's cooking." He thumped his ample chest. "And my heart aches. A fine man! It's the drugs, you know," he added darkly. "These young people, they're crazy on drugs. I tell the police to lock them up. It's illegal, right? But they say they have to wait until they commit a crime. And then you see, they can't find them! A fine man like Tal . . . and all they do is come in here, ask questions! Who did you see, what did you see, was there anything unusual?" He took the mugs of coffee from the waitress's tray and placed them in front of Charlie and Maggie. "But the problem is, it's not unusual! Crime is usual now! I told the police, even here we aren't safe! A fine man like Professor Chandler . . . terrible!"

"So none of you saw anything odd?" asked Maggie.

"Nothing. I was in the kitchen, you know, didn't even see Charlie here come in yesterday. In the kitchen it's very busy. Sometimes I look out the window. Yesterday was a pretty day. But I didn't see anything unusual. You want pancakes? Eggs?"

"Scrambled," said Maggie. "With extra toast and a large orange juice."

"I'll have the same." Charlie nodded. The coffee was hot and strong, George's pride.

"Good appetites," said George approvingly.

"Good food here," replied Maggie. He beamed. She added, "So about yesterday, no one on the street saw anything unusual? Anyone hurrying?"

"Nothing. Only Jack at the shoe store across the street, he saw that lady professor running. He noticed because she was in a suit, not jogging clothes."

"Nora Peterson?"

"Yes, that one. And then a few minutes later Jack heard the shouts, that girl who found him. And Jack said some stranger flew out of the door here and went to help her."

"That was Maggie," said Charlie.

"You? It was you? I'm glad to meet you!" said George. "In that case you know what happened next." He tapped his pad. "So maybe the old fat Greek should go scramble some eggs, eh? Maybe he should stop gossiping?"

"We all want to find out what happened to Tal Chandler," Maggie said.

"Yes. A wonderful, wonderful man." Shaking his head lugubriously, George shuffled back to the kitchen.

Maggie drank some coffee and said, "So Nora running was unusual."

"Maybe. But that's what we all do when we think we're late, right?" Charlie observed. "I was running myself, yesterday morning."

"You sure were!" Maggie grinned, then sobered. "Have you been thinking about what enemies Tal might have had? Or you?"

"Hard to think about anything else." Charlie picked up his mug of coffee and discovered that he'd drunk it already. "But I can't really pin down anything definite. Two general possibilities. It could have been— but I shouldn't make accusations."

"Right, we're just thinking aloud. General possibilities."

"Yes. Well, it could have been his wife."

"Mm. Any special reason you say that?"

"Just . . . well, there are family conflicts sometimes." Aunt Babs crying. Dad, stiff with disgust, walking out the door. Nine-year-old Charlie sobbing, "Wait, wait!"

"True," said Maggie, watching him. "Did you know of any problems between Tal and Anne?"

He pulled his thoughts back to the present. "No. But it's hard to know people really well. And I was thinking that she could have been there earlier than we saw her."

"Yes, that's true too. What's the second general possibility?"

"What we were talking about yesterday. That Tal managed to learn something that someone didn't want known."

"Have you thought of something?"

"Just that some things are . . . not worse, really, but more of a problem in an education department than in other departments. Because we work with children."

"Like what?"

"It's just that no one gets excited any more if a math professor smokes pot or drinks himself to sleep every night. But people who work with little children can't have even the ordinary vices."

"Right. Or suppose there was something . . . well, there have been stories in the newspapers about child molesters. If Tal knew something like that—"

"God, nobody would—not in an education department! Kids are so fragile. So eager to embrace the world but so fragile. We know that!"

"Kids get molested all the same."

"Not by people who know kids. I can't imagine—" Charlie shook his head. He'd never been able to understand how there could be people who would force such horrors onto a child. Yet he knew such people existed. But not in the department! "Anyway," he continued, "I didn't mean anything like that. But good parents are very protective. They want the people who work with their children to be good role models even in small things, and that's good. And you have to look out for the department's reputation. But the main thing is the children. Each child is unique. Being drunk at the wrong time could so easily—" He was squeezing his empty mug ferociously. He eased his grip. "Well, adults can shrug things off. Children can be hurt."

She looked at him silently a moment, the blue eyes so intent on his that he dropped his gaze. She said softly, "You were hurt, weren't you?"

He was saved by the arrival of the eggs and toast. The waitress was nervous, half her attention on George, who stood behind the bar with a critical eye on her. When she'd rattled the plates and cups into place Maggie made an OK sign toward the proprietor, who beamed. Then she drank her orange juice before asking, "Why does Cindy needle you?"

"Cindy?" He broke off. The waitress was back with a coffeepot.

But when she'd left again Maggie said insistently, "And you needle Cindy. It's not just a game."

"Sure it is. Now it is. We had kind of a fight a few years ago, but we get along." He shrugged.

"What was the fight about?"

"Nothing. It's all blown over."

She forked in a mouthful of eggs and mumbled, "You don't want to say what happened?"

Charlie put jam on his toast. "No. Really, it's not relevant. It's over."

"If Tal had learned about it would Cindy be worried?"

"No! There's your proof, you see. Tal *knew!* Tal showed me! It's been years since . . . well, anyway, it's not relevant. Not worth stirring up."

"But there's a lot of emotion around it still." She munched for a moment, then asked, "Okay, Charlie, what would you do if you found out someone in the department was using coke? Or maybe sleeping with his students?"

"Nobody's doing that!"

"We're just supposing. What would you do? Report it to Walensky?"

"No. It would depend. The chairman, maybe. Yeah, I'd probably go see Reinalter."

"And what would Reinalter do?"

"He'd . . . I don't know. Call the person in. Maybe go to the police. He'd make sure it stopped but he'd want to keep it quiet so the scandal wouldn't rub off on the rest of us. And it would, you know, if it got out."

"But the person involved still might lose his job, maybe go to jail."

"Yeah. Depends on how bad it was."

"Okay. Now, this thing with Cindy that's not relevant, does Reinalter know?"

"No." Charlie could feel his jaw muscles clenching.

"And if he did, what would happen to Cindy? Would he say, it's all over, it's not relevant?"

"Maybe."

Her gaze sharpened. "Look, I'm trying to help. I can't help you figure out who's framing you if I don't know anything about you or your possible enemies or the enemies of your enemies."

Hell, he'd thought this high-powered consultant was on his side. Now she reminded him of Aunt Babs, nagging at him to find out why he was late getting home from hockey practice. He thumped his mug down onto the table so hard that coffee splashed out. "Damn." He swabbed at it angrily with a paper napkin. "Okay, look, Bernie Reinalter is really into appearances. It's good for the department, I suppose. But you're right, he might come down pretty hard on Cindy, even after all this time."

"Okay." She sipped some more coffee and leaned back in the booth. She'd finished her breakfast, he saw. He picked up his own toast. She continued, "Next awkward question. Can you tell me about Lorraine?"

"Lorraine?" He ducked his head to hide his growing anger.

"Charlie, I'm sorry. Look, maybe we should just leave it to the police."

"Good idea!" But the fears were nibbling again. The murderer. And almost as bad, Hines with his neutral questions and obsidian eyes. Charlie drained his coffee mug and said in a more conciliatory tone, "Look, Lorraine is at Queens now. Not around here. How could she be involved?"

"I know. It's probably crazy to suggest that she may be trying to get back at you after all this time."

"Not only that—she was very fond of Tal. She wouldn't—"

"Charlie, *everyone* was fond of Tal! You yourself suggested someone who was so fond of him she married him!"

"Oh, hell. I know." He leaned back in the booth, arms crossed, glaring at the sugar container. "Yeah, okay, go ahead. I'll try. What about her?"

"Well, for starts, there's usually some bad feeling when there's a divorce."

"Some." He kept his voice neutral, trying to look at it objectively. "But we respect each other. We're adults. It just didn't work out the way we expected."

"You thought she'd be different than she turned out to be? Or you thought *you'd* be different?"

Charlie took off his glasses, rubbed his nose, blinked nearsightedly down at his plate. "Some of both. You start these things with a vision, you know? How great the world is going to be. Who can tell what goes wrong? Lorraine and I helped each other a lot at first. This project I'm working on now is partly her doing. She said, you've got all these sophisticated ideas about skilled reading. Why work with beginners? Doesn't it make sense to make sure that's really the way skilled readers do it? And she'd heard about someone using video techniques. She put me onto that line of research. She was right: I'm damn good at it. Smart woman, Lorraine." He replaced his glasses. "But personally . . . well, it just didn't work out. Hell, if I knew why I'd have fixed it! After a while we just stopped pretending."

"What was her relationship to Tal?"

"Friendly. No, more than that, really. She took a class or two from him when she was a student here. And after we were married and she got her degree, he hired her at the instructor level. Part-time. Not a great job, but of course there was nothing full-time in her field around here. And it gave her time to finish some research projects. That's what really got her the tenure-track job at Queens."

"Had she done anything . . . well, like Cindy, anything that Tal knew about and that might hurt her career?"

"Lorraine? God, no! Sometimes she smoked pot on weekends. That was it. So did I. So did you, I bet!"

Maggie grinned. "Touché. And I agree, that's not a dark enough secret to inspire a crime, because these days the consequences are about zero. Unless you want to work for the CIA, maybe. Even Bernie Reinalter probably expects his younger faculty to have a little pot in their background."

"Yeah. Nobody's trying for security clearance."

"Good. Is Lorraine's specialty reading too?"

"No, cognitive development. She was doing some work on semantic categories and took my reading seminar the first year I taught it. That's how we met."

"I see. Do you ever talk to her now?"

"Hardly ever. We see each other at conventions sometimes." He pushed his plate away. "Look, if you're finished, let's pay George and get on to campus."

She smiled sunnily. "Good idea. Let's go."

X

The basement of Van Brunt Hall was even blander than the ground floor: white ceiling, white walls, white doors, white vinyl tile. Charlie unlocked his experiment room and switched on the fluorescent lights. Maggie glanced around curiously at the worktable, cardboard boxes of supplies, terminal, and curtained experiment area. "Sorry to put you to the trouble," she said, "but I do a much better job of interpreting scores when I have some idea of what people were actually doing to get the scores."

"Sure," said Charlie. "It's good that you're interested." He'd planned on giving this demonstration yesterday afternoon, after he'd finished introducing her to the computer personnel and explaining his own coded data sheets. But then Tal—*Don't think about that now, it'll just choke you up.* He turned away, switched on the TV and selected a tape. He cleared his throat. "Let me double-check that we've got the right printer attached. Good. The other one's been acting up. Maybe I can get it fixed this afternoon. Okay, now, that's where the subjects sit." He gestured to a chair before the TV.

"I see." Maggie looked at the screen. "Now, I'm a subject. What am I supposed to do?"

"You'll be reading several short paragraphs, and afterward you'll see a set of words, one at a time. You'll press this button if it was one of the words you read. We call it the Yes button." He indicated the bright red button on the remote control fastened to the arm of the chair.

"Got it."

"Now, you sit here and wear these fancy goggles. Pretty much like having your eyes examined." He indicated the chair as he clamped a fresh bite board into the head frame. "This gizmo in front of your nose is a bite board. You bite it."

"Bite it?"

"It keeps your head still. It's important because we'll be photographing and measuring your eye movements by bouncing a light off your cornea and into the camera. If your head moves, it's impossible to tell which letter you were looking at."

"Okay." Maggie plunked herself into the chair and checked the location of the yes button.

"You see the bite board is coated with wax? Your teeth make an impression, so if we have several sessions with the same person we can get things calibrated more quickly." He was adjusting the equipment to her height. "If that feels all right, push the Yes button."

She raised her eyebrows, seemed to decide it wouldn't get any better, and pushed the button.

"Okay, now I'll calibrate the camera. Look at the dot on the screen. As soon as you've fixated it, push the Yes button. That tells the computer the exact coordinates of your individual corneal reflection for that spot. Then it'll show you a new dot. Same thing, look at the dot and push the button." He watched carefully as she responded to a series of dot positions on the screen. Finally the screen read "Thank you!" and Charlie said, "Good. Now, if you're ready to begin, push the Yes button again."

She signaled yes.

"Here we go, then. Read as rapidly and as normally as you can. I know it's hard in this contraption, but try." He started the tape. The short paragraphs, all in capital letters, blinked on and off in sequence. Each was followed by the appropriate set of test words. After ten minutes the tape was done.

"Well," said Maggie, leaning back in her chair, "I like George's cooking better than your bite bar."

Charlie grinned. "No doubt. I'd order chocolate-flavored if they made them. Here, we'll see how you did." He took the record of her answers from the printer and scanned it. "Good. Here's a mistake. We're interested in the mistakes."

"Of course. I've worked with psychologists for years. A perfect score is a dud from your point of view. What did I miss?"

"Burgundies. You said yes, you'd seen the word."

"But I did! In the paragraph about French wines!"

"Here's the tape again." He found the passage and froze it on the screen. Like the others, this sentence was in capital letters: AMONG THE BEST-LOVED WINES OF FRANCE ARE BURGLARIES, BOTH WHITE AND RED.

"God. You're right. Plain old-fashioned proofreader's error."

"Right. We're trying to find out what leads to those errors. Obviously context is one important variable. This sentence is matched with one that reads WHEN DRUG USE INCREASES IN A CITY, SERIOUS CRIMES SUCH AS RAPES AND BURGUNDIES INCREASE TOO."

Maggie chuckled. "Must be really bad wine to count as a serious crime."

Charlie grinned. "Yeah. Gary and I thought the departmental Christmas party served the worst wine we ever had. But we decided even that stuff was only a misdemeanor."

Maggie's attention had returned to the screen. "So I misread that word because of the context? But I remember noticing a few strange words as I read."

"Right. One thing we're checking is whether the location of the eye fixation is involved in misreading. Normally you're seeing about ten letters on each side of your fixation point, plus some peripheral information on the general length of the words coming up next. Let's say your fixation point was somewhere in the word *France.* Your clear span goes through BUR or BURG, and you know something about the length of the word and the shape of it from peripheral information."

Maggie frowned. "When it's all caps, the word shapes are pretty similar."

"We also have conditions with upper and lower case, and later this summer I hope to run one with randomized upper and lower case. Anyway, back to what you were just reading. You see the BURG, plus the peripheral info, plus the meaningful context. And you may be convinced you've read the word BURGUNDIES instead of BURGLARIES. On the other hand, if you happen to fixate inside the word itself, the middle letters LAR will stand out clearly, and you'll read BURGLARIES even if it's not the kind of word you hypothesized."

"I see. I'm zipping along through the paragraph, hypothesize that a word such as BURGUNDIES is coming up next, see some information that supports my hypothesis, and go on without double-checking."

"That's right. After all, most of the time, in most of the stuff you read, you'll be right. No sense in double-checking. Just slows you down."

"I see. So if I'm following instructions, reading rapidly, I'll misread a few of your trick words."

"Exactly. Now, the next question is, why? What are the general sources of misreadings? You just explained my own theory: that a reader has a hypothesis about what meaning is coming up next, and that hypothesis influences reading. That's the theory I like to emphasize."

"If I understand the differences between you and Tal, he'd explain it another way, right?"

"Yes. He'd stress the fact that the word shapes are similar when you have BURGLARIES and BURGUNDIES."

"He'd predict fewer misreadings in the lower case, right? Let's see. In *burglaries* the fourth letter is below the line and the fifth letter is above it. In *Burgundies* the, what, seventh letter is above the line. Plus a capital *B* to start."

"That's right. He's much more interested in the physical layout, on what's really down there on the page."

"So in fact, both of you can explain the misreading I just did. Tal would say the physical clues were poor, and you'd say that I was expecting something about France and wines."

"Right. Of course it's really a matter of emphasis. Both things are going on at the same time, and we both know that. But I just find it more interesting to investigate higher mental processes instead of marks on a page."

"I see."

"Naturally we've got other conditions. Some people see the same sentences in lower case, so the word shapes aren't so similar. Or the same capital-letter words in random order, so there's not as much room for a hypothesis about meaning. We're trying to tease it apart, to find out as much as we can about what's going on when people read, how to help them read effectively." He removed the tape, switched off the apparatus, and waved his hand at it. "Something as complicated as reading has to be investigated one bit at a time. I vowed to myself early on that I wasn't interested in typography or lists of words. All my work involves paragraphs, texts. Even if I'm asking about individual words like BURGUNDIES, it's to see what effect the context has on them."

"I see. Well, thanks for the subject's-eye view of this study." She followed him into the hall. "Was Tal's work similar to yours? I mean, the way he did experiments?"

"In some ways. Of course he didn't have video techniques available. But a lot of his questions were similar. In fact, several years ago he did a study with pairs of sentences similar to the ones you just saw. But his subjects sat down at a table with a pencil. He told them they'd get a point for every correct answer on content questions at the end, plus a five-point bonus if they finished in under ten minutes. And by the way, he said, draw a line under any typos you happen to see. No reward for finding mistakes, though."

"I see. And he tried to find out if meaningful context or word shapes made people miss typos?"

"Yes. Also, he had kind of an interesting condition where words were spelled with random upper and lower case letters. Like 'New York' would have, say, capital E, Y, R instead of—"

He broke off as a door opened almost in his face. "Sorry, didn't mean to ram into you," muttered Bart Bickford, shepherding out a little girl who wore a too-large pink T-shirt. Next to Bart's huge frame she looked tiny, a little stick figure.

"And you know who else I like?" she was saying to him. "Cher!" She gave a clumsy, innocent imitation of a wanton wriggle. Charlie smiled. Children still amazed him, their voracious hunger to learn. Look at this awkward sexless child playing vamp. Or little boys playing war, or cops, or hockey superstars. Or reading. It took a major effort to discourage a child from learning to read, not that adults didn't succeed from time to time . . . Aunt Babs. But most kids struggled on with the letters, the words, the meanings, long after most adults would have quit in despair. As Charlie learned more about the complexities of the feat, he respected children more and more. That tenaciousness, that willingness to work hard. He couldn't remember learning to read, just that he'd always loved it. But he remembered learning to play ice hockey. Just about the age of this girl. He'd spent hours and hours teaching his scrawny legs speed and turns, chasing that elusive puck in the bitter cold, distressing Aunt Babs with his constantly bruised knees and twisted ankles. Not that he'd ever gotten to be good. Only twice, in real games, had he reached that over-heated glow, skating through a haze of red alone with the puck, the way past the goalie shining before him, his teammates screaming approval. But for the most part his rewards had been the tiny increments in his own performance and Coach Wilhelm's enthusiastic praise. Dad hadn't even come to the playoffs. Just as well, maybe. Kindly as he was, the coach had kept him on the sidelines most of the time. By high school Charlie had given it up and concentrated on being a brain. But he still remembered those years of dogged practice.

"And, well, that's all the people I like!" the girl finished enthusiastically.

"That's great!" Bart seemed sincere. He smiled at Maggie and Charlie. "Shelley just told me some great stories. But we have to go now. Her mom's waiting in the parking lot. Come on, Shelley." They headed for the exit.

Maggie pulled open the door to the stairwell, then slowed. Behind her, Charlie almost bumped into her. Then he too heard the low, heated voices. "Look, Wayne, you must have known! Even Cindy Phelps knew! And she says the whole department knew!"

"It was a judgment call, right?" Walensky sounded exasperated. "No need for you to butt in. You've got to understand, Reggie, these academic types are different! Not your average skells that you see downtown. You've got to use a different kind of interrogation or you end up with the dean's office on your back. To say nothing of the ACLU."

"Look, I'm not talking about the third degree, I'm talking about getting the damn information! And if you already know something and decide not to embarrass your academic charges by asking them, at least drop me a hint, all right?" There was a deep sigh, as though Hines was pulling back, trying not to lash out. "Look, Wayne, it's no big deal. They'll have a report for me this afternoon. If the Phelps story seems relevant, I'll have time to talk to everyone."

"Easy for you to say no big deal! You don't have the dean whispering in your ear. 'You got it solved yet? No? Well hurry up. But for heaven's sake don't ask anyone any questions!' "

"Yeah." Hines chuckled humorlessly. "Downtown we've got a few politicians exactly like that. Well, tell your dean whatever you want, but I'm talking to them."

"But take it easy."

"Look, I've got my problems too. Like getting this solved. Don't worry,

I know civil rights law, probably better than you. And I've been to college too, just like your dean. So I won't ruffle any feathers that don't need ruffling. Meanwhile, you know these folks, I'm counting on you for insider information, okay? The sooner we clear up this case, the sooner we'll all be—"

Maggie pulled Charlie into the stairwell and let the door slam behind them as she started up the stairs. She said brightly, "Random upper and lower case letters. I see. That would destroy the familiar word shapes, wouldn't it? Oh, hi, Sergeant Hines, Captain Walensky!"

The two policemen, faces impassive as masks, watched as Maggie and Charlie rounded the turn and climbed toward them. "Hello," said Hines. "I was just on my way to look for you, Professor Fielding. Gary Kramer said you were downstairs. Just a couple of questions."

"Yeah, sure." Charlie stepped up to the landing and forced his shoulders to relax. The police were trying to find the killer, after all. Walensky had been around for years, and even this pushy newcomer Hines wanted to catch the murderer and bring this nightmare to an end. Still, it was a nightmare, knowing that the police were inspecting every word he said, every move he made. And he worried about the friction between them.

Hines opened his notebook civilly enough. "Professor Fielding, you've told me that you were not on the lower path yesterday until after Professor Chandler was shot."

"That's right."

"You suggested that someone might have obtained your memo book, and dropped it nearby." His voice was friendly, almost too hearty, and Charlie realized he was playing to the other policeman.

He nodded, hoping he looked relaxed and confident. "Had to be that way, unless I dropped it from the bridge earlier."

"Now, how would this person be able to get your book?"

Charlie glanced at Maggie. "We were talking about that. I looked at the book at home. By the time I arrived here I was late, so I ran from my car to the office. The whole length of Van Brunt. We thought it might have fallen out of my pocket then. Anyone could have picked it up."

"Anyone who happened to be around Van Brunt Hall," Maggie said.

Hines glanced at her, then back at Charlie. "We'll check into it. Can you think of anyone who might want to cause trouble for you?"

Charlie shook his head. Walensky was frowning now, and Hines seemed to be addressing him instead of Charlie as he explained, "I'm asking because if someone took the trouble to leave the memo book there, there may be animosity toward you."

"Yeah, I know," Charlie said. "My best guess is that it was lying on the floor and someone just took advantage because it was handy."

Hines nodded. "Now, what time did you leave Van Brunt to walk to College Avenue?"

"About twenty of twelve. Maybe a few minutes earlier."

"Did you pass the main office?"

Charlie saw interest kindle in Maggie's expression. "Yes," she said. "But the door was closed."

"That's right," Charlie said. "I figured Cindy and Bernie were both off to lunch."

"Why did you think that?" Walensky asked sharply.

"Because if either one is there, the outer office door is open."

"Always?"

Why was Walensky asking about this point? Did he know something about Cindy? Possibly even Bernie? Charlie answered carefully, "Almost always. Occasionally Bernie will close the door to his inner office when he's there, if he has the budget to get out and doesn't want interruptions, or if he's giving a graduate exam, that kind of thing. But usually when he's there both doors are open. And if Cindy's in the building anywhere, the outer door is open. So if it's closed it means they're both gone."

"You didn't see either of them leave?" Hines asked. His voice was strong, and his hard eyes warned Walensky. The campus policeman gave the smallest of grudging nods, acknowledging that the interview was Hines's again.

Charlie felt like the rope stretched in a tug-of-war. "No, we didn't see them. We were looking at coding sheets in my office."

Maggie shifted her briefcase to her other hand. "I heard that Professor Reinalter was having lunch at the faculty club."

"Mm," said Hines without changing expression.

"At a quarter after. So if he was gone that early—"

"Mm," said Hines again.

"And Cindy was gone too," said Maggie.

Hines looked at Walensky. "Cindy Phelps says she left a few minutes after Professor Reinalter and walked toward the main quad for a brown bag lunch. Did you see her, Professor Fielding?"

"No," said Charlie. Walensky seemed very interested in Hines's question too. "But we were headed the other direction. No reason we'd see her."

Maggie was frowning. "Did she meet someone there?"

Hines looked at her sharply. Despite his preoccupation with Walensky, he wasn't missing anything. "We're checking into it."

"Cindy does like to have lunch alone sometimes," Charlie pointed out. "She says with the kids at home and people in and out of the office all day, it's a luxury to have a minute for herself."

Hines flipped to a fresh page. "Okay. One last question. Do you know anything about guns, Professor Fielding?"

"God, no! Except for what I see in the movies."

"You weren't in the armed forces?"

"No. I had a student deferment for most of the sixties."

Hines nodded and wrote it down. "How about others in the department?"

"In the armed forces? We don't talk much about—wait, I do remember Bart Bickford said once that he'd been in Korea."

"Korea." Hines noted it down, then looked at Walensky, eyebrows arched.

Walensky said defensively, "Ancient history. Most guys have been in the service."

"Anyone else, Professor Fielding?" Hines's voice was steely.

"Well, Bernie Reinalter too, now that I think about it. He and Bart were talking about it once. At a party. Years ago, before . . . well—" He broke off at the black look that clouded Walensky's face.

Hines said smoothly, "Before Professor Bickford decided that Professor Reinalter was trying to pressure him out of the department."

"Uh . . . yes." Did Hines already know everything about this department? Charlie glanced at Walensky and was suddenly depressed.

Hines's pen was poised again. "Now, does Professor Reinalter own a gun? Or anyone else in the department?"

"Well, Bernie goes quail hunting sometimes, he must have a rifle or something. Oh, and Nora! Nora Peterson has a gun. Little pistol, for self-defense."

"Fine. Anyone else?" Hines stood stolidly, unmoving except for the brown hand holding the pen, but the glance that flashed briefly at Walensky seemed to speak triumph.

"No. No, that's all I know about," Charlie said uncomfortably. "But Captain Walensky is right, a lot of professors served in the armed forces. They wouldn't necessarily discuss it around here."

"Of course. Well, thank you, Professor Fielding, I may be talking to you again later."

"Sure. Okay."

Walensky's mouth had a sour cast. "Is Bart Bickford still downstairs?"

"Yes, he just finished with one of his subjects," Maggie told him.

"Well, thank you. I'll be in touch. Let's go, Captain Walensky." Hines started down the stairs, then paused. "Be sure to let me know if you think of anyone who might want to cause trouble for you, Professor Fielding."

"Okay."

Relieved that it was over for a time, Charlie followed Maggie through the door to the ground floor hall. His graduate assistant Gary Kramer, plump and curly haired, popped out of the office next to Charlie's. "Hi!" he exclaimed.

"Hi, Gary," said Maggie.

"How're you doing?" Charlie pulled out his keys.

"Okay." Gary gestured with the plastic videotape container in his hand. "This is the last one with the lower-case paragraphs. I'm ready to start on the all-cap paragraphs now."

"Great!" Charlie unlocked the door, turning to Maggie. "That means you can start on those data sheets too as soon as you're ready."

"Good. So we've got three of the studies ready to go, right? I'll take them down to the computers right away. Unless the cops need something again."

Cops. Damn. Charlie's anger reawakened even as his rational side protested that it was pointless, that they had their job to do. Hines and Walensky seemed a constant presence now, popping in and out of Charlie's life with questions, interrupting his thoughts even when physically they were away. And Walensky, who should be helping, or at least running interference to make sure the department wasn't disrupted, was doing neither. Charlie wanted him to catch the killer quickly, but he was still kowtowing to the administrators, keeping NYSU's reputation clean; that's all he gave a damn about. Charlie remembered Tal's anger two years ago when little Jonathan Hammond was hit by a car. Walensky had spent the precious first few moments after the accident getting in touch with university administrators rather than notifying police and state troopers. Well, he'd called the ambulance, even tried some first aid himself. The newspapers couldn't fault that, not even Tal could fault that. The kid had been badly hurt. But the driver, of course, had never been caught. Damn Walensky anyway. And Hines. And the killer, who might—

"Damn it, Gary, not that one!" Charlie heard himself scream. Gary, at the bookcase, dropped the tape and recoiled as though he'd been slapped.

"Sorry, damn it. Didn't mean to shout. This goddamn thing with Tal . . ." Charlie took off his glasses, rubbed his eyes, put the glasses back on. His voice was under control again. "The study you want is on the third shelf. See them? Brown circles?"

"Got it," said Gary. He pulled the tape, said, "See you later," and eased out of the room.

"God, this thing has me yelling at the students." Charlie slammed his fist into his hand.

"Hey, take it easy." Maggie gave him a pat on the back. "We all feel snappish. It's a damn frustrating situation."

"Yeah. Damn, I wish I could think of who . . . or why . . ."

"Best thing to do is get some work done," said Maggie, brisk as Aunt Babs. "Sometimes answers come when we're thinking about something else."

"They sure as hell aren't coming when I think about the shooting," Charlie admitted.

"I'll be in the computer room. See you later." Maggie breezed out in a flourish of red shirttails. She seemed so strong, so much in control. Charlie dragged himself to his desk.

He needed Deanna. That would help. Deanna was restorative, could make him feel strong and in control with a glance, a touch. Charlie took off his glasses and rubbed his eyes.

He'd met her in February. He didn't play hockey anymore, but still enjoyed skating, the muscular memories of the sport he'd once enjoyed. That slushy Saturday he'd had to drive to Syracuse to pick up a carton of two-inch videotape, and on a whim he'd tossed his skates into the car, deciding to try the huge municipal rink. It was crowded, being Saturday, with beginners stumbling around the edges, boisterous packs of small boys shouting and shoving each other for the benefit of clumsy giggling schoolgirls, more serious skaters like himself trying to avoid them. A few figure skaters worked in the center. He'd almost decided to give up and return to Laconia's modest but less crowded rink when a slender form in figure skates sped past him on the left. She was in white tights and a short neatly darned red skating skirt. Bright brown hair was caught in a white barrette at the nape of her neck. As he watched she executed a beautiful turning leap and arabesque, landing on her right skate to skim backward, facing him now, left leg and arms extended elegantly, cheeks flushed in triumph.

Charlie slowed a fraction to match her speed and clapped his hands in appreciation.

Her eyes met his. She smiled shyly.

A great swelling wave boiled up through Charlie, loins to heart to astonished eyes. Shit, he thought, shit shit shit. But it was too late. She set the air tingling and swamped him with hopeless desire.

And then a second later whimsical fate handed him a crumb of hope after all. One of the rowdy little boys, shoved by his companions, came skidding across Charlie's path and into the backward-coasting leg of the exquisite skater. She staggered back, arms flailing, and almost caught herself on her other skate before falling in a flurry of gleaming skate blades, red skirtlet, and intoxicating white-clad thighs. Charlie was at her side instantly, hand on her elbow, before her expression could change from astonishment. "You okay?" he asked urgently.

"Yeah." She frowned at the boy. "Oh, God, did I hurt him?"

"I certainly hope so!" said Charlie. The lad had struggled to his feet, barked a red-faced "Sorry" at Deanna, and now skated clumsily toward his hooting buddies. She watched him depart, giggled, and stood up deftly with only the slightest pressure on Charlie's yearning hand.

"Don't be mean. He's still learning," she said.

"I'm never mean. But fair's fair." He noticed how her hair sprang back from her temples in a soft spun-copper glow. He said, "How about a hot chocolate? Or a Coke?"

The incredible eyes, fringed with those long, long natural lashes, turned to him again. In them he saw loneliness and need like his own, and wisdom, and caution. "No, thank you. I better not," she said shyly.

"Hey, of course you need something after taking a spill like that. Just to get you going again." And when she glanced at the side bleachers, still hesitating, he struck a melodramatic hand-on-heart pose. "C'mon, you don't want to hurt my feelings!"

No, she didn't want to hurt his feelings. She let him catch her hand and lead her to the refreshment stand. In fact, she was pleased to get the Coke. Her coral lips pursed around the straw, and in a haze of delight Charlie gathered up her little banal comments as though they were precious rubies. Her name was Deanna, she said. She'd moved only recently to the Syracuse suburb of Greenwood, didn't have a lot of friends yet. Yes, she loved movies, *The Sting* and *Rocky* more than *Jaws* or *The Exorcist.* She'd come to the rink today with Betty Giordano—she gestured at a laughing mixed-sex group by the bleachers. The plump, dark-haired one was her friend. But Betty had spotted some guys she knew and she'd gone over to talk to them. She, Deanna, had gone on skating.

"You're very good," Charlie told her. "You must have had a good teacher."

"Yeah. When I was little, in Pittsburgh, there was a great coach at the Y. Miss Donaldson. She was going to put me in her Olympic-rules class."

"What happened?"

"My mom and dad got divorced. We went to live in the country a while."

"No place to skate?"

"There was a pond. It only froze two or three times the whole winter." An adorable pout.

"Well, here you can practice. As long as those brats don't keep knocking you down."

She smiled. "Have to be ready to fall if you're a skater, Miss Donaldson always said."

Oh, he'd fallen, all right, he'd fallen. But he knew he mustn't rush things. She was too shy. She finished her Coke and said something about checking in with Betty. "Sure," he said with a casual salute. "See you around."

But as she tossed her Coke cup into the trash can, she'd given him a look filled with anxiety and hunger, and set his heart singing again. He knew. She knew. They were meant to be together.

Gary tapped at the door. "Uh . . . Charlie?"

Charlie replaced his glasses. "Come on in, Gary," he said warmly. Just thinking about Deanna mended his tattered soul.

"I wanted to double check the coding categories on this new batch of tapes," Gary explained.

"Sure. Have a seat." Charlie pulled his master list from his desk drawer.

Tomorrow, he told himself. He'd see Deanna tomorrow.

XI

Bernie Reinalter tented his fingers and leaned back in his desk chair. "The department will do everything possible to facilitate the processing, Anne."

"I know that, Bernie." He'd invited her into his office, waved her into this seat, told her to make herself comfortable, as though sitting on the student side of the desk could possibly be comfortable. Really wanted her to make *him* comfortable. To sit in the subordinate seat, a desk-width away, under control. No screaming allowed. No weeping either. Merely state your alleged sorrow and your intention of soldiering on as though nothing had occurred. As though your life had not been smashed.

"Are Paul and Rocky coming?" he asked.

"Tomorrow night. Paul may not arrive till Sunday."

"That's good. I'm sure they'll be a great help to you. Smart kids. Well, not kids anymore, really. I tend to remember them before they went off to college." His pale eyes looked into the distance. "I remember Rocky in her baseball cap once at a departmental barbecue. She was probably in junior high about then. I asked her, just teasing, if she was going to major in phys ed in college. 'No,' she said, 'math. To catch a ball you have to solve a differential equation, instantaneously.' " Reinalter smiled. "Cool as a cucumber."

Just like Reinalter to appreciate Rocky's coolness. He was cool himself. Well, sometimes, like right now, he made an effort to be human, but somehow the effect was always as though he spoke from a lofty, chilly height. Reinalter Peak, just north of Mont Blanc. Anne said, "Rocky's still coaching softball."

"Good. Well, I just wanted you to know that we'll do everything possible to help. Officially or unofficially."

Anne said perversely, "Of course when it's murder there are added complications, aren't there?"

He didn't quite flinch at the word, but his blond eyebrows contracted in a frown. "That's true. Of course we're cooperating with the police, trying to clear it up."

"We're all cooperating with the police, Bernie." Anne pulled out a cigarette, lit it, and blew Gallic smoke at his Swiss nose. "And so far I'm doing my damnedest to turn away the reporters."

"I appreciate that, Anne." She'd shaken him at last, and now he leaned forward, suddenly earnest. "You know how important it is to avoid bad publicity."

So that was it. Should have known. "Bernie," said Anne, "someone in this department *murdered* Tal. That's not going to be good publicity, however it comes out."

"Yes, I know. But after all, it is an isolated problem, isn't it? No need to—"

"Don't be silly, Bernie!" Anne had had enough of the subordinate chair. She stood up and tramped around the desk to his wastebasket to tap her cigarette ash. She looked down at Bernie. "There's every need to inspect problems in this department. The police have already searched Tal's office and our home, and they'll be looking at the rest of you too if they can think of any justification at all."

Bernie's eyes flicked down toward the leg of his desk, then up again. "That's true, Anne. But we must still be discreet, don't you agree? I mean, if you're having tax problems, you don't really want it spread across the newspapers, do you?"

Anne almost pitied him. "Hell, Bernie, I don't give a damn. The IRS was wrong on that one. An investigation is exactly what we wanted. And we're not talking much money anyway. Though I can see, in your case—"

She broke off at the shadow of panic in his eyes. She turned to the windows and drew on her cigarette. Lucky Bernie, two big windows overlooking the parking lot. "Look, everybody's being as discreet as possible, seems to me," she said. "Even the police. Walensky's watching every move Hines makes, and vice versa. But we have to tell the truth, even if it's ugly."

"But some things are irrelevant! A waste of time!" A shrill note had entered his voice. He stood up, apparently realizing that it was hard to play the patriarch when even a short matronly woman like Anne could look down on his graying head. He stepped to the other side of the window and drew a deep breath. "And there are things Tal didn't want known."

"Tal devoted his life to truth."

"But he also knew how to keep things in context. A lone fact is not a truth, Anne. Not by itself."

"But it's a piece of the truth." Anne turned to face him. "Look, Bernie, I know some things about this department. Over the years Tal has shared some things with me. Obviously I've never gone running to the newspapers with hot tips about scandals in the education department. I don't intend to start now. But damn it, if you don't tell the cops about your problems back in Iowa, I will!"

Bernie stared at her, frosty as Alpine air. Finally he said, "It's not relevant, Anne. Tal would know that. It can hurt a career. And a department. And slow down the investigation."

"Tell all that to Hines too. He's not stupid. He's not out to ruin careers. He'll keep it in context, as you say. But the context is murder. Tal's murder, Bernie!"

"Anne, I know you're upset, of course you are. But you have to keep a sense of proportion!"

"*My* sense of proportion is fine, Bernie. But what the hell happened to yours?"

Under her glare his eyes shifted away, then back again. "I'll tell him," he muttered at last.

"Good." Anne ground out the cigarette in Bernie's wastebasket. Yesterday, long ago, she might have felt sorry for Bernie, as she felt sorry for young what's-his-name who needed more time for his term paper. But today it didn't matter that Bernie had spent years cultivating an upstanding image for the department and for himself. Nothing mattered. Even finding the murderer and exacting revenge didn't matter. But at least focusing on that task distracted her. Liberated her from deep grief into deep anger. Anger was much more comfortable.

There was a tap on the door. Cindy called, "Professor Reinalter, there are reporters here again. Can you talk to them?"

"Damn," muttered Bernie. "The dean's office is supposed to take care of them."

"Want me to see them?" Anne offered.

Bernie looked shocked. "No, no, of course not. Tell them I'm on my way, Cindy." He reached for his jacket and peered into a little mirror on the inside of his narrow closet door. "Anne, I'll get rid of them quickly. Be right back."

"Thanks, Bernie." She accepted the favor. He was right that she didn't want to talk to reporters.

"When they're gone Cindy can help you with the forms that have to be signed."

"Good."

"See you later." The door closed behind him.

As she stooped to lift her bag, an image flashed across Anne's mind: his quick guilty glance at the leg of the desk when she'd mentioned Hines searching offices. Maybe not at the leg, maybe at the drawer. She pulled the drawer open, surprised at her own detached curiosity. Nothing in it anyway, she saw, just a couple of popular math puzzle magazines, too mass-market to be displayed on a scholar's shelves. Sure didn't take much to embarrass Bernie. She pushed the drawer closed again and waited until she could start signing papers.

* * *

Anne signed the umpteenth form and shoved the stack across Cindy's desk. "Those are done. Ready for the next batch."

"Here you go." Cindy handed new papers to her. "Lundgren says he'll have the rest of the stuff for you Monday, so you can go directly to see him in the personnel office. Won't have to stop by here." Cindy was shuffling the forms into the appropriate piles, stapling and restacking as she spoke. Today she was wearing a white linen suit over a pumpkin-colored knit shirt.

"Okay," said Anne. "Better talk to you today, then."

"Oh?" Cindy paused, her light prominent eyes under the overhang of thickened lashes fixed on Anne.

"Who do you think did it?"

The eyes shifted away. "God. I don't know, Anne. Bart, maybe, or Charlie?"

"Bart, then," said Anne sadly. "Hard to picture. Leaving Charlie's memo book to try to prove that Charlie did it, then making it look like a suicide. God. And then dropping his own pipe by mistake."

Cindy shrugged her white linen-clad shoulders. "Could be," she said. "Or vice-versa."

"Maggie was with Charlie and says he couldn't have done it."

"Could be. But who can you believe in this kind of thing?"

"Cindy, what is it about Charlie? Do you know some way he could have done it?"

"No, no." Cindy's hand rose and fell to the desk again in a gesture of frustration. "He and Maggie weren't together every single minute. But it's hard to think how either one could have done it. On the other hand, Bart is such a peaceable old bear. And Charlie had a motive, after all."

"You think it was Tal's new study? But they've been arguing that same issue for years."

"Yeah, it's a rotten reason. But with everyone else there's no reason at all."

"I know." No reason. No reason at all. So why had it happened? Maybe this was all a cruel dream.

"Anne!" Maggie Ryan swung into the room, ablaze today in a bright red shirt. She dropped her briefcase beside Cindy's desk. "How are you?"

"Angry," said Anne.

"Right. Me too." She touched Anne's elbow and turned to Cindy. "Is there any problem about me staying in the building late tonight? Have to make up some time because I have to take a couple of hours off now."

"Sure, you can work late," said Cindy. "The night watchman comes on around ten and locks up, but your building key will still let you in and out. Where are you going now?"

"Liz wants to take the kids swimming, but when I spoke to her just now she said Will's sniffle is worse. And he's an absolute brat if he misses his nap, even when he's healthy. So she's going to drive by in a few minutes, and I'll take him home for a nap while she and Sarah go off to the park to swim."

"Kids are so inefficient," Anne said. "Paul and Rocky always got sick at different times too. Doubled the problem."

"Better than tripling it," muttered Cindy.

"You have three kids?" Maggie asked.

"Two boys and a girl. And every time a cold hits one of them, I know it'll be three or four weeks of juggling for Mark and me, and sometimes my mother."

"Yeah." Maggie shook her head sympathetically.

"They do get older," Anne said. "After a while they can take care of their own colds. But by then you're worried about them all the time anyway, sick or well. Drugs, dropping out, general teenage stupidity."

"God. Maybe you shouldn't tell us," said Cindy, resting her chin on her hand glumly.

"I remember doing it to my own mom," Maggie said. "God, I put her through a lot. But I sure appreciate her now. Cindy, tell me, is Walensky still investigating this case?"

"Yeah, he came around once. But the black fellow from downtown, what's his name, Hines? He's really working on it. He's been around a lot more."

"I see. I was wondering because I just passed Nora Peterson's office, and a Campus Security cop was in there. He was closing the door."

Anne frowned. "Wonder what he's after? It wasn't Walensky?"

"No, the younger guy. The one who drove us here yesterday. Pete something, Walensky called him."

"Pete Dixon." Anne remembered the name on the gray uniform barring her way yesterday, blocking her from seeing if that too-familiar tweed on the trail was what she feared it was.

"Right. Pete Dixon."

"Interesting," said Cindy. "Walensky's always pretty low-key. Hates publicity. Well, the administrators probably tell him to avoid headlines. But maybe he's following up for a change. Did you see the paper last night?"

Anne said, "I skipped it."

"Well," said Cindy, "there were three front-page photos. One of the gorge, one of Tal, and one of Dean Hughes looking serious and noble. And there's Walensky back in the shadows. You can barely make him out."

"Sounds like the perfect man to work with Dean Hughes," said Maggie. "Hines was nowhere to be seen. But they had a few quotes from a police spokesperson."

"Anything there we didn't know yet?" Anne asked.

"Not a thing. A lot of people refused to comment. Including you."

"Yeah. They called a few times yesterday afternoon and I brushed them off. Took the phone off the hook last night."

"Good plan," said Maggie, then looked up in surprise.

A heavyset balding man in a brown uniform had entered. He bore an invoice, its multicolored leaves and dark carbon sheets crackling in his hand. "Package for Professor Charles Fielding," he announced. Behind him in the hall stood a hand truck bearing a large cardboard box.

Cindy said, "I'll ring him." Her well-groomed fingers punched out a number on the phone. The deliveryman studied the office as he waited, his lively brown eyes sliding from window to cabinets to the three women. His gaze lingered a moment on Eric the plastic head. The man looked familiar to Anne. Probably one of the fellows who had delivered the filing cabinets to the French department last month.

Cindy replaced the receiver. "Professor Fielding isn't in. I can sign for it here, and he can take it down to his office himself."

"Okay," said the deliveryman dubiously. He gestured at the box. "But it's pretty heavy."

"I see." Cindy eyed the hand truck and its load, then stood up and pulled her ring of keys from the drawer. "Well, let's take it down to his office. It isn't far. Be right back," she added to Maggie and Anne as she hurried into the hall. The deliveryman tipped the hand truck onto its wheels and pushed it obediently after Cindy's orange-and-white figure.

"Wonder where Charlie is?" Anne exhaled a cloud of smoke.

"He said something about fixing some equipment this afternoon." Maggie was flipping through one of the file drawers behind Cindy's desk. "A printer, I think."

"Tal always hated working with complicated machines. He said humans were unpredictable enough without adding unpredictable equipment."

"Charlie's a good technician, though. Have you seen his house?" Maggie pulled out a file and checked the name.

"You mean that equipment room he's got? Yes. His office is full of equipment too."

"Right. Actually, I can sympathize. I like to tune up my car myself." She was riffling through the drawer again. "When you deal with people all day it's good to interact with something that obeys the laws of physics in a straightforward way, without layers of psychology on top."

Cindy came back in, one hand fluffing her curls. "Boy, Charlie's getting low on space in there. He's got it organized, but that guy had to push his dolly all the way back by the bookcase before he could unload the—hey! What are you doing?" She darted across to Maggie.

"Looking at my file." Maggie handed a manila folder to Cindy.

"Wanted to see if my health form was in there. I didn't remember if I gave it back to you or not. Will's sniffle reminded me."

Unsmiling, Cindy took the folder, glanced inside, and said, "It's there. All taken care of."

"Okay. Thanks."

Cindy said, "Next time wait and ask me. These aren't public files."

"Sorry, should have thought." Maggie snapped her briefcase closed, dark against her bright red shirt. "Well, I'd better get out to the parking lot. Liz should be here any minute with my runny-nosed son." At the door she turned back to Anne. "Maybe when Liz takes Will again after his nap we can talk for a minute. Will you be finished here?"

"Yes, in a little while. I'll probably go back to my office in Harper."

"Okay. I'll find you." She disappeared down the hall.

Cindy replaced Maggie's folder and Tal's in the file drawer, slammed it closed, and locked it.

Anne picked up her pen to sign Cindy's forms and looked at the door Maggie had just gone through.

With her briefcase.

A briefcase containing two folders from Cindy's locked file.

She hoped they were more informative than the math puzzle magazines that seemed to make Bernie feel so guilty.

.

XII

Anne finished signing the stack of forms and trudged downstairs to the parking lot. She'd drive over to her office in Harper to see if there was anything she should be doing in the French department. One of her young colleagues had had an offer from Princeton, another one thought he might be able to get Jacques Derrida to come give a lecture next year—all that had interested her earlier this week. Eons ago.

She emerged into the parking lot. Ugly utilitarian landscape spread around every building these days. Well, probably wasn't much better in the old days. Before asphalt and internal combustion there was mud and horse manure.

She saw Maggie standing under the roof of the loading area, sliding something into her briefcase and talking to the deliveryman who had brought Charlie's package. Anne waved, and Maggie ran down the two steps and across to greet her. "Finished your paperwork?"

"Only for the moment. Cindy's found an administrator who promises a new supply." She nodded at the deliveryman. "Did you find out anything interesting about Charlie's package?"

"The invoice wasn't very specific. Look, here comes Liz!"

The red Toyota bearing the baby-sitter and two children, one bouncy and one sullen, pulled up near them. "All yours," Liz called as she stretched across Will to unlock the passenger door.

"Okay." Maggie opened the door and unbuckled the child safety seat. "How's everybody?"

In the backseat, Sarah's brown eyes were wide with delight. "Mommy, there's a waterfall where Liz swims!"

"Wim!" echoed Will.

His mother lifted him whimpering from the car, balanced him on her hip, and caressed Sarah's curls. Then Maggie pulled out the baby seat and said, "Have fun, you two. You'll be done in a couple of hours, right?"

"Yes. I'll pick him up at your apartment," Liz said.

"Fine. I'm sure he'll sleep; he's fussy already."

"Wim!" insisted Will tearfully. But the Toyota was already pulling away.

Maggie found a tissue and applied it to Will's runny nose. He twisted his head away in annoyance.

"Kids are such ingrates," Anne observed.

Maggie smiled at the tiny struggling boy. "True. Their opinions are much bigger and stronger than they are."

"Good thing we're set up to love the little critters," Anne said. "When my kids were small I remember marveling that any of us ever reach adulthood. Babies are so low in social graces."

As if to prove her point, Will arched his back and reached for the pavement. "Dow!" he demanded.

"If I put you down, you'll just want to be up again," Maggie reminded him.

"Dow! Dow!"

She glanced around the parking lot. No cars moved. She put the little boy down, and he doddered a few steps away to celebrate his freedom. His mother glanced back at Anne. "You know, Anne, I've been wondering if Cindy couldn't answer some of our questions."

"I doubt it. A few minutes ago I asked her what she thought and she's as lost as we are."

"But she may know part of the answer without realizing it." Maggie's eyes were following her son. "Secretaries have a lot of information."

"Yes," Anne grunted. "I saw you making off with some of her information. Had a chance to look at it yet?"

"Nope. I was going to do it while Will naps. But even so, if we could talk to Cindy while she's away from the office—" Maggie tensed suddenly. Little Will had spotted the deliveryman at the loading dock and was toddling full throttle across the asphalt toward him.

"Da!" he exclaimed.

Maggie started after him, but before she reached him Will had charged up to the loading platform, tripped on the step, and bumped his small chin. He began to bellow, and the deliveryman scooped him up.

"Hey, little guy, it's not that bad," he crooned as Maggie and Anne arrived. Maggie reached for him, but the boy turned away from her and buried his face against the brown uniform. Maggie's eyes met the deliveryman's. It was just an instant, but there was such profound eloquence in their gaze that Anne realized suddenly that things were not what they seemed to be. Recognition dawned.

"Cyrano de Bergerac, I presume," she said.

Maggie grinned at her ruefully. "Nothing like a kid to blow your cover. You're right, Anne. Meet Nick."

"Enchantée," Anne said. "But what the hell is going on?"

"Maggie said things were serious here. I thought maybe I could lend a hand." His voice was different too, Anne noted. Pleasant, but definitely not Cyrano's rolling cadences, nor the working-class gruffness of the deliveryman.

"Tal acted some in college," Anne said. "And never lost his love of it. Thought your Cyrano was great."

"Thanks." Nick smiled. A broad-built, pleasantly homely man, he was still cuddling his little son against his shoulder. The boy's sobs had waned to occasional teary hiccups.

"Well, I'm glad you're here," Anne said. "We're trying to find out what happened because our two sets of hardworking policemen can hardly communicate. And because I can't bear not to try."

"I'll do what I can," Nick promised.

"You don't want people to know you're here?"

"Not yet," Maggie explained. "We'll see if he can find anything by staying in the background."

"Right. You were practically invisible in that uniform."

"Invisible to you professor types." Nick smiled, and Anne was reminded again of the dashing long-nosed Cyrano. "Not to my son. And one of the custodians here had a few questions."

"Time to get you into a new outfit," said Maggie. "Hey, listen, since things have worked out this way, why don't you take Will to the apartment with you? He can have his nap while you change."

"He's ready for one."

"Right. And I can check in the computer room to see if the results of Charlie's first studies are in. It would be good to get that out of the way."

"Okay. Call me in an hour or so." Nick carried Will carefully to a U-Haul van parked near the loading door while Maggie fastened the baby seat into the passenger side. Will protested half-heartedly when his father buckled him in. Maggie grabbed Nick's big hand and squeezed it in farewell, and Anne felt a sudden pang of rage that she could not squeeze Tal's. Unfair that the world had not called a moratorium on affection. It rolled on callously, full of cute babies and people in love and flowers and birds. It should be draped in black, as it was when other princes died.

"Are you okay?" Maggie asked gently. The van had pulled away.

Anne looked up from the pavement she'd been staring at. "No. I'm angry. I want Tal."

"Yes." Maggie hugged her.

"And if I can't have him I want the world to stop. I want all humanity in mourning. I want FBI sharpshooters blasting down whoever killed him."

"I agree! But the best I can do is talk to people. Steal folders."

"Are you going to read them now?"

"Soon," said Maggie. "I want to see if I can talk to a couple of people while they're still around the department. And I do have to check on Charlie's printout."

"I'll come too."

"Sure, if you want to, but it may be dull. I'm going to the computer room first."

"Let's go." Anne hauled open the steel loading door and found herself at the bottom of a wide stair hall. She marched past the steps, energized by her anger, and on through the fire doors into the white corridors of the basement.

Maggie drew even with her. "Fourth door," she said.

The room was filled with terminals, though few people sat at the machines. A big No Smoking sign hung on every wall. Maggie checked a pile of printouts, conferred briefly with a chestnut-haired young woman, then looked back at Anne and made a sour face. "Computer's down," she reported. "They say it'll be back at work in a couple of hours."

"Tal used to go crazy waiting for results."

"Yeah. But usually it's better to go do something else." Maggie breezed back into the hall and held the door for Anne. "Look, there's Bart. Let's talk to him."

Bart turned as they approached, his heavy brow puzzled. "Oh, Maggie. And Anne! God, Anne, how are you doing?"

The truth took too much time. Anne said, "Not bad."

His big face was contorted with concern. "Listen, you know if there's anything we can do—I mean, Libby tried to call you, but the line was busy."

She'd had the phone off the hook. She said, "Sure, Bart, I know you're there if I need you. But there's really not much we can do. Unless you can help us figure out who did it."

"God, I wish I could! It—well, I know it must make everything even worse, Anne, with the detectives always asking questions. It's hard even for me, and for you, on top of everything . . ." He shook his head.

"And the damn reporters."

"Yes. Yes, I guess there would be reporters." His hand strayed to his pocket. He had a pipe in it. Anne could see its shape through the soft tweed. She wondered if he'd had to buy a new one.

"We had an idea and wondered if you could add anything," said Maggie. "They found your pipe in the gorge. Do you know how it got there?"

His deep-set eyes looked away from her, and a spasm of despair crossed his face. Anne was surprised by the depth of the misery written there. "I don't know why," he muttered.

"But you think you know who." Maggie was intent on his face. "You think Charlie did it, trying to frame you. You think I'm covering up for him."

He was uneasy. "Well, I know you work for him—"

"Not for him. With him. The grant pays me as a consultant, independently. Bart, I've been trying to think if there was any way Charlie could have done it, but I've come up with nothing. So I'm asking you to think for a minute. If not Charlie, who?"

"Not Charlie?"

"Look, you're thinking he tried to frame you and dropped his book by mistake when he did it. Well, why couldn't it be you trying to frame him, and dropping your pipe by mistake?"

"Did he say that? Is that why the police have been—"

Anne said impatiently, "Bart, it's one possibility. You're a scientist, think! Each of us knows a few facts. You say your facts make you suspect Charlie. But what if it's not Charlie? What if someone else set up both of you?"

"Both of us. God, that seems so unlikely—but then, it seems unlikely that Charlie would—" He looked into the distance, over Anne's head. "God, you know, at first I was sure it was just a mugger. Then when they found my pipe and Charlie's notebook—well, it was like getting hit twice. Tal, and then Charlie framing me. But why would anyone do this to Charlie and me both?"

"To make sure the police were looking the wrong way," Maggie explained patiently. "Probably hoping that one or the other of you wouldn't have a strong alibi. But it would help if we could figure out who besides Charlie could have taken your pipe."

"I see." Bart looked at them with a spark of hope. "So if we work out who could have taken both the notebook and the pipe, we'll have our answer."

"Except that it's not that easy." Maggie pushed her fingers through her hair. "Charlie's little book was in his outside jacket pocket and could have fallen out anywhere here or on the way to Collegetown."

"So anyone who got the pipe could also get the book." The tweedy shoulders sagged again. "Well, the problem is, I can't narrow it down much more. I had a smoke yesterday morning in the hall. Then I went in and worked on my grant proposal."

"The one Tal was helping with?"

"Yes. After he left I was busy for a couple of hours on it. Then I had to leave to get my photos in Collegetown before meeting him for lunch. When I started down the gorge trail I reached for my pipe and it was gone."

"Okay. You used it this morning, put it away, put it in your pocket. Who did you see after that?"

"You know, Sergeant Hines asked me all this but he didn't explain why," Bart said. "I told him I thought it was Charlie. I thought he was trying to work out how Charlie got the pipe and I wondered why he kept asking about everyone else. Anyway, the first thing that happened was that Charlie almost bumped into me, running down the hall. I saw Cindy in the office, and Tal. Asked to see Bernie but he was too busy." There was a bitter edge in his voice. "So I went to my office. Tal came in, and later I went to check a Piaget reference with Nora in her office. Around eleven I met with a couple of my grad students in my office. While they were there Cindy called, said Bernie had been able to find ten minutes in his schedule and would I come over. So I was in Bernie's office for ten minutes."

"What did you talk about?" Maggie asked brightly.

"Nothing important."

There was a brief pause. Bart fingered the pipe in his pocket. Finally Anne said, "You and Bernie aren't exactly chums."

"You think he—?" A short harsh laugh. "No. I can see him framing me, all right. But Charlie's always been his fair-haired boy. And Tal— God, I keep hitting that, Anne. Everybody liked Tal!"

Wounded, Anne snapped, "In that case someone who liked him shot him. Be logical, Bart!"

"Yes." Chastised, he looked away. Such a big man, *un bouboule,* but so easy to hurt.

"While we're being logical," Maggie said, "let me ask if your pipe could have fallen from your pocket."

"No. Well, maybe it's possible. A couple of times in the past I've leaned over and it's fallen out. But it's unlikely—oh, hell, the whole thing is unlikely, isn't it?"

"Yes." Maggie's arms were folded across her flame-red shirt, and her brows had pulled into a small thoughtful frown. "Well, if you do think of something, be sure to let the police know. But don't let us keep you any longer. I know you're running an experiment now."

"Yes." He smiled at Anne. "Still trying to find out how creative children can be."

"Is this a follow-up to that study you ran two years ago?" Anne asked.

"That was just a pilot study. Had some interesting things in it. But our follow-up study last year didn't work out. The stories were so different the coders couldn't agree on categories. So now we're constraining the kids' stories more, giving them a topic instead of letting them choose. Oh, hell, Anne, you don't want to hear me babble about this!"

Maggie's voice held lively interest. "Anne was telling me that Tal was very impressed by one of the kids in that pilot study. The young Jules Verne, remember, Anne?"

"Jill Baker," Anne said.

Bart nodded. "Yes. That's a good example of the coding problem I was talking about. Jill Baker told some interesting animal stories. I thought they were pretty creative. But one of the coders thought all animal stories were derivative."

"So by giving the kids topics, you'll get your coders to look for creativity in areas other than subject matter?" Maggie asked.

"That's right. Though I hate to limit the children's imagination that way."

"This Jill Baker—did she have brothers and sisters?"

"Let's see." He looked into space again, thinking. "I met the mother. Bobbie Baker, something like that. Seems to me she was divorced and Jill was the only child. Why do you ask?"

Maggie shrugged, the red shirt rising and falling. "Just curiosity. I see my daughter telling stories to her little brother and wonder if it's developing her imagination. Well, Anne, let's go. I have to find Charlie and tell him that the computer's down, with his numbers in it."

"Too bad," said Bart. "Anne, you call us if we can do anything, okay?"

"Okay. See you, Bart."

Maggie picked up her briefcase and they went back down the hall and around the corner. She stopped by an open door. Anne saw that Charlie was in the room, bent over a disassembled machine. He was humming "Over the Rainbow" and gave a start when Maggie spoke. "How's it going?"

"Oh, Maggie! And Anne. Hello." He straightened and pushed his glasses up on his nose.

Maggie put her briefcase on the table next to the apparatus. "Have you found the problem?"

"I've got it narrowed down to two possibilities," Charlie said. "As soon as I check those out I can fix it."

"Good. I figured you must be doing all right if you were humming."

"Yeah." Charlie looked at Anne almost apologetically. "I get absorbed in equipment like this. Forget the real world sometimes."

Anne nodded. Nice of him to apologize, as though he too knew the world should be in mourning. She reached for a cigarette but then hesitated, remembering the signs in the computer room. So much equipment these days needed a smoke-free environment. Including humans, apparently. Well, she'd quit one of these days, but this was hardly the time.

Maggie was telling Charlie about the computer printout problem. "Will you still be around a couple of hours from now?"

"Yes, of course. This contraption will take me another hour at least, and I haven't even checked my mail today."

"Well, I'll stop by again later. Maybe we can go over the results today after all." She picked up her briefcase again. "Good luck with that printer."

"Thanks."

"Next stop, phone booth," said Maggie when they were back in the hall.

"As long as I can smoke," said Anne. "But I thought we were going to look at Cindy's files and return them."

"Yes, if we can. But something else has come up." Maggie shoved open the main doors of the basement and led the way to a bank of outdoor phone booths. Anne lit a Gauloise while Maggie opened the directory. "A lot of Bakers. Do you know where Jill lives, Anne?"

"Jill Baker? I don't know."

"Lives with her mother, Bart said. A name like Bobbie. Roberta, maybe. How about R. M. Baker, 401 Stafford—no, that's on campus, probably a student. Well, we'll try B. E. Baker then. 1731 Pinetree Lane." She slapped the book closed and rejoined Anne.

"So we're going to try to find Jill Baker?"

"We'll just buzz by, then come back here." She replaced the directory and started around the corner toward the parking lot. "Why don't we take my car? That is, if you want to come."

"Sure. But why this sudden interest in Jill Baker?"

"You said her story bothered Tal. And it occurred to me that she'd be home from school by now. School's still in session here, right?"

"Until next week." Anne climbed into the Camaro. Children's toys were scattered across the backseat.

"Okay, let's go. Pinetree Lane is part of that new subdivision on the west hill, right? Forest Park?" Maggie snapped her seatbelt on and turned the ignition.

"Yes. All the streets have names like that. Pinetree, Cherrywood, Oakland. Tal used to call it Parquet Park."

Maggie laughed. "Off to Parquet Park we go. It's not that far from here, if we cut over by Minerva Creek."

"That's right. You know your way around here."

"When I was a grad here I had a lovely rusty old Ford. Springs popping out of the upholstery but it ran well. God, I loved that car. My first. I was always tuning it up, relining the brakes, all that stuff. Drove it all over these hills." Maggie sighed. "The frame finally rusted through and I sold it to a guy for parts. I was moving to New York about then anyway."

"First car, first apartment," said Anne. "Strange how friendly you feel toward them even when they wouldn't do at all anymore. Or first trip abroad. God, I was dumb! But at the time I felt so sophisticated."

"Same here." The blue eyes smiled at Anne. "I was this hick kid from Ohio, thinking, Watch out Paris, here I come! So greedy. Fifteen years old and I wanted to gobble the whole city, everything it had to offer. Art, music, theatre, sports, literature. Love."

"Same with me. I was fourteen. Maybe at that age it's a healthy attitude."

"Maybe." Maggie's voice was serious now. "But you can sure take a bad fall if you aren't careful."

"That can happen anywhere. And you recover from things that happen at fifteen."

"Recover. Well, maybe sometimes." That sidelong glance again, sober this time. "In any case you go on."

"Yes. You go on, you grow." Anne looked out the window. They had descended into the valley from the university hill and were crossing the town toward the road that led up the west hill. "The French understand about going on. They're a lot more forgiving of wild oats than Americans. They've never been Puritans. But of course they expect people to settle down later, make commitments."

"To be *sérieux.*" There was a threat of bitterness in Maggie's voice.

Anne looked at her sharply. "Yes. *Sérieux.*" Untranslatable. It meant serious, yes, but with the emphasis on being a responsible, solid citizen. "But if you were just fifteen, they couldn't have expected that of you."

"No." Maggie took a deep breath and turned into the subdivision, a set of low-slung fifties houses that varied only in paint color and plantings. "Here's Pinetree."

The Baker house was painted yellow, with a rough lawn and overgrown bushes. A well-worn Pinto and a bike sat in the open garage. Anne followed Maggie to the front door.

The woman who answered was a tired-looking thirty-five, blond, in jeans and a pink sweatshirt. "Mrs. Baker?" Maggie asked.

"Yes?" She brushed a wisp of hair from her forehead.

"I'm Maggie Ryan. You're Jill Baker's mother?"

"That's right." She stood very still. "Is there a problem?"

"No, not at all. We're doing a follow-up interview of children who were in Professor Bickford's creativity study a couple of years ago. Sorry we weren't able to reach you in advance. But if Jill's here, we'd like to talk to her for five or ten minutes."

"Oh, yes." The woman relaxed. "Come on in. I'm Barbara Baker. I just got home myself so everything's a mess right now. But you work too, obviously. So you know how it is." She waved them into the kitchen and called down a hall, "Jill! Come here a minute! Visitors!" She rejoined them and asked, "Coffee?"

"Love some," said Maggie. She'd taken a pad from her briefcase and looked very much the earnest researcher.

Barbara Baker poured two mugs from a pot plugged into the range outlet, handed them to Anne and Maggie, and picked up a third mug that was already sitting next to the sink. "What's this follow-up about?"

"We're just checking what the children remember. We'll do a few sample interviews and if they look interesting there may be another full-fledged study." Maggie paused to look at the door. A coltish girl of about twelve was entering, wearing jeans and a powder-blue sweatshirt. She was blond like her mother, with long-lashed blue eyes. She was almost as tall as her mother too, but moved awkwardly, not yet at home in her newly leggy body.

Barbara Baker was leaning against the sink counter. She said, "These people have come to ask you about that project you helped with a couple of years ago. At the university. You remember, the one where you told crazy stories?"

"Yeah?" Jill didn't seem antagonistic, just cautious.

Maggie said, "I'm Maggie and this is Anne. We just wanted to see what kids remember about their stories after two years. That's a pretty long time."

"Yeah," Jill agreed. She flopped down in one of the breakfast chairs and drew up one leg. "It's like a memory test?"

"More like a game. No grades," Maggie reassured her.

"What am I supposed to remember?"

"The stories you told."

"You'll be sorry," Barbara Baker warned. She brought her mug to the table and sat in the fourth chair, giving her daughter's hair an affectionate tousle as she passed. "This one's got a crazy imagination."

"Well, that's exactly what we're looking for," Maggie said. "Jill, can you tell us the stories?"

"Well, I told one about when I was a clown and had a pet chicken," Jill began. She was hugging her knee, glancing up occasionally to check Maggie and Anne's reactions. "We traveled all over the world and came to Laconia. Then we went to the fairgrounds and built a big rocket for the moon. But we didn't have enough money for gasoline."

Barbara laughed. "That part isn't imagination! We got stuck that way a couple of years ago. Jill's father bounced a child support check and there we were, overdrawn too."

"So what did you and the chicken do?" Maggie asked Jill.

"We both got jobs at the mall. But nobody wanted to buy coffee from a chicken, you know? So I got out my clown make-up and made the chicken look like an American eagle. And then everybody felt patriotic and bought coffee. And so we got to go to the moon. I forget how." Jill frowned at the table. "There was some more stuff but I forget."

"That's okay. It's a great story," Maggie said. "You've got a good memory. That was two years ago."

"Tell the other one," Barbara urged. "About the shark."

A shadow crossed Jill's face. "I don't like that one."

"You know what happened? She went off to see *Jaws* with her friends and it scared her to death," her mother explained. "She was, what, nine years old. So she made up a story about it. But she's never liked it."

Maggie said, "You don't have to tell us, Jill. But I'd like to hear it, if you're willing."

Jill was silent a moment, hugging her leg, mouth pressed against her knee. Then she said rapidly, "I went in a room and there was a man with sunglasses and a mustache and a dark slicker and an orange life jacket. I got in a boat. And the water was splashing outside the boat and a shark came. The man said, quick, you're wearing pink, that's what sharks like. So he took my things and showed me how to lie down in the bottom of the boat where the shark couldn't see me." Her voice was flat, staccato. "And I wanted to see the shark but I didn't want to stand up. So he took out my eyeball and held it up over the edge of the boat, and then I could see the water and the shark snapping its teeth. Like looking through the window. And he told me to yell the magic words and the shark would leave. I didn't like the magic words but I was scared. So I yelled, and the shark went away, and he put my eyeball back in. And I got out of the boat and came home."

Anne was shaken. No wonder Tal had brooded over this child's imagination.

Maggie's jaw had tightened. "Thanks, Jill," she said soberly. "I agree with you. The first story is more fun. But I'm really glad you remembered the other one too."

"Didn't forget a thing," said Barbara proudly. "But you know, she still won't wear pink. And she looks so pretty in it."

"Dumb color," Jill muttered with a resentful look at her mother.

"Yeah, she probably made up that story just so she could throw out her pink clothes." Barbara laughed. "Wish she'd waited till she was my size. I'd take them!"

Anne could see that Barbara was trying to lighten her daughter's mood.

"Were there other stories, Jill?" Maggie asked.

"No, we only had time for two. There was something else, like a test we took. Lots of questions. But I don't remember what they were."

"That's okay, we don't need that. One other thing." Maggie pulled out the Christmas party photo. "Do you remember any of these people?"

Jill studied it seriously. "This one's Bart," she said, pointing. "I told the stories to him. And this one's Tal. I saw him after, in the hall, and he wondered why I was crying and I said it was a scary story about sharks. And he said yes, shark stories were very scary. But he said scary stories could be good, if they got us to think about how to be ready if scary things really happened." She frowned at her upraised knee.

"Do you know anyone else in the picture?" Maggie asked.

"No."

"The man in the slicker?"

Jill glanced back at the snapshot. "No." Then the blue eyes flicked up at Maggie in alarm. "I mean, he's not real."

"Right," said Maggie. "Well, that's all. Thank you, Jill, you really helped us."

"Sure." They all walked to the door.

"Oh, Jill!" Maggie was halfway to the driveway. "Could you show me your bike a minute? My daughter wants one and I'd like to know about Raleighs. What you like and what you don't like."

"Okay." Jill joined her in the garage.

Anne got out a Gauloise. "Do you want a cigarette?" she asked Barbara.

"Thanks, no. But you go ahead. Will you tell us the results of this follow-up study?"

It took Anne a second to remember that they were supposed to be working on a new phase of Bart's study. "Of course," she said, and added, "although it may not get very far. This is very preliminary, as you can see."

"Yes."

"Your daughter is delightful. She must be a joy to you."

"Oh, yes." Barbara Baker smiled. "A joy and an exasperation. She does have a wild imagination. You suppose that's because her father left?" She looked suddenly vulnerable.

"Who knows?" Anne said. She wanted to comfort Barbara. Even with an enthusiastic partner like Tal, mothering was filled with doubt and worries. "Probably she's just a bright girl. Maybe a genius."

"Wish her grades showed that!" Barbara smoothed back some stray wisps of blond hair. "She becomes a teenager next year."

"Good luck!" said Anne sincerely. "But she seems a level-headed girl. And it's possible to survive it. My daughter and I did."

"I'm glad to hear that."

Maggie had given Jill's shoulders a friendly squeeze and walked up the driveway. "Hey, let's go!" she called from the driver's side of the Camaro. "Thanks again, Barbara!"

"Sure."

Anne climbed into the passenger seat and mashed her cigarette into the ashtray. She waved at Barbara and Jill as they backed out. Turning from the subdivision toward Minerva Creek, she asked, "What did you and Jill have to say to each other back there?"

Maggie glanced at her briefly, her blue eyes shadowed. "I told her I knew the shark story really happened. But I told her she was right, it was better if her mother and other people thought it was just a story."

"The shark story? Are you crazy?" Anne peered at Maggie suspiciously. "Boats inside rooms and removable eyeballs? Jill just saw that awful film and made up a good story for herself. Or had a nightmare and recounted that."

Maggie sighed as she turned the Camaro into the narrow creek road. "I hope you're right, Anne. I hope to God you're right."

XIII

By four-thirty Charlie had the printer working again. He replaced its housing almost regretfully. It had been good to focus on a different kind of problem. A solvable problem. He slid the printer into its place on the counter and locked the room behind him. Climbing the stairs, he made himself focus on tasks he still had to do: picking up his mail, checking with Gary to see if any problems had arisen with the coding of the fourth study.

He stopped in the main office to check his mailbox and immediately wished he hadn't. Sergeant Hines was propped against the windowsill, his notebook out, talking to Cindy. When Charlie entered he smiled. "Professor Fielding! Just the man I want to see!"

"Oh. Okay." Charlie paused awkwardly at the mail-room door and cast a quick glance at Cindy. What kind of tales had she been inventing now? And where was Walensky? Had he abandoned the field to Hines? Well, Hines alone might be better than having two warring policemen at once.

Hines shifted smoothly to his feet. "If you can talk to me now, we can go to your office."

"Okay. I just came for my mail." At the policeman's nod, Charlie pulled out the half-dozen items in his pigeonhole.

"You got a big box too," Cindy informed him. "I had the guy put it in your office."

"Thanks," said Charlie. "Probably the videotapes I ordered." He looked at Hines. "Ready?"

"Yeah, let's get this over with. Thanks, Mrs. Phelps," he added to Cindy.

All the well-being Charlie had felt while repairing the printer had evaporated. He could feel his neck muscles clenching, his legs stiffening. What a nightmare this was! The horror of Tal's death, plus the damned awkwardness because he'd lost track of his memo book.

He unlocked his office. Cindy was right; there was a big box on his desk. He tossed his mail down beside it, pulled his chair out from behind it so he could see Hines, and gestured at the other chair. "How can I help you?"

The big man sat down, pulled out his notebook, and found his pencil. Charlie wondered where Porter was. Probably back at the police station running FBI checks on everyone, or trying to match fingerprints to unsolved murders, or . . . Hines cleared his throat and Charlie brought himself back to reality. The sergeant had leaned back in the oak chair, long legs extended before him, notebook on his thigh. He said, "I've just got a few questions. Earlier today you mentioned Nora Peterson's gun. Tell me about it."

"I don't know much about it." Hines didn't respond, merely looked up at him expectantly, his pencil still poised. Charlie explained, "I only know about it because last year after that student threatened her, she told us all that she was going to buy a gun."

"You never saw it?"

"Well, in fact, she showed it to us once not long after. Several of us were in the hall and the subject came up. Someone asked about it. Bart, I guess, Professor Bickford. And she brought it out. But I didn't look at it very closely. I don't like guns much." He realized suddenly that Hines doubtless was carrying a gun at this very moment, so he added hastily, "Except of course the police should have them."

"Mm." Hines was writing industriously, still lounging back in the chair. "Where did Professor Peterson keep her gun?"

"Well, that's one of the things that worried me. She kept it in her office. Desk drawer, I think. She said she kept it locked but it still seems a bad idea to me if you have young people around. The university students would be bad enough, but around here there are younger kids too. They come in for experiments, or for the regular preschool program. I mean, you have to be extra careful if there are kids around."

"That's true. I've got kids, and I use a gunlock at home," Hines said. "Do you know if Professor Peterson used one?"

"She never said anything about it," Charlie said. "And I wouldn't know one if I saw it anyway." Where were these questions leading?

"Do you know what drawer she kept it in?"

"Look, what's all this about Nora's gun? Was that the one—my God, was it Nora's gun?"

Hines didn't move, just sat poised patiently to write down Charlie's answer. After a moment Charlie remembered the question. "I don't know which drawer she kept it in. I'm not even sure she kept it in a drawer. But if she did, and if she's got a standard desk like mine, then the only drawer that locks is the top middle."

Hines noted it down, stared at the page for a moment, then pulled in his feet and stood up. He walked across to the window and looked down at the parking lot for a moment. When he turned to Charlie again, backlit by the window, Charlie couldn't read the expression in his dark face. Hines said, "I want you to think about Wednesday morning, Professor Fielding."

"Wednesday morning?"

"Day before yesterday." Hines's voice had changed subtly. It seemed harder, more brittle. "Can you tell me what you did? Start with arriving at the building here."

Charlie's mouth had gone dry. What could this have to do with Tal's murder? Or even with Nora's gun? He said, "There were several things I had to do Wednesday. I was checking with my assistant about finishing the third study. He's the chief coder. And I wanted to get the material ready for the statistician because she was arriving the next day. Had to redo a couple of frequency graphs for her because I only had preliminary ones. And I had to order some—"

Hines broke in. "What time did you arrive Wednesday?"

"About nine. As usual."

"And what did you do first?"

"I unlocked my office. Is that what you mean?"

"Right. You went straight to your office from the parking lot?"

"Yes." Charlie pushed his glasses up on his nose. He had never thought of the sergeant as friendly, but now he was brutally cold.

"And then?" Hines's words were abrupt, jabbing.

"Went into my office. Put my things down. Checked next door to see if my assistant was in, but he wasn't. Came back to my office and started pulling things together for the statistician. For Dr. Ryan."

Hines was writing again. "Good. What next?"

"I started to work on the graphs, and realized I needed a ruler because my assistant had borrowed mine. I checked his office again but he still wasn't there. But down the hall I could see that Nora Peterson's door was open, so I went there and borrowed it. I finished the graphs and—"

"Just a minute, Professor Fielding. Why did you go to Professor Peterson's office to borrow a ruler?"

"I told you, the door was open."

"Wouldn't it be more usual to go to the department office?"

"Not really. It's halfway to the other end of the building. Nora's office is much closer."

"Professor Bickford's office is closer yet."

"But his door wasn't open!" Charlie adjusted his glasses. "He might not even have been there. And even if he was he wouldn't want to be bothered if his door was closed. It's sort of an unwritten rule. If we're willing to talk to people we leave the door partly open."

"Fine, Professor Fielding, fine." Hines was smiling but Charlie got no sense of warmth. The big sergeant was still silhouetted against the glare of the window. "Please go on. You went to Professor Peterson's office."

"Uh, yes. I didn't see her at first so I knocked on the open door. You know the way you do. She said, 'Come on in,' so I stepped in."

"Yes?"

"She was standing on a chair rearranging some books on the top shelf.

She asked what I wanted. I said I wanted to borrow her ruler for half an hour. She said—" Damn. Oh, damn. Charlie rubbed a hand over his chin. He wished the Coach was here to tell him what to do.

"She said what?" Hines's cool voice was relentless.

"She, uh, she said sure, I could borrow it. She said it was in her center top desk drawer and just to help myself."

"And did you?"

"Yes. The drawer wasn't locked."

Hines had stopped writing. Charlie tried to see his expression against the brightness behind him. He seemed to be thoughtful, studying Charlie in turn. Probably looking for signs of guilt—cold sweat, trembling hands. At this rate he'd find them too. Charlie added hoarsely, "I didn't see a gun."

"You didn't? You mean it wasn't in the drawer?"

"No. Maybe. I mean, I didn't see it if it was there. I pulled the drawer open maybe six inches. The ruler was right at the front." He demonstrated, pulling his own drawer out. "I have no idea what might have been in the back of the drawer."

Hines began writing again and Charlie pushed his drawer closed with shaky hands. It was terrifying to see his most innocent actions take on evil shadows from the spotlight of this policeman's suspicion. And why was Hines focused on him? Why not Nora herself? Why not Bart, or Cindy, or—

He'd been talking to Cindy just now. Maybe she'd said something. Or maybe he'd been asking her questions too. Charlie hoped so.

Hines asked, "When did you return the ruler?"

"Return it? I haven't returned it yet." He looked around the box on his desk and spotted it near the front edge. "There it is. Usually I'd have it back by now, but things have been so chaotic."

"Mm." Hines came away from the window, inspected the ruler without touching it, and then sat down in the chair again. "Tell me, Professor Fielding, what is your relationship with Professor Peterson?"

"Relationship? We're colleagues, that's all."

"Do you ever see her outside the office?"

"Well, there are parties, of course. Departmental picnics. Committee lunches. The usual things. All connected with the department."

"Nothing else?"

Charlie closed his eyes a moment. Clearly someone—Cindy?—had been talking too much. He said wearily, "Nothing. Really. At the Halloween party Professor Peterson had a little too much to drink and there was a misunderstanding. But that's all."

"Tell me about the misunderstanding." Hines hadn't softened any. Charlie could see him better now, but his expression was as hard and unyielding as he'd imagined.

"Wasn't much." Charlie licked his lips. "We'd both dressed as early film stars and she was kidding around. Insisted on leaving with me. Probably just as well; she wasn't really in shape to drive. I took her to her door and that was that."

"You didn't go in with her?"

"No. That's where it became clear there had been a misunderstanding. But I just didn't want—I mean, Nora's nice but she's not my type at all."

Hines looked at him shrewdly, as though weighing something, then asked, "Do you think she might hold a grudge?"

"A grudge?" My God, had Nora been the one to tell? No, surely she wouldn't have mentioned this embarrassing incident. He said, "All I know is that we've been able to work as colleagues with no reference to that night. I thought we'd all agreed to forget about it."

"Mm." Hines made a note, flipped back through the book, then said, "Well, that's all for now, Professor Fielding. Tell me if you think of anything more about Professor Peterson or her gun."

"Okay. I will," Charlie promised, standing up as the big policeman exited.

Nora's gun. What the hell could that mean?

From the hall Sergeant Hines's voice said, "Ah, Dr. Ryan! I have a question for you."

"Sure. Fire away."

"How long were you away from Professor Fielding while you mailed your letter yesterday?"

"Three minutes. Maybe five. Not long."

"It's an important point."

"Yes, Sergeant Hines. I know that." Maggie's voice was grim.

"Think it over. Be sure," he advised.

"Okay. What's happened? Is there a new development?"

"There are always developments. We're working on all of them. Have a good day, now." Hines's footsteps receded.

Maggie's curly black head popped around the door frame. "Hi, Charlie. What's going on? May I come in?"

"Yeah. He's after me, isn't he?"

"You mean the question about how long we were out of sight of each other? I doubt if it's personal." She swung into the office, her shirt sizzling red against the bland office background. She sat in the chair Hines had vacated and put her briefcase on the floor. "Probably he's found some new information and has to double-check some of the old."

"Maybe so." Charlie stared at her glumly. A vivid, bony woman, at home in the world, in charge. He wished he felt in charge.

"What was he asking about? Why are you so down?"

"Well, it shouldn't make any difference. I was with you. But he seems to have the idea I took Nora's gun from her desk drawer."

"Nora's gun? You mean Nora's gun shot Tal?"

"Must have. He just spent half an hour grilling me about what I knew about guns, where Nora kept hers, how I could have taken it from her drawer. Et cetera." Charlie shuddered. "I don't know a thing about the damn gun, but when I answered him it sounded suspicious anyway!"

"Yeah. A crime investigation is no lark. Why did he think you could have taken her gun?"

"I don't know what put the idea into his head. But it turned out that Wednesday I went in to borrow a ruler, and she told me to get it out of her drawer. The drawer was unlocked."

"Was the gun in it?"

"I have no idea! The ruler was in the front so I just grabbed it. I didn't even open the drawer far enough to see what else was there."

"Well, then," said Maggie comfortingly, "it could have been anyone else who went in to see her Wednesday. Or other times, if she left the drawer unlocked."

"That's true. But does Hines know it?"

"Oh, I'm sure he knows. He'll be talking to everyone."

"Maybe so." But the memory of the big black sergeant bearing down with his pointed questions was too fresh to dismiss easily.

"Speaking of Nora," Maggie said, "I saw that young campus cop in her office today. Did he talk to you too?"

"No. A young one?"

"He was with us in the gorge, even before Captain Walensky arrived."

"Oh, yeah, I remember. He looked familiar. You're right, I did see him in the building earlier today."

"But I can't find anyone he spoke to this afternoon except Nora. So it's not that Walensky sent him to talk to us, just to Nora."

"Yeah." Charlie remembered the young cop, pictured him talking to Nora. And somewhere in the back of his mind an old image began unreeling: Nora at her desk, cringing, an angry, stringy-haired student pounding on it, Charlie himself hurrying in with Tal to see what the shouting was all about. Charlie grunted, "No!"

"No what?"

"I don't see how this could be. But I'd almost swear that cop is the student who was threatening Nora last year."

"What?"

"Oh, I must be wrong. They're completely different types."

"He and Nora didn't seem to know each other yesterday in the gorge," Maggie said thoughtfully.

"Yeah. I must be wrong. Have you had any other thoughts about all this?"

She was gazing out at the sky, but in a moment she answered, "Nothing earth-shaking. In fact, I've been working on our project. When I got back to campus a few minutes ago your printouts were waiting. Want to take a look?"

"Yes! Let's check them over," Charlie agreed. Maybe they'd take his mind off Hines's attack.

Maggie pulled out the folds of computer paper and flipped them open. "Good news and bad news," she said. "Your main variable of contextual meaning comes through in all three studies. But looking across the studies, the effect of word shape is even stronger. So it looks like you and Tal were both right."

"Well, we both knew that." Yet he was disappointed. He'd hoped his context effect would be more powerful than the word-shape effect. "What about the eye-movement information?" he asked.

She unfolded the printout next to the big box on his desk. "Here we go," she announced, and for the next half hour they pored over the details of the statistics. Not great, but not bad either. A lot of it would be publishable, although people in Tal's word-shape camp would jump on some of the results and parade them around as proofs of their own point of view. Well, that's what science was, an ongoing argument among scientists with nature acting as referee—whenever you could get nature to say anything about the problems. Here, unfortunately, nature was saying word shape was pretty damn important.

"Any chance the remaining studies will change the numbers?" he asked Maggie.

"Probably not a lot. But you never know."

"Well, this gives me a lot to work with. Thanks, Maggie."

"Sure. I'll keep the printout over the weekend and copy it by Monday, if that's okay. Then you can start writing and let me know what other information you need."

"Sounds good."

Maggie slid the printout back into her briefcase, stood and stretched. "Well. See you Monday."

"Okay. Have a good weekend."

She left in a flutter of red shirttails.

Charlie stood up and pushed the box aside. He and Gary would have to move it downstairs Monday. Strange, he thought he'd received that box a couple of weeks ago. Thought it was downstairs already.

He riffled through the long-neglected mail. Mostly announcements of lectures or conferences, a request for a letter of recommendation, two journals. No, one. The other manila envelope had an unfamiliar return address in New York City. He opened it and stared without comprehension at the tabloid inside. Then he saw the circled classified ad and suddenly his legs felt wavery, like legs reflected in water. He sat down abruptly.

He was looking at a copy of *Screw*.

And the ugly ad listed a post office box in Laconia.

What the hell was going on? Who was advertising in *Screw?* Where had this come from?

What should he do about it?

Not tell Hines, he decided instantly. He couldn't face that cold, intelligent questioning again now. But this needed investigation, soon. He picked up his phone and dialed.

"Captain Walensky, please. About the Chandler murder."

"Yessir, just a minute."

After a few seconds Charlie heard, "Walensky."

"Hi, Charlie Fielding here. Listen, I just got something in the mail. I don't know if it's connected to what happened to Tal, but it's very strange."

"Yeah? What is it?"

Charlie lowered his voice even though there was no one in the hall. "It's, um, a copy of *Screw.*"

"Of what?"

"*Screw.* The sex tabloid. And they've circled an ad with a Laconia address."

"Christ. Who sent it to you?"

"I don't know. The return address is New York City."

"I'll be right over. Does anyone else know about this?"

"I just opened it myself."

"Well, I don't have to tell you to keep this quiet until we figure out what's going on." Charlie could hear the worry in Walensky's voice. "If it's connected to the murder it'll come out, of course. If not, we'll do what we can to keep your department out of it. No need to damage your reputations."

"*My* reputation?" Charlie squawked. "I've got nothing to do with this ad!"

"I'm sure you don't. But you understand that if the press hears about it they'll hound you anyway because you received it. So far we've deflected most of them to the dean's office, but we couldn't stop them if they heard about this. You understand?"

"Yes. I understand." Charlie could see visions of flash bulbs and shouted questions, *La Dolce Vita.* "God, why can't someone figure out who killed Tal? Get things back to normal!"

"We're doing our damnedest," said Walensky wearily. "As it is, the dean calls me every couple of hours. Nothing to do but keep the lid on if I can and get on with the investigation. Look, I'll stop by in a few minutes and pick up that *Screw.* Save the envelope too."

"Okay." Charlie replaced the receiver slowly.

What a day.

SATURDAY, JUNE 4, 1977

XIV

Anne pulled the sheets from the dryer, still warm. Seemed like Christmas, why was that? This was June. Oh, the sheets, the blue and yellow sheets she only used when Paul and Rocky visited. Holiday sheets. She trudged up the stairs with the laundry basket. The sheets hadn't been dirty, in fact. But they'd been sitting in the closet since January, so she'd popped them in the laundry to freshen them up. Paul and Rocky probably wouldn't even notice. Or maybe they would, subliminally. Tal said that most mental work was unconscious, not just the elaborate salacious stuff Freud talked about, but also the everyday chores of keeping your balance when you walked, keeping your finger muscles at the right tension when you held a pencil, moving your eyes when you read. Consciously you were thinking about the clever ideas Molière or Rostand was spreading before you, but another part of your mind was quietly piloting your eyes, skipping them across the pages in order to pull out those ideas. She'd helped Tal proofread some of his articles, and it had been strange to read about reading, reflecting on an activity the very instant she performed it.

Back to Tal. That was some submerged part of her mind too, leading her from any thought back to him. But she hadn't wanted to think about him. How had she got here? Oh, the sheets. Paul and Rocky maybe noticing unconsciously that they were fresh. Smell was usually unconscious, hardly registering except to tinge the background emotionally. Maybe Paul and Rocky would smell the fresh-washed sheets and be soothed, not knowing why.

She'd finished Paul's bed. She smoothed down the bedspread and took the other set of sheets to the sofa bed in her own den. This had been Rocky's room once. She'd been shocked when Anne had taken it over. Most young people were prejudiced, believing that their own childhood was sacrosanct, worthy of eternal preservation. But after a day of pouting because her collection of horse magazines was now stored in the basement, Rocky had accepted that being in graduate school in Chicago really didn't leave a lot of days to be home. And yes, she could see that with two parents sharing the downstairs den, it was crowded, bursting with books. But Anne could tell that her daughter was sobered by the realization that she too was subject to inexorable Time. Chapter One was finished. She was now an adult, no longer a child playing at being an adult.

Anne hauled the sofa bed open. Good exercise. Good to find tasks that used muscles instead of mind. Her mind was untrustworthy just now, inefficient, meandering, numbed much of the time but subject to occasional bursts of angry grief. At breakfast she'd automatically poured two glasses of juice, and then the realization that he wouldn't drink his had triggered twenty minutes of helpless sobs.

But she could focus on the investigation, she found. Hines had called this morning, wanting to know if anyone in Tal's department had weapons. Nora's gun was all she could think of. He'd also asked about Tal's term as chairman. Apparently Bernie Reinalter had told him about the problems of heading a department, and Hines had decided to check conflicts involving Tal back then. Anne had told him about the early financial problems but had hesitated to say anything about Bernie's past. Bernie should tell him about that. No need for her to ruin a reputation. So she'd told Hines that she'd get back to him when she'd had a chance to think.

She was still tucking sheets around the unwieldy sofa bed mattress when the doorbell sounded. Must be Maggie. She'd called last night, saying she had some news and wanted to come over this morning to talk to her again. Anne gave the half-made bed a slap. Hell, if she didn't get back to it, Rocky could damn well make it herself.

Maggie was in faded jeans and a crinkly navy shirt today, one of those lightweight no-iron Indian cottons. Looked comfortable. "Lots of news," said Maggie. "And lots of questions."

"No husband and kids today?"

"Nick's doing some background work. And Liz has the kids, bless her. They're getting along well."

"Good." Anne waved her toward the kitchen. "Now, did you find anything in Cindy's files?"

"Found some questions." Maggie sailed through the dining room, dropped her briefcase on the kitchen table, and landed in the same chair she'd used night before last. "Where to start?"

"Coffee?" Anne had taken two mugs from the cupboard, hand-painted French mugs with green leaves and yellow flowers that she and Tal had picked up one sabbatical year.

"Right. Coffee's the best place to start."

"Cream and sugar?"

"Everything, please."

"Okay. Now, start anywhere." She poured the coffee into the mugs.

"Okay. The gun. The gun in Tal's hand belonged to Nora."

"To Nora!" Some of the half-and-half that Anne was pouring into Maggie's mug splashed onto the counter.

"Yes. The one she's had in her desk for months."

"She could have taken the pipe and the memo book, but—"

"There's another odd thing. Remember you told me she got the gun after that scene in her office last year? Tal and Charlie Fielding interrupted and the fellow left."

"That's what Tal said."

"That's what Charlie said too. But he told me yesterday that the threatening student looked like that young campus cop. The one who drove us in Walensky's car."

"A cop? How can he be the stringy-haired student that Tal described?"

"Haircut, uniform." Maggie shrugged.

"But why would Walensky hire him? And why did she say he had a grade problem?"

"Good questions." Maggie put down her mug, half empty. "I'd like to talk to Nora."

Anne stared at Maggie and said, "She could be it, couldn't she? Nora. Her gun."

"Sure. Or it could be anyone else, if they could get at her gun."

Anne said bitterly, "Yes, I know the rest of us aren't out of it. Hines called again this morning. I realize now what he was fishing for. Asked me if I knew of anyone around the department who had a weapon. Naturally I thought of what Tal had said about Nora. So now he knows I could have stolen her gun. Played right into his hands, didn't I?"

Maggie shrugged. "I imagine everyone else he asked said the same thing. It was no secret around the department."

"I guess not," Anne agreed glumly.

"The only other thing I learned about Nora was that she worked her way through college in Illinois, a lot of it at night." Maggie leaned back comfortably, rocking her chair on its hind legs.

"I thought she'd gone to Penn."

"For her Ph.D. Had a fellowship. But as an undergraduate she had a tough life. And you said she helped raise her kid brother."

"Yes, she mentioned that once. Was there anything else in the folder you lifted from Cindy's file?" Anne asked.

"No. That's all I found about her. I mean, she's signed up for the same insurance as everyone else, has warm letters of recommendation from eminent scholars, et cetera." She rocked in her chair again. "There wasn't much in Bart's file either."

"But there was something?"

Maggie nodded. The morning sun slanted across the windowsill and glinted on her black curls, glossy as the starlings on the lawn the other evening. "He was in a hospital in St. Louis about ten years ago. Doesn't say why, just says he was there ten months."

"A hospital."

"St. Charles."

Anne shrugged. "Don't know it. Though ten months sounds like a long time."

"Bad car accident, maybe? Or maybe something mental."

Anne's mouth tightened. "God, you're blunt!"

"Same to you, ma'am. Maybe we should ask Bart about it."

Anne blew a cloud of smoke at the sunbeam. It writhed a moment, then dissipated into thin ghostly traces.

Maggie asked, "Feel squeamish about asking him?"

"Most of these people are *innocent.*"

"Right. But one isn't. One of these secrets may have been the motive. On the other hand, if you prefer, we could just tell Sergeant Hines."

"Even less fun when *he* asks about things." Anne crushed out the cigarette. "I want to find out, damn it."

"Okay. Let's ask. But first, tell me about Cindy."

"What about her?"

"Well, as I say, there wasn't all that much in the folders. But a secretary might notice more. I wondered if she might have the opportunity to blackmail people."

"Cindy? Blackmail? No."

"How can you be so sure?"

Anne sagged in her chair and picked up her empty mug. "I can't, of course. Maybe I'm being squeamish again. But—look," she said with sudden decision, "let's go see her. That's easier than explaining."

"On Saturday?"

"She lives on the Cortland Road. Had us out for a picnic once. Country place. It'll be a nice drive."

"Fine. Nora first, then Cindy." Maggie stood up and closed her brief-case. "We'll use my car, okay?"

"Why not? Let me stop in the bathroom first."

Anne inspected herself in the mirror as she washed her hands. She was surprised to see so little difference. Her graying hair still swirled back from her face, short and businesslike. Her dark eyes in their fan of wrinkles looked tired, yes, underlined by blue pouches, and the corners of her mouth were dragging a little. But there was no visible sign of her inner shock. An Edvard Munch frozen scream, walled over with thick numbness. And that numbness in turn walled over with layers of little tasks. Wash the sheets, make the beds, catch the killer. Busy busy. *Ne te foule pas la rate,* don't overdo, don't sprain your spleen. The French could be graphic.

But what the hell else was there to do? A sprained spleen was a small price to pay for keeping that eternal scream at bay.

When she came out Maggie was examining the departmental directory. "Just getting Bart's address," she said. "If Cindy doesn't know anything about him, we can go see him too."

"Sounds thorough."

"And we should come back here for lunch. I told Nick to call me here if I wasn't home."

"Fine. Let's get moving."

She suddenly found herself scrutinized in that direct, disturbing way that Maggie had. "Do you still want to do this, Anne?"

Anne sighed. "Look, I'm tired, I'm miserable. But I've got to know why it happened. So doing something feels better than staying here trying to stay numb. It's just that my brain wanders off sometimes."

"Your brain is doing fine. Let's go, then."

Nora's apartment was just inside the city limits. The complex consisted of ten two-story brick buildings set at angles to each other and pierced by open stairwells. The access road wound among them, bellying out from time to time into parking lots. Tall trees thick with young foliage surrounded the complex, but the few that grew nearer the buildings were spindly, some with guy wires still attached to their slim trunks.

Nora came to the door. In jeans and a sloppy gray sweater, her gray-streaked hair tied in a loose ponytail instead of its usual bun, she looked younger than she did in her severe campus clothes. "Anne! How are you? And Maggie."

"Hello, Nora."

"What can I do for you?"

She was looking at Anne, so she answered, "We wanted to talk a few minutes. Compare notes."

"About—about what happened? But the police are doing that. I've been talking to Sergeant Hines and Captain Walensky both."

"Yes. They're very busy on this," Maggie said. "But we thought if we compared notes we might jog our memories. That would help them too."

"You want your memory jogged." Nora hesitated, then opened the door wide. "Fine. Not a bad idea. Come on in."

Maggie motioned for Anne to wait. "We've heard about your gun, Nora."

"Yes. I figured that was it. Come on, we'll jog memories."

They followed her into a long white living room with a picture window at the end. Nora grabbed a gray jacket from the charcoal tweed sofa and tossed it into the dining area. "Sit down."

Anne complied, sitting at the other end of the sofa. Maggie was making a quick tour of the room and stopped by an enormous framed print of a rune stone on the side wall. "Love those," she said to Nora. "So mysterious."

Nora nodded. "I like to think one of my ancestors did it. A Norseman or Norsewoman chipping those signs into the stone, long ago."

"Me too." Maggie picked up a photograph sitting on the table below the print. "I've got Viking blood on my mother's side. Always thought that was why I love to go exploring. Family's important, isn't it?" She joined them, sitting in a black chair at Nora's end of the sofa.

"Yes, I suppose it is. Now, you said you wanted to talk about the gun." Nora was sitting on the edge of the sofa, leaning forward stiffly, hands clamped together in her lap. But when she turned to Anne her eyes were soft and concerned. "Anne, are you sure you want to do this?"

"Truth is best, even if it hurts for a while," Anne said. "It's what Tal stood for. And so do I."

"And so do the rest of us," said Maggie.

Nora's head snapped around to stare at her. "Do we really?"

"Of course. Though sometimes it has to be balanced against other great abstractions. Justice, mercy, love."

"Or your pocketbook? Your summer paycheck?"

Maggie leaned forward too, meeting Nora's angry glare. "I'm not lying to protect Charlie Fielding, Nora. I've told the truth as best I could, and I'm trying to learn the rest of the truth. Are you?"

Nora's glance fell. "Yes. Yes, of course. I'm just saying you ought to think very hard about what happened."

"I will. But what makes you so sure Charlie did it?"

"He was Tal's rival. You know that, Anne. And he tried to implicate me by using my gun! No one else would have done that!"

"Bart? Bernie? Cindy?" Maggie asked.

"There's just no reason!" Nora said. "I've been thinking about it, believe me! Right after Tal—right after it happened, I checked my desk drawer. And that's when I realized there was a chance it had been my gun. So I've been going over all the possibilities and nothing else seems reasonable. No one would drag me into it like this!" Her voice had become almost shrill.

"Except Charlie?" Maggie asked.

"Yes. I wouldn't have thought it of him either, but—well, I embarrassed him once. He's been cool to me ever since."

Anne said, "I told Maggie about the Halloween party, Nora."

"I see." Nora looked at her clenched hands.

"What was going on that night, really?" Anne asked. "It's the only time I've ever seen you close to drunk. You must have been under some strain."

"Nothing special. Family—I mean, the man I'd been living with had left, so I was down."

"The fellow in computer science?" Anne said sympathetically, and went on, encouraged by the tiniest of nods from Maggie. "Ray something?"

"Yes, that's right."

"I remember him. Seemed pleasant, but you never know."

"No, you never do. Turned out he just couldn't understand commitments to anyone else. To my work."

"He'd been with you a couple of years, hadn't he?" Anne continued.

"More than that. Look, it had nothing to do with Tal. Believe me, Anne!"

"I believe you. But it led up to your problem with Charlie."

"Only in a vague way. I was feeling low about it, sure. And I drank more than usual and got giggly, and Charlie was doing all those little Chaplin tricks—"

"Yes, I remember," Anne said. "He wasn't a bad mimic, really. All the eyebrow-wriggling and hat-tipping Chaplin did when he saw a pretty girl. And he's usually so shy."

"That was it!" Nora said eagerly. "He'd always seemed half-terrified of me before, but he put on that little mustache and hat and suddenly seemed to be really flirting. And . . . well, I wasn't feeling much like Professor Peterson either. I had my old-fashioned blond wig and a slinky dress. And I started thinking that Charlie was probably lonely too, maybe I should flirt back. So I got him to drive me home." She shrugged without unclasping the hands in her lap. "Well, he switched right off. Even in my foggy state I could tell. Nothing but monosyllables all the way home, and when I asked him if he wanted to come in for coffee he practically pushed me out of the car. By that time I didn't care, but looking back now, I think he was embarrassed. And I don't think he's ever forgiven me."

"You seem civil enough to each other," Maggie said.

"Yes, but there's always that undercurrent. As though he thinks I'm going to assault him."

"And that's why you think he stole your gun?"

"Not just for that, of course." Nora looked straight at Maggie. "Mostly because I saw him take it."

"You saw him?" Anne asked eagerly, and looked at Maggie with doubt for the first time. Had she believed in Charlie's innocence all this time because of the unsupported word of that woman? A woman who had been poor murdered Jackie Edwards's roommate?

"I saw him," Nora said positively. "Wednesday morning he opened the drawer, took something out."

"That's interesting," Maggie said. She was lounging back in the black chair, long legs extended, ankles crossed under the edge of the coffee table. "You were in the room?"

"Yes. His excuse was that he wanted to borrow a ruler. I was shelving books so I told him to get it himself. It was in the same drawer. And then when Tal—when it happened—I looked for the gun, and it was gone!"

"Did you see it in his hand?"

"I—no, I didn't."

"Did you see the ruler?"

"Yes, but he had no reason to hide that! He probably slipped the gun into his pocket so I wouldn't see it."

"Did you look for the gun in your drawer right after he left?"

"No. It never occurred to me anyone would do something like that! I didn't look until late Thursday."

"Did you usually leave your drawer unlocked?"

"When I was in the room, yes. I'd unlock it in the morning."

"Did you lock it when you went to lunch?"

"Yes. Well, usually. I'd lock the office door."

"But not always."

Nora unclenched her hands and gestured helplessly. "How could I know he'd have such a plan in mind?"

"You couldn't, of course. Did you lock it when you left your office for a few minutes? To go to the ladies' room, or to pick up your mail?"

"I usually locked the office door, not the desk." Nora sighed. "All right, it's true I wasn't as careful as I should have been. But it's also true that Charlie was rooting around in that drawer the day before the gun was used!"

Anne didn't know what to think. Had she been right to believe Maggie? But even Nora admitted that other people might have been in her office.

And of course, Nora herself could have taken the gun at any time.

Maggie said, "Anne and I have been thinking that Tal was a very curious person. He'd learned my family connections just in the five minutes we talked. And we thought he might have been killed because he'd figured out someone's secret. Something he wasn't meant to know."

"Secret?" Nora's hands clamped together again.

"Can you think of anyone who has a secret? Someone who'd kill to keep it quiet?"

"I—no, I don't know anyone's secrets. Maybe Charlie's got a secret. But why can't it just be rivalry? If Charlie felt threatened by my movie-star impersonation, why wouldn't he feel threatened by research that contradicted him?"

"Okay." Maggie swooped forward suddenly and placed something on the coffee table where Anne and Nora could see it. It was a silver-framed snapshot of a young woman and a boy of about ten. After a moment Anne realized that the young woman was Nora, her hair long and unkempt in a mid-sixties style. Maggie asked, "Is that your little brother?"

"That? Yes."

"What's his name?"

"Dick. Richard."

Maggie nodded as though pleased. "Tell me about Dick."

"For God's sake, why? He's my little brother, I keep a photo of him. What else is there to say?"

Anne wasn't sure what Maggie was driving at, but she said, "You told me you'd had to raise your brother almost by yourself."

"Well, yes. My mother got very ill when he was nine, and I had to take over."

"How's he doing now?" Maggie asked.

"Fine. He's doing fine."

"He's twenty-two, you said."

"I did?"

"In Plato's, while we were waiting for Tal. Bart asked you how your brother was doing. He said that with drugs and everything it was hard to raise kids these days. You told him Dick was twenty-two and was doing fine."

"Well, I guess I did. It's true."

"Where does your brother work?"

"Look, what does this have to do with anything?"

Maggie leaned back in her chair again. "You evaded Bart's question then. You're evading mine now. Is your brother in trouble?"

"I don't see how this is getting us anywhere." Nora was on her feet. "Anne, I'm not trying to be rude, but this is a waste of everyone's time. Maybe you'd better—"

"Okay, okay, sorry!" Maggie raised her palms in a gesture of appeasement. "I promise not to ask any more questions about Dick Peterson." When Nora looked down at her suspiciously, she repeated, "Honest. It's a promise."

"Well . . ." Nora sat down again. "I still don't see what else we have to say to each other."

"You must have some questions for us," Maggie said.

"Well, Anne, I don't want to be rude," Nora said.

"Go right ahead," Anne told her. "We've certainly asked you some rude questions. It's your turn."

"I wondered if you'd really told the police about the extent of the rivalry between Charlie and Tal."

So she still thought it was Charlie. Anne said, "Yes. I told them. But my impression was that it was just another in a long string of academic controversies that Tal engaged in. He loved it."

"I'm sure from Tal's side that was all it was. If he'd known how seriously Charlie took it—"

"Did he take it that seriously?"

"Well, he must have."

"More seriously than Tal, I'm sure," Anne reflected. "He is young still. But he had a lot of studies going. It didn't look to me as though he'd be ruined if Tal won on one point."

"Maybe not," Nora agreed. "And I'm sure Tal had no reason to think anything else. He certainly wasn't out to ruin Charlie, and couldn't believe anyone would be out to ruin him."

"About your gun," Maggie broke in. "Charlie told me you bought it last year, after someone threatened you in your office."

"Yes." Nora had stiffened again.

"Tal saw him too, didn't he?"

Anne nodded. "He and Charlie went in when they heard the shouting. The student left immediately, Tal said, but you were nervous enough to go ahead and buy the gun."

"That's right," said Nora.

"Just for the office?" Maggie asked.

"No, there's another one I keep in my purse. But I generally put that away while I'm in the office."

"So you had two guns," Maggie said. "What were these threats? Why?"

"Just a grade problem."

"It's more than that, Nora. You don't buy guns because a student is angry. You buy them if you fear serious criminals. Like enforcers."

Nora winced. Anne realized that Maggie had scored a hit, but where had her question come from? She asked, "He was a serious criminal?"

Nora shook her head. "No, no, he wasn't a criminal!"

"Not a criminal," said Maggie. "Okay. So you helped him get the Campus Security job. You talked to Walensky."

"Damn him! He promised he wouldn't tell anyone!" Nora was on her feet again, striding toward the telephone.

"Wait, wait!" Maggie flew after her and laid a hand on her arm. "Nobody told me anything! I'm just putting things together."

"What? What are you putting together?" Nora wheeled to face her.

"All the disturbing things that have happened in the last year to a hardworking professor of child development. Breaking up, buying guns, getting visits from a fellow who dresses first like an angry student and later like a campus cop. But the cop wasn't named Dick Peterson."

Anne understood suddenly. "He was named Pete Dixon," she said.

Nora sagged a little.

Maggie said, "It didn't make much sense at first, all those facts. There was a hollow at the center. But when I realized how evasive you'd become about a brother you were close to, one you'd raised, one you used to tell Tal and Bart about—well, if he was in serious trouble the rest of it made more sense."

"Please don't tell anyone!" Nora begged. "It's life and death!"

"There really are criminals after him, then?"

"He had some drug problems in New York. Ran up a debt. Yes, they're after him." Her eyes were hollow with anxiety. Anne's heart went out to her.

"So you got him to change his name and signed him up with Walensky?" Maggie gestured toward the sofa and Nora let herself be led back to her seat.

"Yes," she said. "It took some work. He wanted money when he came last year, when Tal and Charlie saw him. But I couldn't pay off drug debts. I just couldn't! I realized that's where the other money I'd sent him had gone. So I sent him to a rehabilitation program. He was finally scared enough to take it seriously, I think. We changed his name for protection, and when he got out Walensky took him on."

"You picked Campus Security so he could be armed and so he'd have buddies around?"

"Yes, it seemed safe. And he'd been a security guard off and on in New York City, he said, so I thought he could manage the work. So far he's been fine. Please, don't tell anyone!"

"No need to tell anyone if Walensky already knows all this. Does he?" Anne asked.

"Yes. He was very helpful."

"Well, then, he'll tell Hines whatever's necessary."

"Theoretically he will," Maggie said. She pulled a piece of paper from her pocket and began scribbling on it. "Got an envelope, Nora?"

"Sure. Plain letter size?" Nora started for the desk against the wall.

"Yes." Maggie jumped up and accompanied her. She accepted the envelope, inserted her paper, and sealed it.

"What are you doing?" Nora asked.

"Just a second." Maggie wrote an address on the envelope, helped herself to a stamp from Nora's desk, and pasted it on. "Here, Anne. Please take this out and mail it. I'll meet you at the car in just a minute. I have to explain all this to Nora."

Anne was on the verge of protesting, but something in Maggie's tone caused her to take the letter meekly. "I'll see you later, Nora. Thanks for helping," she said and went out, wondering. The mailbox was at the end of the widened parking area. She lit a Gauloise and then walked across to mail the letter. It was marked "Personal," she saw, and addressed to M. M. Ryan at Ryan and Reade in New York City. By the time she was back at the car Maggie was emerging from the apartment too. "Okay, what was all that about?" Anne asked.

"Maybe unnecessary. But there were a lot of guns in that family," Maggie said, opening the door. "I thought Nora and her brother should be aware that my personal mail won't be opened unless I turn up dead."

"Dead! You think she would—*merde!*" Anne drew a deep lungful of smoke and stubbed out the cigarette in the Camaro's ashtray. "So you mailed this story to yourself, just in case. Surely Nora wouldn't—But if that was her brother in her office last year, he's got a temper."

"He's got a temper, he's got *easy* access to his sister's gun, and if Tal recognized him as the angry student and started asking questions, he'd have motive too." Maggie turned onto the highway and headed for the Cortland Road before adding grimly, "But what worries me most is Nora. She's not overly fond of Charlie, but those accusations aren't grounded in hatred. They're grounded in terror. She's scared to death that little Dicky did it."

XV

The Cortland Road led into the hills through farms where the land rolled gently, woods where steeper slopes made agriculture difficult. Outside the Laconia city limits, the road was lined with small houses on lots snipped from the farms behind. Cindy Phelps lived in a one-story bungalow of white-painted asphalt shingles. It was a drab little house, livened only by a pretty front porch with a swing and a long hedge of spectacular pink peonies along the gravel drive. Maggie pulled over to the edge of the driveway a short distance behind Cindy's Toyota. Anne climbed out and paused to touch one of the massive peony blooms.

"It's gorgeous out here," Maggie said.

Anne followed her gaze and nodded. The hills here rolled down to the lake, sapphire blue on this June day. The scruffiness of the cottages along the road didn't matter because the eye was drawn to the lake, the hazy hills, the white clouds that drifted across the expanse of sky. Anne could see the university towers tiny on a far hill. Behind it her own section of town seemed nothing but trees, and beyond that the cemetery blended into the landscape. She was glad it was on a hill too. Tal liked hills. From a hill, the grandeur of the universe soothed.

She turned and followed Maggie up the cement walk to the porch.

"Well! What brings you two here?" Cindy answered the bell wearing jeans and a Western-style pink-checked shirt. A pink headband held back her tousled curls.

"Got some questions about the department," Anne explained.

"I'd think you two knew everything already," Cindy said. A child peered out the door behind her. She shooed him back in and called, "Back in a minute, Mark." Then she stepped out onto the porch and closed the door firmly behind her. Her sneakers were pink too.

"Everything we learn about it seems to bring up new questions," Maggie said.

"I've noticed that too." Cindy walked to the end of the porch, looked out at the lake, then turned her back on it to sit on the porch railing. "The hell of it is, I can't think why anyone would want to kill Tal."

"I can think of a lot of possible reasons." Maggie was pacing along the length of the porch. "But most of them involve Tal knowing somebody's unpleasant secret."

"That's exactly what I mean," said Cindy. "What secret could he know? And what difference would it make if he did know?"

Anne leaned against the house wall and lit a cigarette. "Thought you might have some ideas."

"Why me? Talk to Bernie."

Maggie's trajectory had brought her to Cindy's end of the porch. "Come off it, Cindy," she said. "You know more about that department than Bernie. You've been there longer and you keep the records. And I notice that you aren't saying people don't have secrets."

"Well, sure. I've been in this mean old world for a while. I know people have things to hide sometimes. Doesn't mean I know what they are." Her rigid shoulders belied her light tone.

Anne tried to ease the tension. "Just thought you might be willing to make some guesses, Cindy. We know that nobody knows for sure."

"Look, Anne, you and I understand each other pretty well. You know there's nothing I wouldn't do for Tal." Cindy's light eyes under the blackened lashes were earnest.

Anne nodded. "I know."

"But I don't know anything that could help. Honestly. And I'm no dummy. I can see where this one's leading." She gave a curt nod at Maggie. "If I say anything about anybody, the next step is to claim I was blackmailing them and Tal found out. So anything I know makes me a suspect too!"

"For God's sake, Cindy!" Anne stamped across the porch to tap ash into the bushes. "You know I don't believe that!"

"Hey, not so fast. *I* might believe it," said Maggie. Still facing Cindy, she had propped a foot on the railing nearby, effectively fencing her in. "I even brought up the possibility to Anne. Right?"

"That's why we're here!" Anne told Cindy. "I wanted to show her that you weren't involved!"

"And how the hell do you expect me to prove that?" Cindy sat tall in her corner, her eyes flicking from Anne to Maggie and back.

"How the hell can any of us prove it?" Anne retorted. "Hines is after me too, Cindy. Looked over all my insurance, talked to all my neighbors."

"I know. I'm sorry, Anne."

"Hines is even checking on Charlie and me," Maggie put in. "And we alibi each other."

"Not all that well," snapped Cindy. "What about that letter you mailed? You and Charlie claim it only took a few minutes out of each other's sight. But add a few more minutes and you're as likely as anyone."

"True. You like Charlie for it, then?" asked Maggie.

Cindy froze for an instant before she said, "What difference does it make if you were really with him?"

"I know it wasn't Charlie. But you and he have a feud going. I'm interested in why."

"So. We're back to dumping on Cindy!" She shifted restlessly on the railing.

"We're not trying to do that!" Anne broke in impatiently. "Maggie, don't play games. Tell her we don't think she did it!"

Maggie took her foot from the railing and turned to face Anne. "I'm telling her the truth, Anne. If you two know something that clears her, you sure haven't told me. Besides, there's a question that bothers me about Cindy."

"What's that?" asked Anne.

"Yesterday she got back from lunch around twelve-thirty. You met her coming in, right?"

"Yes." Anne blew out a puff of smoke. "Unlocking the office door."

"What's this leading up to?" Cindy demanded.

"It's leading up to the fact that you told Anne you'd been at a meeting. But you told Hines you'd had lunch alone."

"I was alone. Quiet spot in the grove."

"Oh, for God's sake!" Anne strode to the end of the porch and hurled the cigarette past Cindy onto the gravel. "We'll never get anywhere if we don't level with each other! Nobody's asking you to tell Hines, Cindy. But tell Maggie so we can get past this and think about Tal!"

"Anne, I'm sorry. But—"

Anne turned on her. "Cindy, I need to know who killed Tal. That's top priority right now. So let's quit this game and move on." She looked back at Maggie. "Cindy was at a meeting. Gamblers Anonymous."

"Damn you!" Cindy stared at her pink sneakers.

"Gamblers Anonymous." Maggie looked at Cindy thoughtfully. "I see. You can't tell Hines who else was there."

"That's it." Cindy tossed back her curls and looked defiantly from Anne to Maggie. "You tell Hines I was at a GA meeting and he'll come hassling me for names. I can't do that to them."

"And Charlie knows you're in GA, and that's why he won't talk," said Maggie. "The gallant type." She took a deep breath and glanced at Anne. "How did you know about Cindy?"

"Tal," said Anne. She moved around the swing and sat on it, half twisted to face them. "A little while after he became chairman he found out. Tried to help."

Maggie looked at Cindy. "Did he help?" Her earlier hostility was gone.

"He helped a lot," Cindy said. "I was just then figuring out that I wasn't getting anywhere except deeper in debt. You know, it's so funny, you can go for years thinking all you need is one more win, and you hardly notice all you're losing while you wait for it. Losing just makes you more sure your luck will turn. But I was finally noticing that the family was getting hurt while I waited for lightning to strike. Tal steered me to GA. Best present anyone ever gave me."

Maggie gazed out at the lake. "So Tal knew for years."

"Yes. Even helped me work out a plan to pay my debts. I'll be even in a couple more years. Maybe get a new car then." She stretched an arm back and fluttered her fingers at the Toyota.

"Who knows about this besides Anne and Charlie?" asked Maggie.

"Nobody, now."

"Your family?"

"No. They just think the university doesn't pay very well. Well, God knows that's true too."

"Does Bernie Reinalter know?"

"God, no!" Cindy's turquoise lids squeezed closed in apprehension. "Mr. Model Manager finds out and my job's on the line."

"Why? You've got the gambling under control now, right?" Maggie said. "You're almost out of debt. Wouldn't he be more understanding?"

"You don't know Bernie."

"True. I don't." Maggie hesitated, then glanced at Anne. "Well, Anne's right. I can't see any point in broadcasting this. But I would like to know if you've had any thoughts about other people in the department."

"Given up on your Cindy-the-blackmailer theory?" Cindy asked.

Maggie spread her hands innocently. "Hey, look, if you tell us, then we'll know it's not worth money to you."

"God, you academics are so logical." Cindy adjusted her pink headband with both manicured hands. "Okay, what are your questions?"

"Do you know anything about Nora Peterson's brother?"

"Brother? Nothing. Unless—" Cindy frowned.

"Want to sit on the swing so Anne doesn't have to twist around?"

"Sure." Cindy joined Anne on the swing. Maggie perched on the porch rail a few feet in front of them, her long legs in the faded jeans stretched out before her. The crinkly navy blue shirt stirred in the occasional breeze. It reminded Anne of a dark bird ruffling its wings. Maggie said, "So you know something about Nora's brother?"

Cindy leaned back in the swing, pink sneakers pushing off gently to match Anne's rhythm. "Funny. When you mentioned a brother I remembered a phone call last year, not long after that student made a scene in her office. I picked up the phone and it turned out the button for her extension was pushed in."

"That must happen from time to time," said Maggie, bland-faced.

"Not as often as it would if *you* had my job," Cindy shot back.

Maggie grinned. "Yeah, you've got me spotted. I'm the epitome of snoopiness. So tell us about this call."

"She was talking to someone she called Dick. Said she'd arranged things, he was to get over to Campus Security in the administration building at two-thirty. He grumbled when she said he'd need a haircut, but she snapped at him, said this was the last time she'd bail him out. Then she said, 'Shhh,' and I figured it was time to get off the line."

"We should have talked to you first," Maggie said. "Yeah, this Dick she was talking to was her brother, and he's now a campus cop. Calls himself Pete Dixon."

"Dixon." Cindy leaned forward abruptly, making Anne's end of the swing wag back and forth. "That's the guy who came by yesterday, right? He's her brother? Why is his name different?"

"There are reasons she wants to keep it quiet. He's got enemies and wants to stay low-profile for a while."

"So he changes his name and comes to the boonies where he has to get haircuts. I see."

"Yes. And Nora gets him a job where he's protected."

Anne frowned. Something didn't fit here. "One thing I don't understand. How could Nora bail him out with a job in Campus Security? Completely separate operation. How could she know Walensky would hire him?"

Cindy peered across at her from under those sooty lashes. "Oh, Walensky's willing to do favors," she said.

"What do you mean?"

"Well, I don't know if this is a regular thing. But a guy I know—all right, he's in GA. Walensky caught him borrowing from one of the fraternities, their petty cash box. Walensky smiled, told the guy he didn't want to ruin his life, maybe they could make arrangements."

"Blackmail?" Anne asked, shocked. "You mean he had to pay off Walensky?"

"He said it was a reasonable amount, one-time. And now he knows a cop is watching."

Maggie said, "Sort of an informal fine-plus-probation."

Cindy nodded. "Yeah, look on the bright side. Keeps everyone's record clear. Also helps Walensky's pocket, and his information network."

"Nora would probably have to pay more than a little for this kind of favor. And Dixon himself—" Maggie stood up, began pacing again in long circles like a hawk's. "Anne, did Tal say anything recently about Nora? Or Walensky?"

"Let me think." Anne leaned back in the swing, closed her eyes. There had been something . . . what? At breakfast Tuesday. A few days ago, an eternity ago. "He didn't say anything specific," she said. "Just that he hardly knew the department anymore. All these projects that Bernie and Nora had, it wasn't like the old days. That was the gist."

"He mentioned Bernie and Nora?"

"That's all I remember now."

"Nothing about Walensky?"

"Not then. But he was always complaining about Walensky, ever since he botched the investigation of that little boy who was hit by the car. The Hammond kid."

"Well—God, this raises some lousy possibilities. Do you suppose Walensky recognized the driver, and slowed the investigation on purpose? If Walensky—" Maggie swung to a halt in front of them, gazing out at the lake, her brow furrowed. "Anne, did Tal ever mention Dixon? Or Nora's brother?"

"No. Just the scene in the office." Anne pulled a Gauloise from the pack and held it a moment, rolling it in her fingers, frowning at its neat gray lettering. "Do you suppose Tal found out who Dixon was? He saw him last year. Maybe he recognized him. Maybe he started asking questions."

"He didn't ask me," said Cindy.

"Would he ask you?" Maggie's gaze shifted from the lake to Cindy.

"He might. He often did, questions about the department. You two aren't the only ones who think I know a lot." She shook her curly mane. "God, I wish I did know as much as you guys think!"

"So do I." Maggie started pacing again, hands thrust deep into her jeans pockets, shoulders hunched. "Hines ought to know all this. Cindy, do you think Tal would try blackmail?"

Anne snapped upright, making the swing lurch, shouting even before she was conscious of her rage. "What kind of idiot question is that?"

"Anne, I'm sorry." Maggie paused again, her compassionate eyes bluer than the sky.

Anne didn't want compassion. "It's a stupid question!"

"It's one Hines will ask."

"Doesn't mean *we've* got to! Waste of time." Anne was still holding the cigarette, had mashed it in her anger. She rolled it smooth in her fingers and lit it. Her hands were shaking. "Maggie, the whole point of asking around ourselves is to save time. Avoid blind alleys. You push this direction and it's over."

"Anyhow," Cindy said, "I know Tal is no blackmailer. Think what he could have done to me!"

"Right!" barked Anne.

Maggie's hands flew to shoulder level, palms out in a gesture of surrender. "Okay. I quit, I quit! Cindy, what can you tell us about Bart Bickford?"

"Big Bart? He wants to get a grant for a new creativity study."

Anne's heart was still pounding. She watched the smoke twisting up from the end of the Gauloise. Calm down, she told herself. Questions have to be asked. Listen to the answers.

"Everybody wants to get a grant," Maggie observed. "Is Bart close to getting one?"

"Yes, I'd think so. Tal thought so. Bart got money for the pilot last year, and he says it's working out. So, if nothing goes wrong—well, you can ask him for details."

"I will," said Maggie. She gazed out at the lake again and added, "Why was he in that St. Louis hospital so long?"

Cindy gave her a long, cold look. "You've been in my files. I thought so."

Maggie shrugged.

Cindy said, "He was being treated for depression. Suicide attempts, the whole bit."

"I see." Maggie swung over to the railing to perch again. "I suppose it's a problem to have that on your record if you're working with kids."

"I don't know if it's a problem or not. But I know Bart is scared stiff that someone will find out. The vita he uses only goes back to the year after he got out."

"Well, it's definitely a problem then. If he worries, it's a problem."

"Tal knew," said Cindy. "He deleted that information from the file when he saw how edgy Bart was. Decided to leave the note on hospitalization, but take out the reason he was there."

Maggie glanced at Anne. Anne blew smoke from her nostrils and glared back at her. Maggie shrugged and turned back to Cindy. "Okay. Now, what about Charlie?"

"Charlie doesn't have anything to do with it. You say so yourself."

"But this feud you have with him," Maggie pursued.

Cindy jumped up from the swing and strode to the front door. "Just forget it. It's over. Charlie isn't involved, you can prove that yourself."

"Could he have a partner?"

Cindy shook her curls. "A loner like Charlie?"

Maggie marched across the porch to stand nose to nose with Cindy. "Cindy, there's more, isn't there? Charlie is keeping quiet about you. Why? You're refusing to talk about him. Why?"

"So we're both playing fair," Cindy retorted. "It's over. Forget it."

"What's over?" demanded Anne. "Why won't you help us? Did you have an affair with Charlie? Is that why Lorraine left?"

"God, no!" said Cindy. Her surprise looked real.

"Well, what the hell do you want us to think?"

Cindy tossed her head. "Doesn't make any difference what I want, does it? We're all going to sit around thinking bad things about each other until this is cleared up."

Anne leaned forward in the swing and jabbed a finger at Cindy. "So help us clear it up!"

Cindy looked at her and shrugged helplessly.

Maggie was still studying Cindy with narrowed eyes. She said suddenly, "You stole money from the department, didn't you?"

Anne exclaimed, "No! She wouldn't!" But in the same instant she saw terror flash through Cindy like a current, and she knew Maggie was right. She stood up and stepped closer to them. "What do you mean, Maggie?"

"She embezzled it," said Maggie.

"You're crazy," said Cindy bravely.

"But . . ." Anne began, then the pieces slipped into place. Tal's worry about Cindy's gambling, the effect on her family, he'd said. His zeal to get her into GA. His worries about the department finances when he first became chairman. Anne said, "Tal saved your job, didn't he? These debts you're paying off—they're to the department?"

"Oh, God." Cindy pushed past Anne and went to stand at the end of the porch again, looking out at the lake. Anne followed and leaned against the corner post of the porch.

"Is it the department you owe?" Anne said insistently.

"Not exactly." Cindy's glance was almost amused. "First I owed Tal."

"Tal?"

"And you, I suppose. He never told you? See, he paid back the department money himself, got the books straight. Then he had me pay him in installments. As soon as my credit rating was back in shape I got a bank loan and paid him off. I don't owe you anything anymore. Nor the department. Just the damn bank."

"Merde." Anne stared out at the blue of the lake.

"You didn't know, Anne?" asked Maggie.

Anne shook her head slowly. "Not this part. How much did he—"

"Sixteen thousand four hundred and seventy," said Cindy.

"Merde," said Anne again. Nine years ago, that had been. He'd probably lifted it from his travel fund. She remembered now, for two years she'd done the trip to Europe alone. He'd said he was too busy now that he was chairman. He'd said he would baby-sit Paul and Rocky while she went. Damn Tal, she wouldn't have screamed at him if he'd told her. Would she? Oh, hell, she probably would have.

"I told him he was a bigger gambler than I was," said Cindy.

"Yeah. Yeah, he was." Anne looked down at her Gauloise. A long tongue of ash protruded from the white stub.

"Why?" asked Maggie, her voice chilly as a north wind. "Why didn't he fire you, Cindy?"

Anne hurled the spent cigarette onto the gravel. "Because he's a damn idiot romantic! The grand folly, the grand gesture. *Quelle sottise! Mais quel geste!*"

"No, seriously." Maggie was still staring at Cindy.

"You think that's not a serious answer?" Cindy's mouth twitched. Her secret out, she seemed more relaxed. "Are you thinking up scandalous explanations, like Anne? You think I turned on my bimbo charms and seduced Tal out of his sixteen thou?"

"Sounds more realistic than Anne's version."

"Well, it's not," Cindy said. She looked from Maggie to Anne, rubbed her palms on her jeans, and said, "Look, promise not to say anything about all this to the people inside and you can come in for a cup of coffee."

Maggie said, "Shouldn't we finish talking out here? Because—"

"Shut up," snapped Anne. This half of the truth she knew. "We're going in."

Maggie glanced at her, eyebrows lifting. "Yessum," she said.

Anne followed Cindy and Maggie through a neat living room with a flowered sofa to the big sunny kitchen-family room that ran across the back of the house. Three children were flopped on the gold carpet before a television cartoon program. "Mark?" said Cindy. "Want you to meet someone from the department. Maggie Ryan."

The children sat up and looked around. A man with reddish-brown hair turned his wheel chair to face them. He smiled warmly with the unscarred half of his face. "Hi," he said, sticking out his hand.

"Hello." Maggie stepped forward without hesitation and took his hand. "Glad to meet you, Mark."

"Anne!" He'd spotted her behind Maggie. "God, that's rough, about Tal."

"Yeah. Thanks, Mark." She took his hand next. His blue eyes were sad and steady. Behind him the gaudy cartoon sputtered and danced. "Nothing to do about it, except find out who did it."

"Yeah." He squeezed her hand. "And go on. That takes some doing too, going on."

"One thing at a time," she said. Her eyes stung. Still holding Mark's hand, she looked defiantly at Maggie.

Maggie was standing very still, checking over the room with a swift glance: the cheerful curtains, the worn chairs, the geraniums in the window, the girl who had moved to her father and was hanging on his shoulder, the framed velvet square thick with decorations, including a Distinguished Flying Cross and two Purple Hearts. She met Anne's gaze and gave a tiny nod.

"Cream and sugar?" asked Cindy brightly from the kitchen end of the room.

They had their coffee. Maggie didn't question Tal's motives again.

XVI

The smell of sweat, buttered popcorn, minty chewing gum. A flickering, tiny figure, graceful in white, pleading, "You're my only hope." Charlie sat very still in the last row, half in a trance. The film was splendid: action-filled, visual, imaginative. And beside him Deanna's warm presence filled him with excitement and well-being.

But his trance kept dissolving as uglier thoughts intruded. Tal's murder. Hines's interrogation. And that copy of *Screw*, sent to him as though someone thought he'd know about the ad. Walensky had questioned him closely on that point when he came to pick it up, but Charlie had finally convinced him that, since he'd had nothing to do with the ad, the sender must have been guessing. "Maybe everyone in Laconia who works with children got a copy," Charlie suggested. "Maybe someone just wants it investigated."

"Well, they got their wish," Walensky said. His Burt Reynolds face looked old, crumbly. "We'll put a watch on the post office box, see what turns up. Of course this kind of investigation is tough. Like drugs. The perpetrator gets a whiff that there's official interest and all the evidence goes down the toilet before we arrive. You understand? I'm telling you not to talk about this to anyone."

"Okay."

"This whole case is a can of worms." Walensky paced over to Charlie's window and scowled at the bushes and parking lot below. "Hines bullying his way around the campus upsetting everyone; the dean screaming for us to arrest someone, anyone; the press hounding us—" He shook his head. "Well, tell me right away if anything else comes up. I'll leave word to put you right through."

"Okay. Should I tell Hines too?"

Walensky looked at him coldly. "You don't give a damn about your department, do you? You think the press won't be dancing if you give them that ad in *Screw*? And telling Hines is the same as telling the press."

"Yeah. Okay. I see. But he hasn't given the newspapers a whole lot."

"Not yet. He's playing by the rules so far, not giving out details. But the reporters already know there are leads pointing to the university. Some secretary starts spinning stories and it hits the fan."

"Okay. But I don't want to hide anything from the investigation."

"You've told me, and Hines will learn what he has to know. We'll get the Chandler killer, don't worry." He paced back to stand in front of Charlie's desk. "God, I thought this place was going to be peaceful! Might as well be back in the Bronx."

"Do you think the killer might have sent it?" Charlie asked, still brooding. "Because he took my memo book and dropped it near, uh, the body. Maybe this is more of the same."

"Maybe." Walensky nodded curtly. "I'll drop a few careful questions to Bart Bickford and Nora Peterson, see if they received copies of this beauty. Only thing is, the envelope is postmarked New York City."

"Lorraine?" Charlie blurted. "But it's been years! Why would she suddenly start hassling me now? And anyway, she wouldn't kill Tal, and anyway, how could she kill him long-distance from Queens?"

"Right, that's what I'm saying. Either the killer moves fast, or there's two of them," Walensky said. "Now, this Ryan woman. She's from New York, right?"

"Yeah. But she just arrived yesterday, just met us!"

"She was here before. She's a cool one," Walensky said. "I worked with the prosecutor on that Triangle Slasher trial because a couple of NYSU kids were victims. He said the defense really raked Ryan over, practically called her a hooker. He said it shook her up but she hung in there."

"Good. She's really trying to help," Charlie said.

"Good." Walensky tucked the *Screw* and its envelope inside his gray jacket and headed for the door. "Well, better get at it. Lot of work to do on this. God, what a can of worms!"

Charlie shifted in his seat. This suburban mall theatre was fairly new, with bristly cherry-colored upholstery that prickled through his thin shirt. It was packed full of people, dim dark shapes before him. Behind his seat, a low wall separated the rows of seats from the rear cross aisle that led to the lobby. The red glow from the exit sign made Deanna's hair shine.

On the screen Luke Skywalker and Threepio sped across a striking desert landscape in a battered land-rocket, searching for the runaway Artoo Deetoo. The audience was rapt. But Charlie's unhappy thoughts reeled on.

After some serious reflection, he'd called Lorraine in Queens, to no avail. Not home. And the message he'd left at her office was still unanswered. Not that he'd been near a phone recently to receive a message. Nor had Maggie. This morning he'd tried to find her too, to probe cautiously if she'd learned anything new. But she wasn't at her home number, nor anywhere in the department. Even her baby-sitter and the children were out somewhere. So he had no leads at all to find Maggie and—

A huge fearsome creature loomed abruptly over Charlie. The audience gasped, and Deanna gasped too. Bless George Lucas. Charlie's worries dissolved. He picked up her hand and was again ensnared in the magic of Deanna and the film. The towering on-screen figure held its ax high. Threepio had fallen off the cliff, and the creature was whacking at Luke Skywalker. Now Luke was down too.

"Oh, no," moaned Deanna. She sat erect and tense in her seat, her hand slipping from his to cover her mouth, eyes glued to the screen. He loved that about her, her ability to lose herself completely in the story and images. Her bright brown hair caught the flickering light of the screen, glinting now golden with the desert sand, now red in the alien sun. He picked up her hand again.

On the screen Alec Guinness, dignified and kindly, had taken over. He was kneeling by the stunned Luke Skywalker, reassuring the nervous little Artoo Deetoo robot. Reassuring Deanna too. She relaxed, tugged her warm hand from under Charlie's, and dove it into the popcorn. Damn Guinness. Charlie glared at the screen a moment, then was caught up again. What a superb actor! His lines were pure exposition, about the history of the Jedi knights and the Force, yet Guinness gave them such weight and sorrow that they seemed profound.

Lucas had done a splendid job on this film. No wonder it was taking the country by storm, so that even in this shopping-mall theatre in a suburb of Syracuse, Charlie had had to stand in line for an hour to get the tickets. People of all ages had stood with him: several fond young couples in denim, a silent silver-haired pair in pastel polyester, a balding university type in an Aran sweater, a cowboy-booted young father occasionally visited by spouse and small children. There were lots of slightly older children doing the standing-in-line on their own, if constant giggles and shoves and trips to restrooms or nearby shops, after instructing the next guy to "Save my place, okay?" could be called standing in line.

The parking lot filled up, the acres of varicolored enamel and chrome sparkling in the June sunlight. About noon it had become warm enough even in the shade of the mall arcade for Charlie to take off his windbreaker. He'd noticed that the Aran sweater had come off too.

At last, he'd reached the box office and obtained the precious tickets. He stood by the door and waited. And prayed. Deanna had been skittish this morning. A casual meeting would be best, he'd decided, and he'd lurked like a lovesick adolescent near her apartment building until he saw her come out. Alone, thank God. She was in jeans and a sunny yellow T-shirt, walking purposefully toward the little crossroads shopping center two blocks from her building. He fell into step beside her.

"Hi," he said.

"Oh—hi." She was surprised, smiling her shy smile, pleased yet hesitant. Go easy, Charlie.

"Doing anything special today?" he asked.

"I have to get some groceries now."

"Yeah. Know what you mean. Maybe this afternoon?"

"No, I don't think so." But her timid glance was desperate for his understanding. "I mean, I've got so much to do."

"Deanna, hey, you know I love you." He swallowed, his palms damp. He rubbed them against his jeans. "So if there's a problem, we should talk about it."

"No, that's okay." One narrow shoulder shrugged, too casually. "I just can't see you today."

"Okay, look. No strings attached, I promise. We'll just see a movie at the Greenwood, okay?"

"You promise?" She wavered a moment, glancing at him, then coyly down again.

"Of course."

But then she shook her head at the sidewalk. "I've really got a lot to do."

"Star Wars?"

That did it. Excitement sparked in her eyes. Yet she protested weakly, "But it takes forever to get tickets . . ."

"You just get everything done and show up there at twelve-thirty. I'll have the tickets, okay?"

"Well, okay." She looked at the watch strapped onto her delicate wrist. "Oh, God, I'll have to rush!"

"See you at twelve-thirty!" He headed for the theatre.

She was a couple of minutes late, but they were able to find seats in the last row, on the aisle. He'd bought popcorn. Deanna had a bottomless appetite, and popcorn was always an accompaniment of their moviegoing. Charlie didn't mind. As a kid he'd loved popcorn too, and the buttery smell of it was now half-nostalgic, half-infused with the sweet electricity of Deanna's presence beside him.

"Oh, my God!" exclaimed Deanna as a gasp ran through the audience. Amazing creatures filled the screen. A silly honky-tonk tune was being played by big fetuslike musicians dressed in black. A surly bartender served an astonishing array of customers—God, what imagination had gone into this! Charlie was amazed and delighted. Scaly creatures and slimy creatures, one-eyed and many-eyed creatures, beaked and fanged and cobra-headed creatures, gigantic insect creatures and manateelike creatures, all huddled over bizarre drinks. An unpleasant human with a blasted nose was picking a fight with Luke. Old Obi-Wan Kenobi was talking to a hulking monster that seemed to be a giant gorilla dressed in Yorkshire terrier pelts. But when the noseless man swatted Luke across the room, Obi-Wan Kenobi's laser sword hummed and sliced off a limb. Deanna clapped both hands to her eyes in delighted disgust.

Charlie could restrain himself no longer. He slid his arm around her slim waist, slipping his hand under her sunny T-shirt to the warm downiness of her skin beneath.

"You promised!" she whispered fiercely, wriggling under his ecstatic hand. The popcorn fell to the floor.

"C'mon, you can see better if you sit on my lap," he murmured, and pulled her toward him. She resisted sweetly, bowing her head and pushing against his arm. She liked playing coy. But he understood her, loved her seductive wriggles, loved the intoxicating little games she played.

Something clamped onto Charlie's shoulder. Deanna twisted away from him, out into the aisle. What the hell? Charlie leaned across her abandoned seat, saw her running across the rear aisle toward the red-glowing exit sign. But the grip on his shoulder had tightened. He looked up.

The big balding man in the Aran sweater was leaning across the half wall behind the seats, his powerful hand pressing Charlie down.

Charlie didn't think. He dove down, wrenching free of the heavy grasp, and pitched himself into the aisle like a runner from a starting block. Popcorn crunched under his soles. He sprinted toward the door that was still closing from Deanna's departure. In the lobby he saw her disappearing through the glass doors that led to the parking lot. But as he approached those doors, thought returned and he hesitated. Following Deanna was reflex, like gasping for air when drowning. But the big man was right behind him. He mustn't lead that brute to his darling.

But it turned out he had little choice. The man caught him by the elbow but instead of restraining him rushed him out the glass doors with the skill of a professional bouncer. Charlie looked frantically around for her and finally spotted the yellow T-shirt and bright brown hair. She'd come on her bike. The man stopped him a few steps from the theatre doors, and together they watched her speed across the parking lot, standing up on the pedals for power, pumping hard to pick up speed. Hurry, Deanna, Charlie urged silently. Get out of his sight. Had she noticed this man behind them? Is that why she had run?

Charlie wasn't resisting anymore, but the muscular hand still clamped viciously on his arm as they gazed at Deanna's slender retreating figure. Finally the big man glanced at Charlie. "Tell me, Professor Fielding," he asked courteously, "how old is your little girlfriend? Ten?"

XVII

A huge stack of mail awaited Anne inside the front door slot. She let
Maggie and Cindy pass, then scooped up the pile and took it to the
kitchen table. "Coffee's in the cabinet over the sink," she said, dumping
the letters down. Bills, notes. Maggie went to start the coffee, and Anne
pulled out French bread, cheese, and pâté.

Cindy spread her arms. "What a treat! I'm usually the one to make the
coffee. Occupational hazard."

"Don't crow yet," said Anne, slicing the bread. "Plates are in the
cabinet up there. The one next to the sink."

Cindy sighed theatrically and set the table. She had succumbed to
urging from Anne and Maggie to come by for a sandwich. "Okay, I've got
to pick up some groceries anyway," she'd said. "And hell, you're right. I
keep worrying about this mess too. It's kind of good to talk about it with
somebody besides those wooden-faced cops."

Anne put the *moutarde de Meaux* and the little *cornichons* onto the table,
opened a bottle of Beaujolais, and looked again at the pile of mail. She
pulled the tall kitchen wastebasket over next to her chair and sat down.
Cindy and Maggie joined her at the table.

"Coffee'll be ready by the time we're done," said Maggie. "May I?" She
brandished her knife.

"Sure. Dive in." Anne tossed a couple of flyers into the wastebasket.
Much of the stack seemed to be condolence notes. She set them aside to
read later.

Maggie put a slice of pâté onto some bread, hesitated, then placed it on
Anne's plate. "Eat," she commanded, cutting herself a new slice.

"God, you're as bad as my neighbors," grumbled Anne, but she abandoned the mail, speared a *cornichon,* and began eating.

"So," said Cindy to Maggie, "what are your questions?"

"Well," said Maggie, her mouth full, "let's see. We've probably said
what we can for now about Nora and her brother. And about Bart. You
say Charlie's out—"

"Right," said Cindy. "You say so too!"

"—unless he was working with someone else. So maybe we should
talk about Bernie."

"Bernie?"

"Did you see him leave for lunch, Cindy?"

"Yep. At twenty of. He had lunch at the faculty club with those Oriental computer guys."

"And when did he get back?"

"He didn't show up again until two-thirty or so, just before you and all the cops arrived."

"So the computer guys alibi him."

"Yeah. Except—well, the cops know this. He wasn't supposed to meet them until twelve-thirty."

Maggie glanced up, alert. "It took him fifty minutes to walk a quarter mile to the faculty club?"

"He always leaves early," explained Cindy with a shrug of her pink-checked shoulder. "Hates being late, plus he loves his little glass of something before lunch."

"That's true," said Anne. "Bernie drinks a lot. Never shows, though. He just gets quieter and quieter."

"More and more uptight," agreed Cindy. "Can't imagine why he bothers. I like it to loosen me up." She saluted them with her wineglass and took a swallow.

Anne asked, "Cindy, did Bernie ever say anything about that problem he had in Iowa? The arrest?"

"No. Not to me."

"Cindy, don't be coy," said Maggie impatiently. "Did you learn anything about it, by any other means?"

"God, you've got me on some kind of pedestal of nosiness!"

"There's a whole crowd of us up here on that particular pedestal," coaxed Maggie. "It's a good cause."

"Yeah, okay, I heard bits of Tal's conversation with his friend from Iowa," Cindy admitted. "But the case was dropped, you know."

"We know," said Anne. "But we still wonder what it was about. All Tal told me was that a couple of prostitutes had accused him of being a client."

"Well," said Cindy. She took another sip of wine, put the glass down, turned it a couple of times with her fingers. "Well. It seems one of them mentioned chains and whips."

"Oh, boy," said Anne. Clean, mild, uptight Bernie? "But of course the case was dismissed," she reminded them feebly.

"And he's been a good boy for ten years now," said Maggie.

"Publicly, at least," said Cindy.

Maggie looked at her sharply. "What do you mean?"

Cindy shrugged. "Nothing serious. He keeps magazines in his bottom drawer."

"So what?" said Anne. "I saw those magazines yesterday."

"He showed you?" asked Cindy in disbelief.

"No. Just thought he was acting furtive about that drawer. So when he left I peeked."

"Good for you," said Maggie.

"But all he had was math puzzle magazines."

"Oh," said Cindy. "You didn't look inside, then."

"What's inside?"

"Porn. Bondage. Just what you'd expect if the Iowa story was true."

"Oh, boy," said Anne again.

"He threw them away yesterday," Cindy added. "Anne must have scared him."

"Yeah." Maggie had gobbled her sandwich quickly and was now leaning back in her chair, balancing her empty wineglass in both hands, frowning at it. "Cindy, you have to admit, you've got a lot of dirt on these people."

Cindy nodded.

Maggie glanced warily at Anne. "And so did Tal."

"Yes," said Anne.

Maggie's gaze shifted back to Cindy. "More than he kept in the official records. More than he told his wife."

"Really wasn't my business," Anne pointed out. "Things have happened in the French department that I didn't bother to tell Tal."

"Yeah." Maggie was still looking at Cindy. "And yet, with you, he never—?"

"Never," said Cindy.

"Of course he knew you had no money."

"Less than none," said Cindy. "Literally."

Anne suddenly realized what they were talking about. She banged the table with her fist. "Leave it, Maggie!"

"Anne, you can't have it both ways! Either we try to find out what happened, or we forget it. Believe me, the cops will be asking the same questions."

"But it's a waste of time!"

"Probably." Maggie shrugged. "But look, even if Tal wasn't blackmailing anyone, suppose someone thought he might be planning to?"

"Why would they think that? After all these years?"

"Maybe they'd just learned that he knew something they didn't want known. It might seem threatening."

"But they should have known he'd tell me! Unless—" Anne thought, "unless he planned to bury it. The way he buried Bernie's past. Or Cindy's, um, loan . . ."

Maggie twirled her wineglass. "Yeah."

"Or unless he didn't know for sure. He might not tell me if he was just guessing."

"Right. But either way, we want to find out. If Tal didn't tell you, it may well be the secret that led to murder. If he did—well, you may be in danger too."

The phone jangled.

Damn, probably another reporter. Anne got up angrily to silence it. "Yes?"

"Professor Chandler?" A man's voice. Pleasant enough.

"Yes?" she barked.

"Sorry to bother you, but is Maggie Ryan there?"

"Yes. Maggie?" She held the receiver out stiffly, at arm's length. Maggie bounded across the room to take it.

Still shaking, Anne stumped back to her chair. Could Maggie be right? Could she be in danger too? Hell, she didn't want to think about it. She sure as hell wasn't going to quit looking for the truth. She picked up the mail again.

"Hello?" Maggie said. "Nick! Hi . . . Oh, damn. Damn!" Her fist punched the wall. "Yeah, I'll try. Where's her mother? . . . I see, works on weekends. Well, I'll try to get in touch with her too . . . One other thing. He'll have a secret collection, I'd put money on it. Try to find out about it . . . No, meet us at Charlie's office, about an hour. He's got a projector there. I'd like to see if that film you lifted from his office yesterday is really what it seemed to be when we held it up to the light."

She replaced the receiver and closed her eyes a moment. Then she muttered *"Espèce de merde!"* and turned back to Cindy and Anne. Cindy was standing by the sink now, scraping dishes.

"Hey, guys," Maggie said, jabbing her hand through her curly hair and surveying them sadly a moment.

"Yeah? What?" Anne said gruffly. She put aside a note from Tal's sister and ripped open the next envelope. Handwritten, with no return address. A stupid crank letter, *Tell Lambert 6/2 = 8/18. Gazette V.* The result of getting your name in the paper was receiving this kind of—

Maggie asked, "Did you know Charlie Fielding is a child molester?"

"Christ!" whispered Anne. The letter dropped into her lap.

"No!" Cindy's head jerked up to stare at Maggie. "That's—that's over!" She bowed over the sink again.

"You knew?" Maggie was across the room in two strides, grabbing Cindy's arm and spinning her around to face her. A plate thumped onto the vinyl and rolled into a corner. "You *knew!* You asshole, you've known for years, haven't you?"

"No—"

"And you didn't say anything!"

"Cut it out!" shouted Cindy. She was prying at Maggie's fingers, trying to loosen them from her arm. "You don't know a damn thing!"

"Wrong. I know several damn things! I know you and Charlie Fielding hate each other, but you've been protecting each other like best friends.

So I figure if Charlie won't tell that you embezzled from the department, even when someone's murdered and he's one of the suspects—well, then *you* must have a real threat to dangle over him. This is it, right? You knew!"

"It's over, damn it! I've almost paid it off! And as for Charlie, it was only the one time—"

"Cindy." Maggie's voice was cold as an arctic wind. "Charlie was in Syracuse today, in a movie theatre, feeling up a ten-year-old girl."

"What?" Cindy stopped digging at Maggie's fingers to stare at her. "What?"

"Today. A ten year old."

"But—he promised! And he got married, even—"

"God. That long ago?" Disgusted, Maggie loosed Cindy's arm and stuck her hands in her pockets. Shoulders hunched, she stalked across the kitchen to lean against the refrigerator. "Cindy, maybe you don't know that most child molesters don't change. I spent a depressing hour in your library yesterday looking at the statistics. They keep doing it. To dozens of kids over a lifetime. Hundreds. Psychologists are trying, but they just don't know how to fix them."

"But how could he? Damn it, people can change! You think it was easy for me to quit gambling? What does he think—"

"I don't know what he thinks." Maggie sounded very weary to Anne. "But it's time to hear what *you* think, Cindy. The whole thing. Start with how you found out about him."

Cindy bowed her head. The mass of highlighted ringlets fell forward from the pink headband, half hiding her face. "It was a few weeks after Tal had found out about . . . what I'd done. Charlie was working on follow-ups to his thesis back then. Something about reading in older grade-school kids. Well, some administrative order had come down about changing the locks in the building, and I went down late one afternoon to the experiment rooms to see which set of keys worked. The schedules were posted on the doors, and Charlie was supposed to be finished. I didn't even think twice, just unlocked the door, and there they were, half undressed, him and this fifth grader—" Cindy's hand went to her face and she shuddered.

"Jesus. What did you do?" Maggie's fists were clenched in her pockets, the denim taut over knobby knuckles.

"I stepped in, closed the door behind me, and said, 'Honey, I've come to drive you home now. Get your jeans back on, okay?' She was scared, poor little thing, whispering, 'Don't tell, please, don't tell!' Charlie said, 'It's not what you think, Cindy!' and I said, 'Yeah, sure.' And then he said, 'You know, Tal asked me to look at a page or two of the departmental ledgers a couple of months ago, Cindy. I couldn't help noticing some problems.' "

"Jesus," murmured Maggie again.

"So what could I do? I said, 'It's paid back. And I've been in GA for six weeks now. I'm turning my life around. You turn yours around too and my mouth will stay shut as long as yours. But no longer. I promise.' And he looked at little Melanie, that was her name, and said, 'I promise.' I thought—" Cindy raised her head. Tears had run down her cheeks, leaving pale trace lines in her makeup. "That filthy slimeball!"

"Yeah, and you too!" Maggie's fists came out of her pockets to thump the refrigerator door angrily. "All those years, little girls were in danger—"

"Hey, wait a minute! To me, *my* kids come first! To say nothing of the bravest guy ever shot down in that shitty war! What about the danger to them, Miss Know-It-All? You think I should have said, 'Oh, sorry, Mark, we gotta give up my job and sell the house and go on welfare?'"

Anne sat dazed, their words crackling around her.

Maggie protested, "But those poor kids—"

"Shut up!" Cindy's lashes were beaded with tears. "How the hell was I supposed to know? I don't have a fancy Ph.D. like you. *He* was the one with the goddamn Ph.D.! I didn't know I was supposed to look up any goddamn statistics. He said he'd quit. He knuckled right under about little Melanie, didn't put up any fight at all. If he had—"

"Yeah, what about Melanie? You just let her deal with it all by herself? You didn't tell her parents?"

"Damn right I didn't tell her parents! She begged me all the way home not to tell. Her dad would beat her, she said. And if she told her mom she'd just get drunk and tell her dad, and then he'd beat her." She drew a deep breath. "She said Charlie was the only person who loved her. The only one who thought she was nice. I was sick, Maggie. Sick!"

"Yeah, okay, *I'm* sick now!"

"So what would you have done? Be honest!"

Cindy and Maggie glared at each other. Anne sat still, unable to understand, unable to believe.

Maggie's eyes dropped first. "I would have—hell, I don't know, Cindy. I wouldn't have told Melanie's parents, you're right. Wouldn't have done any good to call the cops on him either because it would need Melanie to make a case."

"There! See?"

"But I would have derailed Charlie Fielding, somehow."

"Easy to say," Cindy scoffed. "What would you have done? Poison his coffee?"

Maggie flapped a hand at her in frustration. "Hell, I don't know, Cindy. If I didn't know that these guys don't quit . . . well, you're right, maybe I would have believed Charlie too. Hell, he probably believed it himself, at the moment."

Cindy's anger wilted at the conciliatory words. She said in a small voice, "If only Bernie wasn't such a tight-ass—"

"Yeah." Maggie glanced at Anne, and her gaze sharpened. "Anne. Are you okay?"

"Yes," said Anne. But Maggie, frowning, stepped closer and felt her forehead.

"You're pale," she said.

Anne made an effort. "So quit springing shocks on an old woman," she said. She groped in her pocket and pulled out her cigarettes. The note in her lap drifted to the floor, and Maggie retrieved it. Anne lit her Gauloise and took a deep lung-scorching drag on it. *To hell with life anyway. Full of crank letters and pain and child molesters. Who needs it?*

Cindy had been standing by the sink lost in thought, one carefully manicured hand massaging the knuckles of the other. She said, "I'll do it, Maggie. I'll tell Hines. You're right, we can't let him keep on and on. Maybe Bernie will be reasonable—oh, hell, he won't be. We know that. But I'm good, I can go somewhere else. Work my way up again."

Anne cleared her throat and tried to focus on Cindy's problem. "You're willing to risk your job? But Tal worked so hard to make sure you kept it!"

"But Maggie's right. I thought he'd quit. But if he's still doing it . . . God, I keep thinking of little Melanie, how he took advantage of that little lonely beat-up girl, made her think she had to pay that price for love . . ."

"But what price would she have to pay for justice?" Maggie asked soberly. Her hand was resting on Anne's shoulder. "When that rapist attacked me I had to go to court. Had to tell the story over and over, to a dozen different people, most of them skeptical. What would that do to a kid? And his lawyer attacked me too, in public, in front of the judge and jury and reporters, everyone. Said I was the one who seduced that poor vulnerable man. Said I asked for it. Said I was a slut and a liar. If the rapist hadn't slashed me with a knife, he might have been let off."

"But that man had killed people!" Anne exclaimed, and then wondered at herself for even caring. Nothing mattered. Yet some vestigial bit of the old Anne was still protesting.

"Didn't stop his lawyer from attacking my character," Maggie said. "Okay, maybe in this case he wouldn't call Melanie a slut, but he'd certainly call her a liar. Wonderful imagination, he'd say. And the same with that little girl in Syracuse, and maybe Jill Baker—"

"Jill Baker? No!" Anne protested.

"Maybe."

"Look, what are you saying?" Cindy asked. "A minute ago you said I should have stopped Charlie. Well, you were right. But now you're saying I shouldn't!"

Maggie squeezed Anne's shoulder and placed the fallen note on the table next to her. "No, not exactly. I'm just saying there are drawbacks to telling Hines. Anne, listen, are you up to another trip to campus? Because there may be another way."

XVIII

The man in the Aran sweater hung up the phone. His name was Nick, he'd said, and near as Charlie could make out, he was some kind of private eye. He climbed back into the driver's seat and checked Charlie's bonds. A careful man. Charlie was tied into the passenger seat of his own car, wrists crossed behind him. They'd stopped on the highway at an isolated service station with a roadside phone booth, and Nick had left him for a moment to make a call. Charlie had wriggled strenuously, but the ropes were secure. He'd yelled a time or two, hoping that the garage attendant might help him, but Nick had parked far from the building and left the windows closed tight. No one could hear him. He couldn't even reach the horn with his forehead.

"Well, Charlie," said Nick, inserting the ignition key, "tell me about her."

"I already did," Charlie pointed out sullenly. "You know her name, where she lives, where her mother works. What else is there to say?" He was not about to tell this stranger any details, damn it, the quick light touch of Deanna's little mouth, the downy curve of her back . . .

Nick said mildly, "I'd like to hear your side of the story."

Charlie looked at him suspiciously. "Who hired you?" he demanded. "Deanna's mother?"

"No. Doesn't look to me as though she has that kind of money."

"Is this connected with the murder at NYSU?"

"You could say that, yes. I'm here because of Tal Chandler."

"But Tal didn't know!"

"Didn't know what?"

Charlie was silent.

Nick said, "When we came out of the theatre you said, 'It's not what you think.' "

"Well, it's not."

"Tell me, Charlie, what do I think?"

Charlie glanced at the man next to him—solid, muscular, jaw set firmly, sharp brown eyes checking him from time to time. He said he was not a cop. Well, he was probably telling the truth about that. Cops read you your rights, and they had handcuffs if they wanted to arrest someone. Charlie was not under arrest. He wondered who had sent him. He seemed cultured and intelligent, and his underlying violence seemed well controlled. Could he understand? So few understood. "Well," Charlie said cautiously, "you probably think I'm one of those filthy guys who molests children."

"The thought did occur to me," Nick admitted. "You say you're not?"

"God, no! Those people—my God, they ought to be—" Charlie caught himself. "Uh, are you—"

"Well, no, my personal taste runs more to women," said Nick. "But I can try to understand."

Charlie said, "Well, I know there are guys who abuse children. Force themselves on them. God, I can't understand how anyone could do that. It's a betrayal, you know? Ordinary children are so innocent, so vulnerable. So much damage can be done! Those guys should be locked up for life."

"I agree with you so far."

"Well, you see, I'm not one of them," Charlie said.

"Could you explain?" Nick said courteously. "I do agree with what you said about the vulnerability of children. The immense damage that can result from abuse."

"Yes." Is that why he had tied Charlie up? Charlie glanced at his captor. He didn't know what to believe. Nick had overpowered him easily, had tied him up with no nonsense; but since then he'd been sympathetic, almost pleasant. Now he was driving sedately at the speed limit, eyes on the road, lumpy profile unworried. Only the tight grip of his big hands on the steering wheel betrayed any tension. He'd shown no disgust, only a sympathetic curiosity. Maybe he did understand something about children. Maybe he could understand about Deanna.

And if he understood, he might let Charlie go.

Nick flicked a glance at him and added, "You said *ordinary* children."

"Yes." Charlie licked his lips and stared straight ahead at the road. Did he dare explain? Except for Coach Wilhelm, he'd never found anyone who really understood.

"Some children are not ordinary?" Nick prompted.

"Every now and then, there's—well, it's hard to explain."

"A girl who is not ordinary?"

"A girl who is . . . very special." He hated having his hands bound. His glasses were slipping down his nose. "Look, I don't think you can understand."

"I can't understand why you think you weren't molesting her."

"Because she—well, with most girls maybe that's what it would be," Charlie admitted. "Of course I'd never ask that of most girls. But Deanna is—well, special."

"How?"

"It's—well, for example, Bart Bickford in our department is working with creative children. Some of them are amazing, imaginations far beyond the usual child. Or in sports . . . I remember a boy I used to play hockey with, brilliant even when we were kids. Or there are children who are musical prodigies. Rare, just one out of thousands, but by the time they're ten or twelve they're ready to perform concerts with adults."

The knuckles whitened on the steering wheel. "So your theory is that the same is true of sex? Some little girls are prodigies, ready to perform with adults?"

"No, not just sex. Love. Total love. A girl who has a talent for love should be allowed to love."

Nick didn't answer, just shook his head.

He seemed intelligent. Charlie tried another tack. "This is nothing new, for God's sake! Do you know how old Dante's Beatrice was when he first saw her? She was nine! Juliet was thirteen!"

"Romeo wasn't thirty-six, like you!" snapped Nick. "And when Beatrice was nine, so was Dante."

"But he could tell!"

"He could tell?" Nick paused, and when he spoke again his words had lost their angry edge. "I am trying to understand, Charlie. You are saying there's a way to distinguish a . . . prodigy, you call her, from ordinary children. How?"

"Oh, you can tell. A girl has a special look about her. You can sense the —the hunger."

"She flirts with you?"

"No, no! Not at first. Most are very timid, little fawns. No one understands them so they're lonely. But they look at you and you know."

"No. I don't know," Nick said apologetically, shifting in his seat and glancing at Charlie in a puzzled way. "I didn't notice anything special about Deanna. She seemed like a shy little girl, extremely anxious to please, who wanted to be agreeable but really didn't want to spend time with you."

The words bruised. Charlie tried to stay under control. "That's not true! It was just that she had a lot to do, she said! She came to the film in the end!"

"Ordinary kids would too! It's obvious that Deanna's mother is struggling as it is, probably can't give Deanna much spending money. Someone offering an expensive ticket to a movie everyone in school is talking about . . . well, a kid doesn't have to be a prodigy to want to see *Star Wars.*"

"That's not it!" Charlie was almost screaming, hauling on his wrist bonds. He wanted to pound Nick into silence, to stop those false words. Words from his waking nightmares, from those moments afterward when he felt like the filth of the earth. "I love her! And she loves me! Don't you understand?"

"No. I don't," said Nick obstinately. "She desperately wanted to see the movie, that was clear. She was trying not to hurt your feelings. But she wouldn't agree to come with you until you promised to leave her alone."

Charlie's heart felt like a stone. "You—heard that?"

"I've been watching you for hours."

"Damn! And you waited until—"

"Hell, I was hoping that she was your niece, maybe, and that you'd have a nice platonic afternoon at *Star Wars*. But she was so upset when you touched her—"

"No, she wasn't! Damn it, you don't understand! She just likes to act a little coy sometimes."

"Coy! Christ!" exploded Nick, thumping the wheel with the heel of his hand. He scowled out at the green countryside that sloped from the highway down to the distant lake.

Charlie looked down at his knees. He'd hoped that something in Nick's experience might have helped him understand. He'd seemed sympathetic. But he was as blind as the others. Charlie said stiffly, "You're taking me to be arrested, aren't you?"

"Yes."

"I'm sorry you don't believe me."

"Oh, I believe that *you* believe it," said Nick. "Christ!" But then in a moment he added more gently, "It must be hard for you to know that your little prodigies grow up so soon."

Charlie glanced at him warily. "Yes."

"And you'd have no record of them. Maybe snapshots, that's all."

"Oh, no! I've got records. A beautiful collection!"

"A collection?"

"Photos, little gifts they've given me, even a couple of short films. But you wouldn't understand," he added belatedly. He shouldn't talk about his secret collection, treasures sacred to his dearest memories. Melanie's sock and Deanna's little panties were far more precious than Judy Garland's pinafore.

"I understand wanting to remember." But Nick's voice was tight.

Anger surged through Charlie again. "I don't abuse children! How many times do I have to say it? I protect them, for God's sake! But if I can, I help someone special achieve her potential!"

"Yeah, I know, and if the poor kid is lonely enough and confused enough not to scream, you talk yourself into believing that she's one of your so-called prodigies, that she likes it."

"You don't understand!"

"I do understand. You find a lonely little girl starved for affection. And you offer her affection, and *Star Wars* tickets, and popcorn. But if she accepts, she finds that the price of affection is soul-destroying."

"Not true! It's fulfilling for her! She loves to please me!"

"Most kids love to please adults. But not that way! Didn't you see her run away, for God's sake? A kid doesn't skip out on *Star Wars* and tear off like that unless she's running for her life. To save her very self."

"I told you, she likes to be coy!"

"Christ." Nick sounded weary. He glanced at Charlie as they turned off the highway onto the road that led to College Avenue. "Professor Fielding, expert on reading and on misreading. I'm told you believe that many misreadings occur because the reader has a strong hypothesis about what word is coming next, and doesn't check to see what the letters really are."

"Yes."

"Yet you don't see that your wrong hypothesis about these children is blinding you to their real needs. The expert Professor Fielding can't tell when he himself is misreading a child."

Misreading? Ridiculous. Charlie's nightmares writhed beneath his mental protests, but he fought them down. He was no filthy child molester. He wasn't! He hadn't misread Deanna, she just enjoyed playing hard-to-get. He could tell. And he hadn't misread sweet Melanie. No. Nor downy Janine. Nor Wendy, back when he'd been in high school. Nor Ellie . . . Nick just didn't understand.

They were crossing the College Avenue bridge. Charlie wriggled his wrists and asked uneasily, "Where are we going?"

"To your office, Charlie."

"But why?"

"To decide what to do next."

Nick said nothing more as they turned into the largely deserted parking lot and found a place near Charlie's end of the building. Nick undid the rope from the seat back but didn't remove the wrist bonds. He hauled Charlie from the car, locked the door, pocketed Charlie's keys, and marched him into Van Brunt and up the steps to the first floor.

The office door was slightly ajar and voices came from within.

"What the hell is going on?" Charlie demanded, halting at this further violation.

Nick pressed him roughly through the door and closed it behind them.

Cindy Phelps and Anne Chandler were sitting in two of the chairs. Maggie was perched on the edge of Charlie's desk, threading film into his projector. "Hi, Nick. Charlie, I see you've met my husband. You're just in time for our screening. Cute little film we unearthed in a videotape container here."

Charlie's unwilling eyes found the plastic box on the desk.

It was one of the containers his blundering assistant had almost taken yesterday.

Nick pushed Charlie down into the third chair and remained standing behind him, one hand on his shoulder. At a nod from Maggie he reached across to the wall switch next to the door and killed the lights. The screen had been set up across the room, above the television, so the image was small but clear.

Establishing shot of a pretty beach. Blue sky. Then throbbing music and pink letters spelling out BABY JAWS. Cut to a pair of chubby legs splashing in the water, a happy giggle. Then waves, a child's shrieks, a red stain in the water. A little body on the sand, ketchup on arm and face, and most horribly, a blue eyeball lying near his head.

"My God," said Cindy, "that's Eric's eye."

"Eric?" asked Nick.

"The take-apart head on the office shelf. I'd recognize that blank stare anywhere."

Anne Chandler said in a strained voice, "Is that the little Hammond boy?"

They fell silent as a new image filled the screen: back view of a paunchy, muscular man in an official-looking tan uniform. "I'll catch that shark," he said, with a clumsy theatrical clenching of his fists. "I'll catch that child-eating shark! But—I need bait!"

Cut to a lovely blond, blue-eyed girl. She was dressed in pink jeans and a lighter pink T-shirt. Anne Chandler gasped, "Jill! That's Jill Baker!" She scooted to the front edge of her chair, eyes intent on the scene.

Jill was frowning, "I don't like this," she mumbled. Then, more clearly, "I want to go home."

Nick murmured, "That's not acting. She meant that."

"Use whatever they give you, right, Charlie?" Maggie's voice was like vinegar.

The official tan shirt was putting on a dark slicker, careful not to show his face. "You and me against the world," he was saying. Cut to the exterior of a boat. Then to Jill, still protesting, saying she didn't like sharks. Charlie looked at his shoes. He was ashamed. Jill was not special, she was an ordinary child, she didn't like it. He should have tried harder to keep her out of it. But damn it, he'd done all he could. And he'd saved her from some of the scenes they'd asked for . . .

Jill was in the boat now. "I want to go home," she repeated. On the sound track a song faded in, "Show Me the Way to Go Home." The man, face still hidden, explained to Jill that she must sacrifice her clothes to serve as shark bait.

Nick's hand tightened on Charlie's shoulder at the next shot. Jill huddled naked in the bottom of the boat. Then a shot of the water, the slicker-clad arm swishing pink clothing through the waves. Then purposely murky shots of the shark, violent amidst foam and shadows, intercut with lingering views of Jill stretching to peer through a porthole. "I know that shark!" Maggie said. "It's plastic and it's sitting on your living room shelf."

Nick said, "She doesn't seem aware of the camera."

"We shot through a one-way mirror," said Charlie. "She never knew I was there."

"All she knew was that no one would ever believe she was telling the truth," said Maggie.

A hasty shot of the muscular man firing a gun. The shark thrashed in red water. Then there were bubbles, then calm. A voice-over explained that the girl was grateful to her hero. Too bad they'd had to use the voice-over, Charlie thought clinically, but the damn kid hadn't given them much that was usable. But they'd got her to do the main scene, anyway. Here came the shots of her groveling in the boat, glancing up fearfully at the porthole, and crying out the obscenity they had taught her.

"What the hell!" exploded Anne Chandler. "She wouldn't say that!"

"The magic word," said Maggie bitterly. "Remember she told us there was a magic word to make the shark go away?"

"Good God," growled Anne.

The voice-over explained the girl's gratitude, and the footage was repeated in case anyone had missed it. Cut to the man, removing the slicker to reveal his muscular back. As he tossed it aside the light caught the back of his upper arm. "What was that?" Maggie asked. No one answered.

The rest of the film had no dialogue, just their few usable shots of Jill respliced in various combinations with occasional views of the man's bare back. Damn fool was an exhibitionist. Didn't really care about kids. It was all done against the soundtrack "Show Me the Way to Go Home." They all watched in silence until Charlie cleared his throat and said, "He, uh, he never actually touched her."

"Great," snapped Maggie. "You must be real proud." She switched off the projector light and began rewinding the reel.

"Look," Charlie said, eager to explain, "I didn't want to upset her, so—"

"Didn't want to upset her?" Maggie exploded.

Nick flicked on the room lights, and the sudden brilliance caught Charlie full in the face. Anne Chandler and Cindy shifted their chairs around to face him. Maggie dropped the *Baby Jaws* reel into her briefcase and walked around his chair to stand in front of the screen. In her navy blue shirt, shoulders hunched vulturelike, arms crossed, she reminded Charlie of the Disney sorceror returning to annihilate his cringing apprentice. In memory the fly crawled across Aunt Babs's face.

Charlie pulled himself together and faced the blue glare of Maggie's eyes. "I didn't upset Jill! I helped every way I could because she was just a kid . . . couldn't understand."

"God, Charlie. You really believe that, don't you?" He was surprised to hear pity in her voice.

Cindy said, "Charlie, tell me, did your wife find out about Melanie? Is that why she left?"

"No. No, not really."

"She found a little white sock. And a copy of *Screw* he'd hidden, with an ad with a Laconia box number," said Nick.

"Damn that ad—" Charlie suddenly realized what Nick had said. "Lorraine told you that? Lorraine sent you?"

"No, no. I was coming anyway. So I stopped by to see her, to ask if she knew of any reason someone might be trying to frame you. First she said she knew nothing. But I pointed out someone was after you and anything she knew would help. She got very upset. She said she'd left you years ago and you hadn't told her a thing. She'd talked you into research with adults, she said, and she'd been sure her suspicions were wrong, and she didn't want to know anything more, but if I did maybe I should look at *Screw*. By then she was crying so I left her alone."

"Damn. You sent me that *Screw?*"

Maggie said, "We thought you'd try to destroy evidence and lead us to it, or at least you'd try to contact any partners you might have. Well, you must have covered your traces at the post office pretty well, since you turned it right over to the police. You looked innocent as pie. I almost thought we were on the wrong track. But since then I've learned that Walensky was probably already blackmailing you. Right? And Nick lifted this film when he delivered a box here yesterday. I squinted at enough of it last night to know we'd better keep an eye on you. And then Nick caught you with Deanna."

Charlie asked miserably, "Why couldn't you leave it to the police?"

Anne snorted. "They aren't very gentle with children. Tell me, are you the one who hit the little Hammond boy and broke his legs? That was him lying on the beach with the plastic eye, right?"

"Yeah, but he wasn't hurt then!" Charlie shuddered. "That all went wrong! See, the kid wasn't hurt at all in that scene but he didn't like the ketchup, and—well, no, I didn't hit him."

"Whether you did or not, we'd better decide what to do with you, Charlie," Maggie said briskly.

"I—look, I never wanted to make those films anyway. I stood up for the kids, didn't let him touch them. Really!" he insisted as Nick's hand tightened. "He just wanted the money, wanted to show off a little. He didn't touch them!"

"That's real nifty," Maggie said, "but we'll get to that in a few minutes. You see, somebody did touch Deanna and Melanie. That has to stop."

"All right. It's not the way you think it is, but I'll stop."

"You said that before!" said Cindy, her voice dark with scorn. "You promised me the same thing years ago. It's time to lock you up."

Stupid woman. Charlie shot back, "If I go to jail, Cindy, so do you!"

Fear flashed in Cindy's eyes, but she tossed her head and said, "I doubt it. The money's back and I've been clear for years. So I'm ready to risk it if it means getting you behind bars."

"Stupid move, Cindy. You'll be out of a job too."

"Hey, Charlie, you know I'm a gambler. If you get locked up, it looks like a win to me."

There was no reasoning with her. The point of despair deep in his ribcage was growing, sending out spidery arms to chill his bones. Then he remembered what had worried Cindy most years before. He said, "It's no favor to Melanie to bring it up again!"

But it was Maggie who answered. "Glad you see it that way," she said genially. "We agree, courtrooms are pretty brutal places for victims. I know, I've been there. Now Jill might be strong enough to testify if she gets some solid counseling. But even there I'd hate to make her go through it."

"Yeah!" He turned eagerly to Maggie. "You do understand! So, well, I'll stay away from little girls."

"Even the special ones?" asked Nick.

Charlie hesitated.

Maggie shook her head hopelessly. "God, Charlie, you still think it's okay sometimes! I wish we knew how to reach you, but—Look, you're abusing children, it's as simple as that. We've got to stop the damage. The only answer I can see is to lock you up."

"You'd hurt the children? Dragging them into court?"

"No, no. We're going to lock you up for murdering Tal Chandler."

XIX

It took a moment for her words to register. Then Charlie squawked, "Me? For murdering Tal Chandler?" He looked wildly at the others. They were shocked too.

"But he didn't!" Anne exclaimed. "Because—"

"Hush!" Maggie raised a palm to interrupt her. "Think about the children, Anne! Let me explain how he did it, okay? Look at his motive first. We know how long he's been working on this research project. How important it is to his career. And suddenly this emeritus professor, retired and then some, is writing a paper that cuts at the root assumptions of the project."

Charlie shook his head. "Impossible! No one will believe that a professor would—"

"Quiet!" snapped Anne Chandler. "Let her finish."

"You see, Charlie," Maggie went on, "we've remembered some interesting facts. Cindy and Anne both remember how Tal said his new study might hurt your work. Right?"

Cindy and Anne nodded.

"I can report that statistically, the effect you're basing your theory on is very weak, and in fact there's evidence for Tal's theory in your studies too. So it's obvious that if you were going to get your stuff published, Tal's findings would have to be kept quiet. But he was going to report them at the MPA meeting next month."

Nick was leaning against the closed door, arms crossed. "Why didn't he just destroy Tal's research instead of murdering him?" he asked. Charlie looked at him gratefully.

But Maggie had an answer. "Because that would point directly to Charlie. By staging another crime and leaving evidence that threw suspicion on others in the department, he hoped to deflect interest from his own motives."

"And his Chaplin memo book?" asked Anne.

"That could have fallen out of his jacket pocket, just as he's been saying all along. Probably when he pulled out Nora's gun from the same pocket. Cindy, don't you remember this morning, the bulge in his jacket pocket? It clunked against the door frame when he came into the office."

Cindy looked coolly into Charlie's eyes. "By golly, I do remember. Clunk."

"Right," said Maggie. "On the other hand, Bart and Nora won't remember anything in his pocket in the restaurant. By then he'd left it in the gorge."

"In the gorge? But—" Charlie began.

Nick cut him off. "When did he have time to go into the gorge?"

Maggie smiled apologetically. "Well, you see, I thought I'd only been in the post office for a minute or two. But now I remember that I paused to leaf through a little newspaper that they had on the table. A summer supplement, exhibits and parks and theatre, you know. The Syracuse Farm Theatre was listed, I remember. Could have been twenty minutes before I met him again."

"God!" Charlie stumbled to his feet. "This is unbelievable! You're saying that—Maggie, for God's sake, you were with me, you know it wasn't that long! You know I didn't kill Tal!"

Maggie's restraining hand on his arm was gentle. "I know you're damaged, Charlie. I don't know how you got that way but don't you see? You'll hurt one child after another all your life! We have to protect the children!"

She didn't understand about the girls, that was the problem. Stupidly assumed that Deanna and Melanie had been hurt, when they'd been so happy to have such a special relationship. Women were bitches, if you trusted them they left you in the lurch, alone, out of control. Mother. Aunt Babs. Lorraine. Now Maggie. Charlie said, "Look, if you frame me for this, don't think you're keeping the kids out of court! I'll tell about the girls! Name, names, everything!"

Anne Chandler stood up abruptly, trembling with anger. "You do that, Charlie Fielding, and I'll explain something else that happens to be true. Tal suspected that something very wrong was going on in his department. He was worried about the Hammond boy. About Jill's story. Told me about it. Didn't know who, of course, so he couldn't tell me that. But he knew something was deeply wrong, and if he'd found out—"

"A jury will think that's another reason that you killed him," Maggie explained gently. "Really, Charlie, it's to your advantage not to mention the girls."

Charlie sat back down. It was true, people would be eager to believe that someone who liked little girls was a killer. People didn't understand. It would make things worse in a trial if he told.

Nick said softly, "You know what happens to child molesters in prison, Charlie? You know about Short-Eyes?"

Short-Eyes. God, that's what they'd think, the other prisoners! They were now filming that horrible play, based on the real-life tortures that other prisoners inflict on molesters. He hated molesters too, had thought of it as a sort of rough justice. But if these academic people didn't understand that he wasn't a molester, how could he expect criminals to understand? He did not want to go to prison as Short-Eyes.

"Okay," he said desperately. "I'll leave the kids out of it. But you can't get away with this! I'll tell them you framed me!"

"Go right ahead," said Maggie. "Tell them that the wife of the victim, the departmental secretary, and a New York statistician you'd never met before all got together to frame you."

"Well, it's true—" Charlie faltered.

"It's also true that a man in a slicker told Jill Baker to take off her things and yell magic words to fend off sharks," Maggie snapped. "But who believed her?" Then she combed her fingers through her black curls and spoke more softly. "I'm sorry, Charlie. But I don't know how else to stop you."

Charlie stared down at his shoes. He was trapped. She was right, no one would believe him, it was too insane. If those three stuck to this story . . . And it was true, telling about the girls would make things worse for him. Much, much worse. If he told the truth, if he said Maggie had made it up to keep him away from the children, the lawyers would just turn it around and say that Tal had found out and Charlie had killed him to keep him quiet. It would make him look even guiltier. And then in prison . . . Or suppose he somehow got released. If people knew about the girls, no one would hire him. And worse yet, he would be watched. It would be even more difficult to find the next little Deanna or Melanie.

He came back to the present to discover that Anne Chandler and Cindy had left for home. They didn't want the police to find them all here together. It would look less like a conspiracy if they were interviewed separately. "I'll see you soon, Sergeant Hines," Maggie was saying. She replaced the telephone receiver.

Hines. He mustn't let Hines find out about the girls. He mustn't let anyone find out.

God, Hines would search his house.

If Hines found his secret collection, he'd find out. He might even destroy the collection, destroy the precious memories. Charlie had to get his collection to a safe place. How?

Salvation rapped on the door, then unlocked it. "Fielding?" said Walensky, then paused, taking in the scene.

Thank God it wasn't Hines.

Walensky stepped in, closing the door behind him carefully. "What's going on? Fielding, why are you tied up?"

"They did it," Charlie confessed, thrusting his wrists toward Walensky. Walensky untied them.

"Wait!" Maggie said. "Professor Fielding is the one who killed Tal Chandler!"

"No! No, I didn't!" Charlie rubbed his wrists.

Walensky looked neutrally at Maggie. "How could he? You're the one who said he was with you almost the whole time."

"I thought he was. But now that I've thought things over, I've decided that I must have been in the post office longer than I said at first. See, I stopped to read something. So it was fifteen, maybe twenty minutes."

"I see."

"And Cindy Phelps thinks the gun was in his jacket pocket Thursday morning."

Charlie shook his head. "It's not true! None of it is true!"

"That's for the court to decide," said Nick.

Walensky glanced at Charlie and unsnapped his holster. "I hate to say this, Professor Fielding, but he's right." His voice was hard.

"My God, you don't believe them, do you? But you've known me for years!"

"Look, what can I do? Nora Peterson says she saw you take the damn gun, Fielding. Bickford's been saying you did it from the beginning. And now your alibi disappears." He looked at Charlie thoughtfully. "Of course the jury will probably sympathize. You've never even assaulted anyone before. Nice young man, worried about his job, overstressed, no danger to society." There was a flash of hatred in his face as he added, "No doubt you thought you had a good reason to kill that old man! And never thought of the consequences!"

Charlie was shocked. Walensky believed her, so easily!

Maggie said hastily, "It was a professional reason! His research was threatened by Tal Chandler's work. I'm the project statistician and I've seen his results. And of course, you could check with Anne Chandler."

"A professional reason. I see." Walensky squinted at the bookcase. "Fielding, you told me your results are on videotape, right? Maybe we'd better impound those."

Nick said, "Isn't it more important to get Professor Fielding's statement?"

"It's all important," Walensky bristled. He pulled the plastic lining bag from Charlie's metal wastebasket and began to pitch videotapes into it.

Walensky had given him an opening, Charlie realized suddenly. Should he make a break for it? But then he remembered that his car keys were in Nick's pocket. And Nick had moved away from the bookcase and was watching him alertly.

Maggie's eyes were on Walensky. "Here, I'll help," she offered, and scooped some experimental tapes from Charlie's shelves.

"No, thanks, Miss Ryan. This is police business." Walensky moved toward the boxes that hid the films.

"Well, at least let me stack them for you!" Maggie didn't want the films in police custody, Charlie realized. She was still trying to shield the children. She pulled the incriminating boxes out and began to straighten the experimental tapes left in the bag.

Charlie saw Walensky register the way she had sorted them. She looked up from her task, met the captain's narrowed eyes, and recognition sparked between them. "The man in the slicker!" she gasped. "So it's not just that you're blackmailing Charlie. You're in this personally!"

"I'm sorry you force me to do this the messy way," Walensky said regretfully. His automatic was suddenly in his hand. "Over against the window wall. All of you." The gun was steady on Maggie, and she promptly obeyed, backing toward the window, almost stumbling over her briefcase. Nick joined her at the opposite side of the window.

But Charlie hesitated. "Look, I'm on your side!"

"Yeah? Then how did she see the film?"

"She found it herself! And anyway, it doesn't matter, because she's not going to say anything about the kids or the films. She doesn't want them to have to testify in court."

A hard little smile tensed Walensky's face. "Right, Miss Ryan. You were cross-examined in a sex crime once yourself, weren't you?"

"Wasn't much fun," Maggie said neutrally. "Nothing I'd wish on a little kid. It's like abusing them all over again."

"So you want to keep them out of court. Fine," Walensky mused. "Maybe we can come to an agreement. Fielding, I don't know why you haven't left."

"Nick has my car keys!"

Walensky sighed regretfully, like Coach Wilhelm when Charlie had muffed a play. "Toss them over." He waved the gun and Nick complied. Charlie scrambled to pick them up. Walensky said, "You'll get one more chance to break out of custody. But since you're still here, you might as well get the right films into that bag. We need to have a little bonfire. That's why I came tonight, you know. All my copies got incinerated the moment you told me someone had sent you that *Screw* with my ad circled. But then I got to thinking, you're such a pack rat, you wouldn't have the brains to destroy the masters. So let's do it now."

"Okay." Walensky was right, they had to go. Charlie glanced nervously at Nick and Maggie but they were standing quietly by the window, watching. He sorted the plastic cases of films into the bag and knotted the top. "So much work," he said sadly.

"Gotta cut your losses," Walensky said.

"Yeah. Oh, she's got another one of them in her briefcase," Charlie remembered. He started toward Maggie.

"Stop!" barked Walensky. "Don't get between them and me!"

"Oh." Charlie jumped back.

"Miss Ryan, throw your briefcase over to Fielding."

"Okay," said Maggie agreeably. She picked up the briefcase, obediently sighted at Charlie, and swung her arm back to toss it to him. Instead it smashed through the windowpane behind her and disappeared outside.

"Oh, God! Sorry!" Maggie's hand flew to her mouth in apparent shock.

"Damn!" Volcanic anger seethed in Walensky's eyes but he stayed in control. "Well, we'll get it on the way out. Fielding, is there anything else in this office? Any records?"

"Oh. Yes, I've got an inventory." Charlie scrabbled in his file cabinet and found an old data set. The inventory was nestled among the other sheets. "Here it is. There's nothing else in the office."

"Okay." With his left hand, Walensky pulled a lighter from his pocket and tossed it onto Charlie's desk, startling him. He controlled his twanging nerves and dropped the inventory into the wastebasket before lighting it. It took four tries before the paper caught and flared into black ash.

Charlie nodded at Nick and Maggie. "What are you going to do with them?"

"Depends on how cooperative they are," Walensky said. "If worse comes to worst, well, we all know accidents happen to little children sometimes."

Charlie shivered. He didn't want any more children hurt. He said urgently, "Please, listen to him! He means it! The little Hammond boy didn't like the ketchup and when we started home he kept looking back saying, 'Bad place.' We were afraid his parents would get suspicious, and Walensky said if he'd been hit by a car, of course he'd say 'bad place.' And he took the kid out and ran over his legs very carefully."

Maggie's eyes dilated, but she said calmly, "Tell us what you want us to do." Why was she so calm? Charlie himself felt jumpy as a silent movie.

"For now you know nothing. Just stay with the status quo," said Walensky. "If you implicate us in any way your kids will suffer. But I'm sure we'll find a way to work together."

The sound of a far-off siren drifted through the broken window. "Listen!" Charlie exclaimed. "She called Hines, you know. Just before you arrived."

"Jesus, Fielding!" Walensky exploded. "When are you going to start giving me the facts I need to know? Pitch those films out the window and let's get out." When Charlie had complied he added, "Is there anything else you haven't told me?"

Nick spoke for the first time. "What about your secret collection, Charlie?"

"Oh, God, that's right! I've got to move my private collection from home to a safer place. Hines might search my house."

"No problem there." Walensky was backing toward the door. "I took care of everything. When I couldn't get you on the phone this afternoon I figured I'd better make sure Hines couldn't find anything. So I let myself into your house and broke open the filing cabinet you showed me. Don't worry. Your collection got incinerated along with my stuff. Come on, let's go."

For a moment Charlie couldn't understand. He stood rooted where he was, staring at Walensky. Then he gasped, "Incinerated? You burned it?"

"Yeah, right. You got nothing to worry about. Let's go, now."

"You burned my collection? All of it?"

"Not the movie stuff in your living room, no. That's harmless. I just burned that one drawer you showed me."

Black rage welled up in Charlie. All the sacred relics of those lost, golden afternoons with little Melanie, little Janine. Gone, forever gone, like the pure unclouded children now grown into gross adulthood. "You burned it?" Charlie screamed. "Burned it?" He lunged at Walensky. A haze of red veiled everything but the gun and the man who had destroyed his life's work, his life's love. He saw his own hands wrenching at Walensky's, saw the surprise on Walensky's face, heard the crack as the gun fired, felt the hard steel recoiling in his own hand. He fired again and again until the gun made nothing but clicking sounds that could barely be heard through the screaming in his head.

Someone was tugging him backward. Nick. The red haze was retreating. Maggie was scrambling from behind the big steel desk as though she'd been hiding there. She knelt by Walensky. The captain was on the floor, his head and chest ribboned with tatters of red like Sonny Corleone in *The Godfather,* like Bonnie and Clyde. He was making ugly wheezing sounds.

Someone else was holding Charlie now. Officer Porter, that's who it was, handcuffing him.

Paramedics burst into the room and surrounded Walensky. Maggie backed toward the broken window.

Sergeant Hines was looking at Walensky, shaking his head. "What the hell happened here?"

"I—I shot him," Charlie said, explaining to himself as much as to Hines.

"Why?"

"He burned—"

Maggie broke loudly into his sentence. "We were explaining to Captain Walensky that Charlie Fielding killed Tal Chandler."

"Chandler too?" Hines looked at him, but this time Charlie didn't answer because he was remembering now. Short-Eyes. He mustn't tell. And Walensky's words, *The jury will sympathize . . . You've never even assaulted anyone before.*

Now they'd think he'd assaulted two. Killed two. Or tried to. The paramedics were carrying Walensky out.

Hines asked, "Think he'll make it?"

The paramedic holding the door open said, "With brain injuries like this? If he's lucky he'll die. But his vital signs are strong, poor bastard, so we'll have to put him on the machines. Just don't be expecting him to testify."

Charlie stared at the floor, trying not to see the spattered blood, listening to Maggie explain how he had shot Walensky, and shot Tal Chandler. Hines was careful, checking each point she made, and by the time they were ready to lead Charlie to the squad car he knew her story was almost impossible to refute. Walensky might live, so that would be a lesser charge. Even so, her story meant that Charlie would be locked away a long, long time for killing Tal.

But one tiny cheering thought occurred to him at last. Maybe they wouldn't charge him with Tal's murder after all. There was still Bart's pipe. The prosecution would say Charlie had left it to frame Bart. But it was still a loose end of sorts. And Hines was a professional, a plodding, thorough kind of detective. Hines would keep looking.

And if he kept looking, he might find the one thing Maggie couldn't explain away. He might find the real killer.

Whoever it was.

XX

After Sergeant Hines and the man from the district attorney's office left, Anne checked her watch. Plenty of time to start a grocery list. She had the refrigerator open, counting eggs, when the doorbell rang again.

"Hi," she said to Nick and Maggie and the children. "I hoped you folks would stop by."

"Your daughter's coming tonight, right?" Maggie asked.

"In about an hour. I'll meet her at the airport and bring her home. Meanwhile, if certain bright-eyed little persons would like to swing some more . . ."

Sarah's delighted smile was answer enough. They went out to sit in the late afternoon sun. The children ran from the terrace to the swing set.

As soon as they were out of earshot Anne lit a cigarette and said, "I heard that Charlie shot Walensky."

"It was terrifying," Maggie said soberly. "Walensky was his partner. The man in the slicker. And Charlie said he was the one who hit the Hammond kid."

"God, no wonder Tal couldn't get him to investigate!"

"Right. When he told Charlie he'd burned the photos and mementos of his little girlfriends, Charlie went berserk. Blindsided Walensky, got the gun from him, emptied it out before Nick could reach them."

"God. And I was worried that no one would believe Charlie would shoot someone!"

"Yes. It pretty much guarantees that he'll get a long sentence, and we won't have to bring the girls into it. They threw the films into the bushes, but Nick got them out before the police noticed them."

Anne shook her head. "Hines said Walensky wasn't dead."

"No. I guess in Charlie's state he wasn't shooting straight. Slight wounds in the shoulder and hip, but two wounds high in the forehead . . ."

"The forehead. So he'll probably end up a vegetable." Anne shuddered. "Time was I was ready to hang whoever hit the Hammond kid. But this . . . Tal used to say that the worst fate would be to damage your mind and have your body stay alive. He said he'd rather be shot in the brain stem."

"Well," said Maggie carefully, "he got his wish."

Anne tapped her cigarette against the ashtray and said softly, "So. You figured out who really killed Tal."

"Yes," Maggie said gently. "That's why we can use it against Charlie."

"Damn bastard," said Anne.

"Yes."

"How did you find out?"

"It took a while," Maggie said. "From the beginning the death seemed so—theatrical. It was right on the border between two police jurisdictions. And there were so many clues, all pointing at different people, all with dark secrets that Tal might have known. Yet you kept saying it was the children that really troubled him—Jill Baker, the Hammond boy."

"Yes. He knew there was a problem."

"But he didn't know who, and it's terrible to accuse an innocent person. Walensky was discreet, but he was so discreet he sometimes refused to investigate, Tal thought. Probably ignored some of Tal's other suggestions too. So the goal of the killing was to pull a competent outside police force onto Walensky's turf. Walensky would keep things discreet, but someone had to be willing to take a hard squint at the education department."

"That's right," said Anne.

"But I wasn't certain until I saw the note."

"Yes. That's what told me too."

"Lambert is Tal's doctor?"

"Yes."

Maggie looked across the table at Nick. "Anne got a note in this morning's mail. The first part said, 'Tell Lambert 6/2 = 8/18.' 6/2 is June second, Thursday, the last medical examination he had. They must have done some kind of test."

"X rays," said Anne. "You know Tal. A million questions, always looking over John Lambert's shoulder at his own charts. John was a good sport about it. Taught Tal to read them. I remember him coming home last year, saying how good his August eighteenth X rays looked."

"So he exchanged last year's good X rays for the latest ones somehow."

"Wouldn't be hard," Anne said. "Lambert and his partners don't run a high-security office. The technicians label the X rays with little stickers and put them in your file. You generally have to wait a while alone in the examination room, with your file in a holder on the door so the doctor can look it over before he comes in. Tal's peeked a couple of times in the past. He could have switched the sticky labels on the X rays if he saw the latest ones looked bad."

"I see," said Nick. "He looked at his X rays, saw he was doing badly—"

"Doomed is the word," said Anne crisply. "If it started spreading again, he knew that was it. No more tricks in Lambert's bag."

"So he expected to die soon. And he exchanged the X-ray labels to trick his doctor."

"Yes." Anne watched the smoke spiraling up from her cigarette into the twilit air. "Tricked his doctor. Tricked me. Told his friends he was celebrating. Spilled coffee on Nora's desk so he could sneak her gun from the drawer. Stole a few other items to leave in the gorge. Made some big suspicious footprints and threw away the boots. And then he took Nora's gun in his right hand and shot himself in the head."

They were all quiet a moment. Then Maggie said, "He accomplished his goal. Cops came from every side. Stumbling over each other to investigate the department, and investigate each other."

"And investigate me," said Anne. "Hines gave me the third degree. Hell, so did you, Dr. Ryan." She glared at Maggie.

"Hey, can't blame Tal for that," said Maggie. "He'd set it up carefully. He knew someone in the department was hurting children, and that Walensky was reluctant to investigate. I think on his own he'd narrowed it down to four: Charlie; Nora's wild brother; Bart, who ran the experiment Jill was in; and maybe Bernie with his former arrest. So he asked them all to lunch at Plato's, so they'd be at the right place at the right time. He couldn't get Bernie, but as head of the department he'd certainly be questioned too. And there were two people he thought were protected by lunch appointments on the other side of campus. You, of course, Anne."

"Yes. And then I canceled it, like a fool." But he had planned for her. He had. She held the thought like a small warm ember in her heart.

"And Cindy. Her meeting wasn't the ideal source of alibis, but in case of need someone or other would come forward to help her out. I imagine Tal thought the question wouldn't arise, because he'd left clues pointing to the other people. He thought Cindy was protected. And you."

"Always the damn romantic hero. Protecting damsels." Anne let smoke stream from her nostrils. She'd always had a secret sympathy for the dragons, herself. "Never occurred to him that the damsels might prefer to have him around a little longer."

Nick said, "He was facing an ugly end, Anne."

"Oh, God, I know. But there must have been some other way!"

He rubbed his bald head. "We men are cowardly creatures, Anne. We're not bad at facing quick and glorious deaths. But to go on—that requires a different kind of courage. Deeper."

"Cindy's husband is right." Maggie's arm was around Anne's shoulders. "It's tough to go on. But people are asked to go on all the time, especially women. Hurts like hell. But generally, somehow, we find that deeper courage."

"Yeah." Anne stared down at the floor.

"There was a second part of the note," Maggie reminded her gently. "He said, 'Gazette Five.' That's part of the message too."

Anne nodded. Cyrano's Gazette: act five, scene five. His death scene. His farewell to the beloved Roxane. She said gruffly, "Damn romantic hero."

Nick's brown eyes were liquid, profound. He quoted softly, " 'Always my heart is with you, always yours. And in the next world I shall love you still, beyond measure, as long as time endures.' "

Anne's chin was trembling. She took a deep pull on the Gauloise.

"What he did helped a lot of little girls," murmured Maggie. "If we can see it through the courts for him."

"Oh, yeah. I'll see it through. I'll go on. But God, that is so like Tal, making the grand gesture. *Quel geste!*" She snorted, suddenly furious. "Damn the man, cheating me of weeks of him!"

Maggie squeezed her shoulders.

"Still, what a gesture!" Nick insisted. " 'Despite you all, old enemies who round me loom, I bear aloft unstained, unyielding—my white plume!' "

Men. Anne ground out her cigarette, straightened up, and prepared to go on.